D0753054

JoH

N 11 17

POWDER BURN

Center Point
Large Print

Also by William W. Johnstone and
J. A. Johnstone and available from
Center Point Large Print:

Those Jensen Boys!
Rimfire
Twelve Dead Men
Brotherhood of Evil
The Trail West
Monahan's Massacre
Will Tanner, U.S. Deputy Marshal
A Stranger in Town
Tyranny
Black Friday

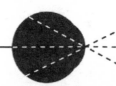

**This Large Print Book carries the
Seal of Approval of N.A.V.H.**

A WILL TANNER
U.S. DEPUTY MARSHAL
WESTERN

POWDER BURN

William W. Johnstone
with J. A. Johnstone

CENTER POINT LARGE PRINT
THORNDIKE, MAINE

This Center Point Large Print edition
is published in the year 2017 by arrangement with
Kensington Publishing Corp.

Following the death of William W. Johnstone, the Johnstone family is working with a carefully selected writer to organize and complete Mr. Johnstone's outlines and many unfinished manuscripts to create additional novels in all of his series like The Last Gunfighter, Mountain Man, and Eagles, among others. This novel was inspired by Mr. Johnstone's superb storytelling.

The text of this Large Print edition is unabridged.
In other aspects, this book may vary from the original edition.
Printed in the United States of America on permanent paper.
Set in 16-point Times New Roman type.

ISBN: 978-1-68324-451-6

Library of Congress Cataloging-in-Publication Data

Names: Johnstone, William W., author. | Johnstone, J. A., author.
Title: Powder burn : a Will Tanner U.S. Deputy Marshal western / William W. Johnstone with J. A. Johnstone.
Description: Center Point Large Print edition. | Thorndike, Maine : Center Point Large Print, 2017.
Identifiers: LCCN 2017016725 | ISBN 9781683244516 (hardcover : alk. paper)
Subjects: LCSH: Large type books. | GSAFD: Western stories.
Classification: LCC PS3560.O415 P677 2017 | DDC 813/.54—dc23
LC record available at https://lccn.loc.gov/2017016725

POWDER BURN

CHAPTER 1

It was a cold December day when Mike Lynch walked out of the gate at Arkansas State Prison in Little Rock. Outside, he turned to look back at the stone walls that had imprisoned him for the past decade. They had been long, hard years of bitter regret, not for the life of lawlessness he had lived, but for the fact that he had been caught. "You're a free man now," said Ed Todd, the guard who had escorted Mike to the gate. "Did that time locked up inside teach you anything?" There was no attempt to hide the sarcasm in the question. Todd was one of the older guards at the prison. He had been among the early hires, so he had seen a lot of convicts released. Most of them returned to the life of crime that landed them in prison in the first place. He didn't expect much different from this one.

"Yeah, I learned somethin'," Mike Lynch answered. "I learned I'd better be more careful, so I don't get caught next time." He flipped the collar of the ill-fitting coat up against the cold breeze that swept across the stone wall, and pulled the floppy, wide-brimmed wool felt hat he had been issued down firmly on his head.

"Huh," Todd grunted scornfully. "I give you six months, maybe less, you'll be back."

"The hell I will," Lynch shot back. "And you'd best say a little prayer for the lawman that tries to bring me in."

"That's awful big talk for a man just set free," Todd said. "Matter of fact, a judge might take that to be a threat against an officer of the law. Maybe I might take you back inside."

Lynch knew the guard was bluffing, amusing himself by trying to get his goat. "I expect you'd better look out your mouth don't make a claim your body can't back up, old man. You ain't got nobody to help you outside that wall."

Todd smirked in contempt for the brash ex-convict. "Big talk, prison ain't learned you nothin' a-tall, has it? Where you headed now?"

"Wherever the hell I want," Lynch said.

Todd shook his head. "Probably go straight to a saloon and spend that little bit of money the state gave you." Tired of bantering with the cocksure ex-convict, he turned and walked back in the gate.

"That's a good idea, Todd," Lynch called after him. "I think I'll go find me a saloon." A drink of whiskey was not his first priority, but he had to admit it wasn't far down the list. The problem was, as Todd had mentioned, he was seriously short of money. On his release, he was given a suit of clothes and $10, then shown the door. He was a free man, but one on foot with over three hundred miles to get where he was going.

He needed a horse and a gun for sure if he was going to make it all the way to Tishomingo in Oklahoma Indian Territory. That's where his father sent word that he would meet him.

Jack Lynch, known more commonly as Scorpion Jack by the outlaws he rode with, had managed to stay one step ahead of the law in Colorado and Kansas for the past several years. He could not risk a return to Arkansas after he was charged with the murder of a U.S. Deputy Marshal and the two possemen with him. So he sent word for his son to make his way to a trading post he was sure to remember. It wasn't necessary to name the place, for when Mike was a boy, he had spent several months with his father at Lem Stark's place on Blue River in Indian Territory. Although it had been some time since Jack Lynch and his men had escaped from Arkansas, he was under no impression that the U.S. Marshals Service had given up on capturing him. For that reason, Mike was very much aware of the probability that he might pick up a tail when he left prison, hoping he might lead them to his father. With that in mind, he started down the road, heading for Fort Smith and the Oklahoma border.

The sun was still hovering over the horizon when Mike came upon what appeared to be a camp on the bank of a creek. He paused to look it over before proceeding. There was apparently only one person and one horse beside the dark water of the creek. There had been no attempt to make the camp out of sight of the common road, and there was a big campfire blazing away. A traveler on the road would hardly miss it. Mike couldn't help grinning at the opportunity presented him. *I reckon I ain't gonna go without some coffee and supper tonight after all,* he thought. "Hello, the camp," he called out when he was still a few dozen yards away. "You got an extra cup of coffee for a tired traveler?"

"Why, sure, friend," a voice came back. "Come on in." The man got up from where he had been sitting and backed away a little from the firelight.

Mike took a good look around as he left the road and walked the short distance along the bank to the fire. He felt satisfied that the man was alone, and he didn't seem overly cautious when a stranger on foot suddenly appeared on the road. *That's because he's been sitting here waiting for me to show up.* The thought struck him suddenly. What if, instead of the tail he was expecting, the man was a deputy marshal, hoping to pump him for information on where he was heading and hoping he would lead him to his father. He would have had to leapfrog around him to arrange this casual encounter. "I sure do appreciate the hospitality," Mike said. "I'm a little short of supplies right now." He glanced at the man's horse as he walked past it. It was a well-built sorrel with a broad chest and strong legs. *A typical sign of a deputy marshal,* he thought. *They always ride a good horse.*

"My name's Bob Hardy," the man said. "Be glad to share some coffee with you, and some grub, too." He stepped back in a little closer to the fire. "Where you headed? On foot like you are, have you got far to go?"

"A ways yet," Mike said.

"Well, set yourself down and help me eat some of this bacon and hardtack," Hardy said. "Grab that extra tin plate there."

Smug in the satisfaction that he could see through the lawman's clumsy attempt to set him at ease, Mike helped himself to the generous amount of sowbelly in the frying pan. "You cooked up a lot of bacon," he couldn't resist commenting. "Was you expectin' company, or do you just have a big appetite?"

Deputy Marshal Bob Hardy hesitated a moment before answering when he realized that it might seem like more than a man would have fried for himself. "No, I reckon I wasn't thinkin' when I sliced off that meat." He forced a chuckle. "But ain't it lucky I did?"

"You're campin' a little early," Mike went on. "It'll be a couple of hours before hard dark. I wasn't lookin' to stop for the night for a while yet myself."

"It is a might early," Hardy allowed. "But I needed to stop and rest my horse, so I figured I might as well make camp."

Mike glanced at the sorrel again, thinking the horse didn't appear to be tired at all. *You might as well open your coat and show me that badge you're wearing,* he thought. "Which way you headed?" he asked instead.

"I was headed toward Little Rock," Hardy said. "But I ain't set on nowhere in particular. What about you? You ain't never said where you're goin'. Must not be far, since you're walkin'." The deputy was hoping to find out that Mike was meeting someone close by.

"It's a little ways yet, like I said," Mike replied. "I'm on foot, without no supplies because I had a little piece of bad luck a while back. But it ain't too far to walk when a man's got a good horse and supplies waitin' for him down the road."

This garnered Hardy's interest right away. "Well, that sounds like you ain't expectin' to be walkin' much farther. How long you figure it'll take? Maybe I can give you a ride wherever it is you're goin'."

" 'Preciate it, but you said you was headin' to Little Rock. I'm headin' toward Fort Smith."

"No trouble a-tall," Hardy hurriedly replied. "Like I said, I ain't particular right now which direction I'm headin' in."

If there had been any doubts about the

intentions of his host, Hardy's eagerness to help him dispelled them. "I thank you very much, Mr. Hardy," Mike said. "But I reckon it's best if I just go on by myself. I've gotta cut off the road up ahead to get to a friend's place, and he's a peculiar feller. He's liable to take a shot at a stranger on a horse ridin' down through the trees." He flashed a wide grin at Hardy. "I wouldn't want nothin' like that to happen to a friendly feller like yourself." He ate the last of his bacon and gulped the remainder of his coffee, then got to his feet. "Matter of fact, I reckon if I don't set around this fire any longer, I can make it to my friend's cabin before it gets too dark to see. So I'd best be gettin' along."

"I reckon you know what's best," Hardy said. "Hope everything's gonna turn out like you expect."

"Thank you, sir," Mike replied respectfully. "I'm pretty sure it will." He took the hand Hardy offered, thanked him again for the coffee, and headed back along the creek to the road, satisfied that he had the lawman hooked like a fish.

As he continued down the road, the daylight began to fade rapidly as evening set in. His concern was that it might become too dark for Hardy to follow him if he didn't find a good ambush spot before long. A quarter of a mile farther on he came upon the perfect place. The road took a sharp turn at the base of a low ridge covered with pines. Some distance beyond the turn, he discovered a game trail that crossed the road and led back toward the ridge. It was made to order for what he intended. He almost laughed at the thought. The path could well appear to lead to a cabin or a camp on the far side of the ridge. Now he had to make sure the deputy saw him leave the road to follow the game trail. He glanced back toward the curve behind him. There was no sign of Hardy. He hadn't reached the turn yet, or he was hiding while he watched him. Mike wasn't sure how much of a gap the deputy had maintained, but it couldn't have been very far, because of the poor light. And it was getting poorer every minute. He decided Hardy had to be watching him, so he paused before the game trail and pretended to look up and down the road, as if making sure no one saw him. Then he hurried along the narrow path and disappeared into the pines.

Un-huh, Hardy thought as he watched the ex-convict hesitating before leaving the road. *If I had waited much longer, I might have lost him in the dark.* He remained where he was for a couple of minutes more so as not to be seen when he left the trees that shielded him. When he reached the narrow game trail, he took a few moments to make sure Mike was not lingering there, having possibly seen that he was being followed. Then he stepped down from the saddle and led his horse a short distance into the trees before tying it to a young pine, thinking it better to pursue his prey on foot.

Proceeding cautiously, he followed the winding trail that seemed to be leading toward the ridge. The darkness within the pine trees made it difficult to see very far ahead of him, and he reminded himself that he had no notion as to who, or how many, might be at the end of this trail. What if the man's father, old Jack Lynch, himself, had slipped back into Arkansas, and he and his gang were waiting for his son? *I sure as hell should have considered that before I started,* Hardy thought. His plan to tail Mike Lynch without a couple of possemen now occurred to him as a little foolhardy. In spite of the tense atmosphere of the dark forest closing in on him, he was struck by the irony when he realized that the word *foolhardy,* when split apart became his name and *fool*. It created a mental distraction for only a second, but that was enough to cause him to fail to see the stout pine limb that caught him full in the face, crushing his nose.

Mike wasted no time following up the massive blow delivered by the pine limb. Hardy went down on his back, stunned by the attack and unable to defend himself against a second blow that landed beside his head with sufficient force to break the limb in two. Like a crazed cougar, Mike Lynch was immediately on top of the

15

smaller man, pinning him to the ground while he drew the .44 from Hardy's holster. With the barrel of the weapon barely inches from the unfortunate lawman's forehead, Mike fired a bullet into Hardy's brain.

Straddled atop his victim's body, Mike listened to hear any sounds that might indicate he had been wrong in thinking Hardy was alone. When there was no sign that the sound of the shot had summoned anyone, Mike got off the body and proceeded to strip it of everything of any value to him. He was pleased to find that the lawman had a little money in his pocket. Still concerned that there might have been more lawmen following up behind Hardy, Mike did not linger. He took only a moment to consider stripping the body of its clothes, but he saw right away that they were much too small to fit. It was especially disappointing to find the boots too small as well. He would have hoped to trade them for the prison work shoes he wore. *Wouldn't want anybody to see me wearing a dead man's clothes, anyway,* he told himself. "Right now, I need to get as far away from this place as fast as I can," he announced to the corpse staring up at him. To confirm his original suspicions, he took a moment to reach down and pull Hardy's coat open. "I'll see you in hell, Deputy," he said when he saw the badge pinned to Hardy's vest.

Back at the start of the trail, he found the sorrel

tied to a young pine. "Now, I reckon we're gonna see just how stout a horse you are," he said to the horse and stepped up into the saddle. With no thought of sparing the patient mount, he kicked it hard into a full gallop down the dark road, anxious to leave all traces of his evil deed behind him as quickly as possible. As he rode through the night, he reveled in the realization that, like his infamous father, he too had sent one of the government's deputy marshals to his grave. It gave him a sense of pride and a closer feeling of kinship with his pa.

The sorrel was willing, but was soon straining to the point of foundering, and Mike was forced to let up on the lathered horse. With concern for nothing other than reaching Indian Territory as quickly as possible, he rested the horse only when the weary animal began to stumble. He set out once again when the sorrel appeared somewhat recovered from the grueling pace. Holding the gelding to a steady lope, he rode on through the night, and morning saw the abused horse once again stumbling. "Damn you!" Mike swore. "Don't you quit on me!" He pushed the weary sorrel on through the morning until he came to a small settlement of farms. Passing through them, the horse began to balk, barely continuing until nearing the last in the cluster of homes, where it finally came to a halt, refusing to go farther. No amount of cursing and whipping could persuade it to move. Mike dismounted, forced to let the horse rest, only to have to jump quickly aside to keep from being crushed when the sorrel fell over dead. His initial reaction was to curse the horse for its failure.

Back on foot again, he looked around him, not sure where he was, but thinking that surely he must be less than a day's ride from Fort Smith—if he had a horse. He cursed the sorrel again. It seemed a shame to leave a fine saddle, but he didn't care for the notion of lugging it all the way to Fort Smith. So he removed the saddlebags and a coil of rope and started out once again on foot.

He had put several miles between himself and Hardy's dead sorrel when an opportunity to ride again presented itself. He had come to a section where the fields of a large farm came right up to the road he was walking on. At the far end of one of the fields, he could see several men working to clear some additional land. His initial reaction was to slip into the trees on the opposite side of the road to avoid being seen, returning to the road only after he was sure he was clear. Looking out across the rolling fields he now passed, he saw a house and barn in the distance. They looked to be located near the creek he could see ahead of him. "Hot damn!" he blurted suddenly when some movement in a pasture below the barn caught his eye. He stopped abruptly to make sure. It was horses, all right, a dozen or more. "And just when I need one," he muttered. He turned around and looked back the way he had come. He could no longer see the men working in the field, but he figured they most likely came from the farm buildings he had just spotted. There was no decision to be made, and no hesitation to head for the herd of horses in the pasture. Preferably, he would pick out a nice horse for himself and ride off without anyone knowing. But even if he was spotted stealing a horse, he was now armed with Hardy's weapons, so he wasn't worried about anyone left at the farmhouse stopping him.

When he got to the pasture by the creek, he took a few moments to watch the horses, as well as keeping an eye on the barn and the house. He realized then that there was another house beyond the one he had seen from the road. It was smaller than the one closest to the barn. The only activity he saw was when a woman came from the house and went to the outhouse. While he waited for her to complete her business, he took the time to select his pick of the horses, settling on a flea-bitten gray that showed a lot of spirit. He shifted his gaze back to the outhouse. "Come on, lady," he complained softly. "You gonna spend the day in there?" It seemed an unusual amount of time to get the job done. When finally, the door opened and she reappeared, it occurred to him that in that lengthy session in the toilet, there had still been no sign of any other activity around the barn. "If I was sure you were the only one left at the house," he muttered, "I might take an extra minute or two and pay you a visit." It was only wishful thinking, however, for he was in a hurry to get to Fort Smith. The situation was enough to encourage him to think about sneaking over to the barn with the possibility of finding a bridle and saddle. "First, I'll get me that speckled gray," he said.

The horse showed no sign of resistance, plodding slowly forth to meet him when he approached. Mike looped the rope he had taken from Hardy's saddle over the gray's head and led the horse into the trees lining the creek. Having decided there was no one around to even attempt to stop him, he tied the horse to a small tree and proceeded to the barn, where he found a bridle and saddle conveniently waiting for him sitting on the top rail of the last stall. He couldn't help smiling—it was almost too easy. He didn't even have to go to the tack room, where saddles and other tack were usually kept. And as he hurried back along the creek, his new saddle on his shoulder, he was almost of a mind to knock on the kitchen door to get a closer look at the woman.

It was no more than a half-day's ride to Fort Smith from the farm that had unknowingly provided him with a fine riding horse and saddle. Mike Lynch had not been sure of the distance, but he knew where to go when he got there. So he headed straight through town and rode down to the river near the docks and the ferry slips until he found a battered old two-story building with a sign that identified it as Jake's Place. He figured that to be the best place to stay the night before heading out again in the morning for Tishomingo. Jake's was a popular saloon for men on the wrong side of the law, according to what some of his fellow inmates at Arkansas State Prison had told him. He was feeling a little less pressure now that he had gotten away with no apparent pursuit. And thanks to Deputy Marshal Bob Hardy, he could afford to rent a room upstairs and have a couple of drinks with some supper. He pulled the gray up before the hitching rail, dismounted, and went inside, where Jake Cochran welcomed him—just like his fellow prisoners said he would.

CHAPTER 2

"Will Tanner," Sally Evening Star murmured, her usually solemn face taking on a smile when she caught sight of the lone rider leading a couple of horses down the path toward the house. "Gonna need more potatoes." She put the pan of potatoes she had been peeling down on a chair and walked to the edge of the porch to get a better look. It was Will, all right. It would be hard to mistake the easy way he moved with his horse's motion, almost as if they were one. And he was still riding that big buckskin gelding named Buster. "Will Tanner," Sally repeated softly, her smile breaking into a wide grin as she turned toward the front door to fetch Miss Jean.

The widow Hightower, known more familiarly as Miss Jean, was in the kitchen, helping her sister-in-law prepare supper when Sally came through the doorway. "We got company for supper," Sally announced.

"Oh?" Marjorie Ward responded. "Who's the company?"

Looking at Miss Jean, Sally answered, "Will Tanner," then waited for the reaction she knew would follow.

Miss Jean didn't disappoint her. "Will's here?" she exclaimed. "Well, for goodness' sakes, I thought he had forgotten his way to Ward's Corner." She placed the stack of dishes she was holding on the corner of the table and quickly followed Sally down the hall toward the front door. At first glimpse of the tall sandy-haired rider she was immediately reminded of her late husband. Jim Hightower had always been proud of the young boy he had taken in to raise. And while she felt sure Jim would have preferred that Will would remain in Texas to run the ranch he had worked so hard to help build, at least Will still owned the J-Bar-J. Actually, he owned only half of the ranch, since he had split the owner-ship with Shorty Watts, fifty-fifty. Miss Jean was confident that Will's fifty percent was heavier than Shorty's fifty. She suspected that that was the way Shorty saw it, since he was always hoping Will would return to Sulphur Springs when he grew weary of chasing outlaws for Judge Isaac Parker's federal district court.

At the sight of the frail little woman standing on the porch, Will raised his hand in greeting and turned Buster toward the two waiting to greet him. "Think a fellow could get a cup of coffee around here, and maybe a biscuit to go with it?" he asked as he pulled his horses up before the porch.

"I don't know," Miss Jean returned. "The folks who own this house are mighty particular about who they share food with." She smiled at the

23

still-grinning Osage woman standing beside her, and joked. "They went out of their way to take Sally and me in. Didn't they, Sally?"

Will stepped down to receive a welcoming hug from the woman who had been like a mother to him for so long. When he thought about it sometimes, it occurred to him that Miss Jean never hugged him when he was a boy. This gesture of affection had begun only after her husband's death. After a brief embrace, Will stepped back and held her at arm's length. "Looks like they're treatin' you pretty good here," he said. "You must be behavin' yourself."

"We only get on her once in a while when she kicks up her heels too high," Marjorie Ward teased as she stepped out the door to join them. "How are you doing, Will?"

"Can't complain," Will replied. "I brought a couple more horses to put with my others while I've got a little free time. I might have more than Henry and Hank wanna fool with now, about fourteen if I've got my figures right. These two oughta make sixteen. So if things at the courthouse stay pretty quiet till after Christmas, I'm thinkin' about moving my horses down to the J-Bar-J." Marjorie's husband, Henry, was a farmer and not into the business of raising cattle and horses, so Will figured he'd welcome the chance to rid himself of the care of Will's growing horse herd.

"I'm sure it's all right with Henry if you leave them here for as long as you need to," Marjorie said. "My daughter's boys, Jimmy and Thomas, have sorta taken over the job of looking after the horses. Keeps them out of mischief."

"Well, I surely do appreciate it," Will said.

"You'd best take care of your horses now," Marjorie said. "We're getting ready to put supper on the table as soon as Sally cooks the potatoes. Henry and the menfolk will be showing up to eat before long, and you don't wanna get left out."

"Yes, ma'am, I'll get right to it." He stepped up into the saddle and turned his horses toward the barn and the pasture behind it.

There were two houses built close beside Sawyer's Creek, the larger one belonged to Henry Ward Jr. and was home to him, his wife, Marjorie, and their son, Henry III, who was called Hank. Hank was nearing his thirty-fifth birthday and had never married. The smaller cabin belonged to Henry and Marjorie's daughter, Helen, her husband, Jim Smithwick, and their two teenage boys. The Ward and Smithwick families farmed a rich piece of land just under four hundred acres in size. Will couldn't help admiring the success the two families had enjoyed as he led his horses to the barn where he would leave his saddle. After that, he turned them loose to graze with his other horses in a six-acre pasture behind the barn.

He stood there for a few minutes, watching

Buster as the big buckskin trotted to the creek to drink. Then he walked out into the pasture a little way to look over the rest of his horses where they were bunched together near the creek. They were all good stock, for he kept only the good ones, and all had been acquired through the arrests of outlaws, many of whom were killed in the process. Just as a matter of habit, he started counting the horses. Coming up one short, he counted them again, but could still count only fifteen, not counting Buster. *Maybe,* he thought, *one of the boys is riding one.* He shrugged and turned to walk back to the house. As he walked, he realized which horse was missing. It was a flea-bitten gray that he had been especially impressed by. A strong, sturdy horse, and he was not surprised that one of the boys would pick the gray to ride.

Even though the two families lived in their separate houses, they still maintained a tradition of eating supper together at the main house, so the evening meal was a noisy occasion that always fascinated Will on his infrequent visits. This evening was no different, and Will was greeted warmly by the men of the two families. After supper, when the young boys left the older folks to sit and talk while the coffee was finished up, Will told Henry about his plans to move his horses to Texas. "I reckon you didn't think I was

26

ever gonna take 'em off your hands," he said.

"They ain't been no trouble a-tall," Jim Smithwick spoke up. "You don't need to be in a hurry to move 'em. Jimmy and Thomas have been watchin' 'em."

" 'Preciate that, Jim," Will said. "Tell you the truth, I was thinkin' about lettin' your boys pick a horse outta the herd for their own. I figure I owe 'em at least that much for takin' care of 'em. I noticed one of the horses wasn't there, so maybe somebody already picked a favorite, that flea-bitten gray. I ain't surprised. That's the one I woulda picked, myself."

His statement was met with blank stares, then Hank spoke. "I didn't think anybody had cut out any of those horses to ride. Have they, Jim?"

"No, not that I know of," Jim replied. He looked at Will. "You say that gray is missin'?" When Will nodded, Jim continued. "It musta wandered off somewhere. They usually stay pretty much in a bunch. We'll go look for it if it don't show up tonight."

"Nothin' to worry about," Will said. "I'll go look for it in the morning." He wasn't concerned about the horse. He felt sure the horse would wander back to the others, since horses tend to feel safer in the herd. He would concern himself with it in the morning. At least, that's what he thought until Jim's younger son, Thomas, came back from the barn.

"What did you do with your good saddle, Pa?" Thomas asked. "It ain't by the back stall where you always keep it."

"It ain't?" Jim responded. "Well, somebody musta moved it. Ask your brother, he's always settin' on it."

"Jimmy was with me in the tack room," Thomas said. "Ain't neither one of us moved it, and it ain't in the tack room, either."

"You just didn't look in the right place," his father said. "I haven't moved it, ain't had no reason to. I saw it there this mornin' on the top rail of the back stall, right where it always is. It couldn'ta just walked off by itself." He seemed not overly concerned about it.

Will, on the other hand, was more than curious. A missing horse, and now a missing saddle, that added up to something worth looking into. "How 'bout bridles, Thomas. Any bridles missin'?"

"I don't know," the boy answered. "I didn't look to see if any bridles were gone."

"I expect we'd best do that now," Will said. "Come on, I'll go to the barn with you and you can show me where your pa's saddle usually sets."

"He probably just didn't look in the right place," Jim insisted, but then realized that Will was deadly serious. He became immediately concerned as well. "You don't think . . ." he started, but didn't finish. "I'll go with you," he said.

It didn't take long to determine that the saddle in question was definitely gone, and one of Jim's newer bridles was missing as well. Jim pointed to the top rail of the stall. "Right there is where it was this mornin'," he said. "And the bridle was hangin' on the saddle horn." He scratched his head, bewildered.

As unlikely as it seemed, there was no reasonable answer other than one of the horses had been stolen. That conclusion was difficult for Jim and Hank to accept because there had been no trouble from horse thieves since before the end of the Civil War. Due no doubt to being in the business of chasing horse thieves and cattle rustlers, Will accepted the possibility at once and turned his focus toward catching the perpetrator. It might be a difficult thing to do. He didn't know how much head start the thief had, but at least he knew it was sometime after breakfast and morning chores when the saddle was stolen from the barn. He also had no description of the person he was looking for, but he was certain he could recognize the horse. *I like that gray,* he thought, *and I'm damn sure gonna go after the son of a bitch that stole him.*

The fact that only one horse had been taken, plus the theft of a saddle and bridle, made it easy to assume that probably it was a one-man job. The thief needed transportation and he came upon a herd of grazing horses that obviously were not closely watched. A gang of rustlers could have easily driven off the entire herd in broad daylight after realizing all the men at the farm were off working in the fields. A lone thief could have come to the same conclusion, slipped into the back of the barn, and taken what he needed without fear of being caught. As a matter of habit, Will began a search of the tracks close to the stall. There were many—of all sizes, some old, some new—people and horses. They had nothing to tell him—there was too much confusion of footprints. He went to the back door of the barn to see if he would have better luck where the thief probably entered. About to conclude it was a waste of time and wouldn't tell him anything that would help him, anyway, he paused when one print caught his eye. Next to the door post where a rat or some other varmint had been digging a hole, there was a clear print in the loose dirt. It was from a man's shoe and was of the approximate size of one that could have been left by Hank or Jim. The thing that made it stand out, however, was the clear impression of an X in the rear center of the heel. *Little Rock* was the thought that immediately leaped to his mind. Marshal Dan Stone had told him of a trial practice at Arkansas State Prison to help identify inmates. The shoe repair shop had undergone a program where heels on the prison work shoes were replaced with heels bearing an X burned into them like a brand. According to Dan, the program was short-lived, for they found that the heels were soon worn down so that the X was no longer there. Now Will knew that his horse thief was either an escapee or recently released from prison. And Jim was just unlucky that he had passed his farm. There was nothing he could do about it tonight, so he would see what he could find in the morning.

The women were upset to learn that someone had brazenly gone into the barn to steal while the men were all working in the fields. "What if one of us had happened to go out to the barn for something and bumped into him?" Marjorie asked. "With none of you men here," she added.

Henry and Jim did their best to allay their fears, assuring them that it was a case of a man on foot seeing an opportunity to ride, and nothing more sinister than that. Miss Jean seemed almost unconcerned about it, saying there were a lot of cowardly people in the world, and they were the ones always sneaking into barns and henhouses. She was more disappointed that Will would have to leave right away to go after the thief. "I know you have to go after the thief," she said to him, "but I don't think you've got much chance of catching him."

"You may be right," Will said. "The first thing I'll have to do is figure out which way he's

31

headed. He musta been walkin' on the road to Fort Smith, so I'll have to find out if he's headed there, or goin' the other way, toward Little Rock. I'm willin' to bet he ain't headin' toward Arkansas State Prison."

"Well, I'm sorry you can't stay around and visit for a little while at least, but I understand." She affected an impish smile for him. "If somebody hadn't stole one of your horses, I know you'd have come up with some other reason to go."

"I need to get back to Fort Smith pretty quick, anyway," Will said. "Maybe I'll catch up with my flea-bitten gray if he's headin' that way. But I'll be back before long to take those horses off your hands."

Will was up early the next morning, sitting at the kitchen table with Miss Jean and Sally Evening Star, drinking coffee and eating a biscuit with a thick slice of sowbelly inside it. He found it amazing that the two women still got up in the morning before everybody else, just as they had for so many years on the J-Bar-J in Texas. He had planned to get started before breakfast, but the two women insisted on feeding him before he set out to recover his horse. Buster was already saddled, and Will consented to linger over his coffee cup only until the sun's first rays crept across the creek and gave him enough light to look for signs. When it was time, he said his good-byes to Miss Jean and Sally and started his search, beginning at the back door of the barn.

He had to rely a great deal on guesswork, for there was no real trail that could be distinguished from the many prints around the barn. Trying to think as the horse thief might have, he picked the most likely path to strike the Fort Smith road that would provide the best chance of escaping without being seen from the house. He had decided to assume the thief's destination was Fort Smith, thinking that if he came up empty, he'd search in the opposite direction. His hunch paid off. He found what he was looking for on the bank of the creek a hundred yards of so from the house. Several prints of the *X*-marked work shoe, along with a pattern of hoofprints told him that this was where he saddled the horse he had stolen. From that point, he followed a single trail that crossed over the creek and continued on in a straight line to the Fort Smith road.

He realized his chances of catching his man were slim, but he at least felt confident that he knew where the man was heading. The thief might have an opportunity to get some new clothes, maybe buy some new boots, but if that gray horse was somewhere in Fort Smith, Will was going to find him. He turned Buster's head toward Fort Smith and nudged him into a gentle lope, a gait the gelding could sustain for a long time.

It was not yet noon when Will rode into the east end of Fort Smith. As he rode along the main street, he looked for the gray horse at the hitching posts he passed. He had no way of knowing if the man he pursued had any money or not, but he paid special attention to the saloons and general stores as he rode by. He spotted several gray horses, but not the distinctive flea-bitten gray he sought. But Fort Smith was a big town, so he began a search of the cross streets, starting with Garrison Avenue, where he stopped to check the stable at the hotel. There was no sign of the horse, so he continued on, riding along streets outside the business sections of town before heading to Vern Tuttle's stables, where he kept a couple of extra horses. It was getting along into the afternoon and Buster had done a day's work already, so Will decided to give the big buckskin time to rest. Vern was forking hay into the stalls, even though it was close to the time when he left the barn to get his supper at the Morning Glory. Vern always ate his supper early. He said he wanted to get there while the biscuits were fresh out of the oven.

"Howdy, Will," Vern greeted him. "You didn't stay long at Ward's Corner. I thought you said you'd be gone over that way for two or three days."

Will explained the reason he was back so soon

34

and asked Vern if he had seen a horse matching the gray in town the day before. "No, I ain't," Vern answered. "Could be he just rode right on through, and I ain't been no place but right here and the Mornin' Glory." He stroked his chin thoughtfully. "Could be he mighta holed up at that dump Jake Cochran runs down near the ferry slips. He wouldn't be the first horse thief that holed up there."

"Could be," Will replied. "I was thinkin' about ridin' down there after I got a fresh horse. I don't know why I didn't go see Jake when I first got here." He pulled the saddle off Buster and turned him out in the corral. "Wouldn't hurt to give him a ration of oats," he said. "I'll throw my saddle on the bay." It was easy to say he should have checked Jake's saloon first, but he had not assumed the man he was looking for was heading for anyplace in particular in Fort Smith. If he had been incarcerated at the state prison, he might not have even known that Jake's was a favorite hangout for many men of questionable backgrounds. Will had frankly counted on spotting the gray horse at one of the first saloons he came to, instead of spending a day searching every little street and lane in Fort Smith. He had purposely decided not to report in to the U.S. Marshal's office until he found his horse, in case Dan Stone had a job for him that couldn't wait. Telling Vern he'd most likely be back before he closed the stables that night, Will rode off toward the river.

Well, like I said, Will thought, *I shoulda rode straight down here to begin with.* He pulled the bay gelding up short and sat for few minutes to look at the three horses standing in the small corral behind a weathered building near the river's edge. "I believe I know you," he muttered to himself as he looked hard at the flea-bitten gray horse that plodded slowly over to the side of the corral. *Probably hungry,* he thought, *and there sure ain't nothing to graze on in that mud hole they put you in. I'll be back to get you.* In his mind, there was one thing worse than a horse thief, and that was a horse thief that didn't take proper care of his horse.

He didn't see anyone around the back of the two-story building that housed the saloon with some rental rooms upstairs. So he dismounted and walked into a small shack that he figured might be used as a tack room. Inside, he found that he had guessed right, for there were three saddles thrown against one wall of the shack. He struck a match in order to examine the saddles in the darkness of the small enclosure. Jim Smithwick's saddle was easily picked out, since it was the only one of the three that looked to be in almost-new condition and was the only one with Stagg rigging around the saddle horn. To be certain, Will looked on the left stirrup leather to find the initials *J.S.* There wasn't much doubt after that. He picked up the saddle and went back outside to the corral, where he stood for a moment to make sure he was still alone. The lack of loud noise from inside the saloon told him that it wasn't a typical day at Jake's. Since there was little chance he would be interrupted, unless someone had to use the outhouse, which was next to the corner of the corral, he proceeded to lead the gray out and saddle it. When that was done, he led his two horses around to the front of the saloon to find the horse thief.

Stepping quietly inside the door, his rifle in hand, he wasn't noticed right away by the few patrons in the saloon. So he took the opportunity to look the room over, glancing at Jake Cochran at the far end of the bar talking to an older man drinking beer. Will shifted his gaze toward the row of tables against the side wall where four men sat playing cards. Seated at a table next to them, one man was alone, watching the game. Will's gaze settled upon the lone man. He wore a battered hat and an ill-fitting jacket, like one that might have been provided for him by someone who wasn't overly concerned about the fit. *Like one that might have been given to him when he was released from prison,* Will thought. Confident that he had found his horse thief, he pushed on through the door.

Just then aware someone had walked in, Jake looked around. "Will Tanner," he grumbled, irritated by the sight of the lawman. "Somethin' I can do for you?"

"Howdy, Jake," Will returned. "How's business?" He kept an eye on the lone man at the second table, who was now showing signs of discomfort. He had evidently picked up on Jake's unfriendly reception to Will and gotten the feeling that he might be a lawman.

"Pretty good, as long as not too many lawmen start hangin' around," Jake replied. "You don't usually come to my place to get a drink. You lookin' for somebody?"

Will smiled at Jake's attempt to alert his customers that Will was a deputy marshal, in case one or more of them were on the run. None of the four men playing cards paid much attention to the tall stranger, but the lone man shifted nervously in his chair, as if to get a position to more easily get to the pistol strapped on his hip. Will walked directly up to face him. "I reckon I don't have to waste time tellin' you how fast you'd be dead if you reached for that gun. Jammed up against the arm of that chair like that, it'd be pretty hard to draw it," he said. "You'd most likely shoot yourself in the leg, tryin' to clear the holster. So why don't you just place your hands on the table in front of you, and we'll make this as easy as possible."

It was obvious to the man that Will was right. He had no chance of drawing the weapon before Will shot him, so he had no choice but to comply. "Whaddaya botherin' me for?" he complained. "I ain't done nothin'. I just rode into town this mornin'."

"Well, we've got a little problem there," Will said. "You see, you rode in on a stolen horse. Stole him off a farm in Ward's Corner, and we don't suffer horse thieves lightly in this district, especially when the horse you stole happens to be mine." Will glanced briefly at the four men at the next table to make sure there was no interference from that quarter. The card game had come to a stop, but there was no reaction from the players beyond wide-eyed surprise. Another quick glance told him that a scowling Jake Cochran had better sense than to give the well-known deputy any trouble. "Now, I want you to get up outta that chair, but keep your hands on the table," Will said. The man stood up as directed and stood hunched over with both hands still planted flat on the table. Will stepped behind him to remove the pistol from his holster.

It was at this moment, when the weapon was not clear of his holster, that the outlaw decided to make his move. He had just been released from prison after serving time for cattle rustling. If they sent him back for stealing a horse, he might be there for life. But there was also a little matter of a dead deputy lying in a pine thicket, and his dead horse left in the middle of the road. That was more likely a rope around his neck. And just when he was so close to slipping across the river into Indian Territory. He had to make an attempt to escape. Feeling his pistol slipping up out of his holster, he suddenly whirled around in a move to strike the deputy in the head. Wary of such a desperate attempt, Will blocked the blow with one arm and drove his fist into the side of the man's head, causing him to collapse across the table. Before he could recover, Will pulled the reluctant pistol from the man's holster, cocked it, and pointed it at the man's face. "Are you done?" he asked.

His head still reeling from the powerful right hand to the side of his head, the outlaw was not inclined to try again. Convinced he might fair even worse if he resisted further, he went peacefully when Will motioned him toward the door. "He owes me money!" Jake exclaimed. "Who's gonna pay the bill he ran up?"

"I reckon that'll be on the house," Will answered. "Maybe you can send the bill to the state prison in Little Rock." Outside, his prisoner was surprised to find the horse he had stolen saddled and waiting at the hitching rail. Seeing the gray ready to ride, the outlaw saw one more opportunity to possibly escape if he was quick enough to jump into the saddle and gallop. The deputy showed no indication that he was in a hurry to climb on his horse. So he went directly to the gray and reached up to grab the saddle horn. "Nope," Will said, and motioned him away from the horse. "You're gonna walk over to the courthouse." He then motioned for him to start walking up the road from the docks while he stepped up into the saddle. The few folks who happened to be out on the road leading up from the river paused to gawk at the strange sight as a deputy riding a bay and leading a gray herded a man on foot toward the courthouse.

When they arrived at the jail under the courthouse, they met Sid Randolph coming out on his way to supper. "Well, I'll be—" Sid started. "Whatcha got there, Will?"

"We got us a horse thief," Will replied. He dismounted, his Winchester still trained on his prisoner. "What's your name?" he asked the sullen ex-convict.

His prisoner didn't answer until prodded in the back with Will's rifle. "John Smith," he grunted.

Will shook his head. "I doubt that, but I reckon we'll find out after we check with the folks over in Little Rock. I thought he might enjoy a little stay in your hotel while we do. He's wearin' some work shoes with X's on the heels, so we'll see if they're missin' anybody."

"I'll be glad to have him as a guest," Sid replied. "I'll have one of my guards escort him in." He walked back to the door and called out, "Roy!" In a couple of minutes, a guard showed up to take charge of the prisoner.

"I served my time," the prisoner protested. "I got my release. I didn't bust outta prison."

"And stole a horse first thing," Will said, shaking his head in sarcastic amazement. "You musta liked it back there in Little Rock."

It was a moment of panic for Mike Lynch. He realized finally that he was going to go back to prison, no matter what, and they were bound to find out how he came by the money in his pocket. And that was going to lead to a hanging for murder. "You're makin' a big mistake, mister," he pleaded with Will. "I never stole no horse. I bought that horse from a feller between here and Ward's Corner."

"Is that a fact?" Will replied. "Well, why didn't you say so? Just show me your bill of sale and that'll settle this whole misunderstanding."

"I ain't got no bill of sale," Lynch said. "I just gave him the money and he gave me the horse."

"What was his name?" Will asked.

"Hell, I don't know," Lynch said, getting more and more frantic by the moment, knowing that his father was waiting for him in Indian Territory. He was so close to slipping over the river. If only he hadn't decided he'd like one last drink of whiskey, he would have already been in Oklahoma. "I didn't ask him his name. I was on foot. I needed a horse, and he needed to sell one."

"Well, now, there you go," Will said, well aware that every word out of the man's mouth was a lie. "You shoulda got a bill of sale from him. But Sid, here, can fix you up with a place to stay till we can run this fellow down." He nodded to the guard. "Take him on in, Roy."

Lynch realized his goose was cooked. He knew that if he went inside that jail, he was never coming out again. Roy took him by the arm and started to escort him to the door, but Lynch resisted. When Lynch balked, Sid stepped forward to lend a hand. Seeing this as his only chance, Lynch pretended to stumble and lose his balance. Sid, without thinking, stooped to help him. When he did, Lynch was able to jerk the gun out of Sid's holster. Armed now, Lynch immediately spun around to level the pistol at Will. With a cartridge already chambered in his Winchester, Will cut him down before he had time to cock the pistol.

"My Lord, my Lord . . ." Roy repeated over and over, visibly shaken by what had just happened. They were the only words uttered for a moment or two as the three lawmen stared in stunned disbelief at the dying man writhing in pain at their feet.

Will was as shocked as Sid and Roy. He had misjudged the desperation of the man, never thinking he would make such a foolish move.

But when Lynch leveled the pistol at him, he had reacted without conscious thought. Before Will could decide whether to send for Doc Peters or the coroner, Lynch relaxed in death. "Damn," Will muttered softly, still finding it difficult to believe his arrest had resulted in killing the culprit. "I reckon I'll take him to Ed Kittridge." With a hand from Sid Randolph, he lifted Lynch's body up and laid it across the saddle on the gray. Then he led it away from the jail while the two guards, as well as a man standing beside a wagon across the street, stared after him, still amazed by what had just happened.

Kittridge was eating his supper in the kitchen behind his office, but interrupted it to accept the body. Will had already gone through Lynch's pockets and was surprised to find $30. A welcome find, he thought, because as a deputy marshal, it was his responsibility to pay for burying any outlaw he killed. Out in the territory, he would have simply dug a hole and dumped the body in it. In town, however, he would have to pay for the burial. "A nameless outlaw," he said to Kittridge, "so there ain't gonna be no funeral. Just give me the cheapest box you can nail together." When he had settled up with Kittridge, Will took his horses to the stable.

Knowing he was going to have to report

his actions to Dan Stone, he came back to the courthouse to look for the marshal. He was surprised that Dan had not come down to the jail level when he heard the shot from his rifle. Several people upstairs over the jail had come out to gawk at the dead man, but Dan Stone was not one of them. When Will went to his office, he found that Dan had already gone home. "I reckon I'll report in the mornin'," Will thought, and turned his steps toward the Morning Glory Saloon. He knew he could just as well go home to the boardinghouse, but he had told Ruth that he would be gone for a couple of days. So they weren't expecting him for supper. Besides, he felt like he might like a drink or two after the happenings of the day just ended.

"Howdy, Will," Gus Johnson greeted him when he walked in the Morning Glory.

"Gus," Will returned.

"Whaddle you have?" Gus asked. "Shot of whiskey or something to eat?"

"I reckon I'll have both," Will replied. "What's Mammy cookin' tonight?"

"Soup beans and pork chops," Gus said, "and you picked a good night to eat here. Mammy made some corn bread, too. Want her to fix you a plate?"

"Yes, sir," Will answered. "That suits my taste just right."

He stood at the bar and made small talk with Gus for a while until the scrawny little gray-haired woman brought him a plate of food. As usual, it was piled high when she was told it was for Will. And as usual, Lucy Tyler came over to join him when he sat down at a table. "You want coffee?" Mammy asked.

"Yes, ma'am," Will answered. Before long, Gus came over, pulled a chair out, and sat down with them, causing Will to comment, "Looks like it's a slow night."

"I reckon," Gus said. He and Lucy watched Will eat until a couple of fellows drifted in and Gus went back to tend bar. Lucy remained until a few more of the regulars came in to drink and play cards. She got up then and paused to give Will an inquiring glance, even though he never had engaged her services. As usual, he gave her a smile and shook his head.

"I hope somebody down at that boardin'house is takin' care of your natural needs," she said in parting. " 'Cause if they ain't, you're gonna dry up worse than Mammy."

"Reckon so," Will said. Her comment sent his thoughts to Sophie Bennett, for no reason he had a right to, for Sophie was committed to take care of another fellow's needs. He had quit trying to tell himself that it didn't bother him. He watched Lucy as she walked over to a table where a card game was getting started. *One of these nights I might surprise you,* he thought. He gulped down the last of his coffee, paid Gus, and left to go home.

"I heard you shot a man last evening," Dan Stone said when Will walked into his office the next morning. "Any particular reason?"

"He was gonna shoot me if I didn't," Will replied.

"Always a good reason," Stone said, "but I hope there's more to the story than that."

Will went on to fill his boss in on the circumstances that led up to his having to cut his prisoner down on a public street right in the middle of town. "Out of all the farms and towns between here and Little Rock, that fellow was unlucky enough to steal a horse that belonged to a U.S. Deputy Marshal," Stone said, shaking his head. "Well, since it seems pretty likely he just got out of prison, maybe we'll find out who he is. I'll wire Little Rock and see if they've had anybody released or escape during the last week or so. If he was released after serving his time, like he claimed, maybe they can identify him for us." He looked at Will and grinned. "Wouldn't it be something if his name really was John Smith?" Back to business again, he said, "Knowing those folks over at state prison, I'd say it'll take a little time before they get word back to me. I expect there'll have to be a hearing on the matter to satisfy Judge Parker, but I need somebody to ride down to Durant with Alvin Greeley to pick up a prisoner, and you showed up at the right time. There ain't nobody else in town right now. Fellow named Jim Dockery, they say he killed a Choctaw woman he was living with. So they got him locked up in a smokehouse down in Durant."

"That'll take three and a half days, maybe a little less, to get down there," Will reminded him. "That's if we don't take a jail wagon. That would take a week."

"I know it, but I can get the judge to hold off on the hearing till you get back. There were witnesses that saw you had no choice but to shoot this fellow yesterday, right?"

"Yep," Will said, "two pretty good witnesses at that."

Dan smiled. "Yeah, I know. I talked to Sid Randolph this morning already and he said it was self-defense, pure and simple. He said if he and Roy hadn't got in the way, the fellow wouldn't have gotten his hand on a gun in the first place."

"None of us expected it," Will said. "I was arrestin' him for stealin' a horse. I didn't think he would take a chance like that. There might be more to this than we've found out so far." He shrugged, then paused a moment while he thought about the assignment just given him. Alvin Greeley was a good man, as far as Will had heard. One of Stone's more experienced deputies,

48

Greeley had been in the Marshals Service a long time. Will didn't mind going along as a posseman, even though he usually preferred working alone. Alvin would be sure to take a cook and a wagon to transport this Dockery fellow back to Fort Smith. He was pretty stringent about going by the rules. *Maybe it'll be nice to have a cook along for a change,* Will thought.

CHAPTER 3

Will found Alvin Greeley waiting for him at Vern Tuttle's stable early the next morning. Alvin had left word with Dan Stone for Will to meet him at half past six, so Will made it a point to be there a little earlier. In spite of that, he was greeted somewhat curtly with an air of impatience, as if he was late. They exchanged a brief howdy with a businesslike handshake. "I was hopin' to get a decent start on the day," Greeley complained first thing.

Will got the impression that Greeley implied they were getting a late start because he was late. "We coulda left earlier," he said. "Dan Stone told me to be here at six-thirty, and accordin' to my railroad watch, that ain't till fifteen minutes from now." He nodded to Vern, who was coming from the back of the barn, then turned back to Greeley. "I figured you'd most likely take a cook with a wagon. I don't see him nowhere."

"He'll be here before long, I reckon," Greeley said. "Somethin' musta held him up. I know for a fact that he got all his supplies loaded yesterday." He paused, then said, "I reckon you'll be responsible for all your supplies."

"That's right," Will said. "I've got everything I'll need right here in Vern's back room. I'll take a packhorse. Won't take but a minute to load it, and then I reckon we'll just lay around and wait for your cook to get here." He studied the rangy deputy's face, most of it hidden by a heavy black beard streaked with gray that bore witness to more than eleven years as a lawman. He had an angular body, lean with large bony hands. A broken shoulder, the result of a shoot-out some years back, had not healed correctly and caused him to slump to one side. Will had never had occasion to work with him before, but knew him by reputation. Greeley enjoyed the respect usually afforded a deputy who had survived long years of service. Will had formed no previous opinions about the man, preferring to judge him based upon his actual experience working with him. This was not the case with Greeley.

Greeley wasn't ready to trust a deputy marshal who always seemed to work alone, and Will Tanner had rapidly gained a reputation as a loner. There was something else about Tanner that bothered Greeley. It seemed to him that he had a high ratio of kills compared to arrests, considering he'd worn the badge for only a couple of years. That opinion was made even stronger when he heard about the shooting at the jail the night before. According to what he had been told, Tanner's prisoner had stolen a horse. That didn't seem a legitimate reason to shoot the man down. Come to find out, it was a horse that belonged

51

to Tanner that the man had stolen. Maybe that was the real reason he got shot before he had a chance to stand before the judge. The incident didn't seem to bother Dan Stone when Alvin said as much to him about it, however. He said Tanner had just happened to find himself in a desperate situation that had left little choice other than to shoot his way out or be gunned down himself. Stone didn't disclose the fact that he purposely sent Will on jobs that were potentially more dangerous than the average arrest, especially if the perpetrator was a known gunman. In spite of the confidence Dan Stone apparently had in the younger deputy, Alvin was determined that Will would have to prove himself to him. Further thought on the matter was interrupted with the arrival of Horace Watson and his wagon.

"Good mornin'," Horace called out cheerfully. "You boys waitin' for me?" He climbed down and extended his hand to Will. "You're Will Tanner, ain't you?" Will took the hand offered and said that he was. "Glad to meetcha." He nodded to Greeley then. "You didn't say Will was ridin' with us."

"I didn't know till yesterday," Greeley said.

"Well, I'll cook you up some good chuck," Horace said, directing his comment to Will.

"I'll be the deputy in charge," Greeley was quick to advise. "Tanner's comin' along as a posseman." He shifted his gaze toward Will to see his reaction, but there was none as Will busied himself loading his packhorse. He didn't really care who was in charge, and if it was important to Greeley, Will was content to let him call the shots. It was a routine assignment at most. The Choctaw Lighthorse had arrested the offender and locked him up. The deputies' job was a simple pick-up and transport assignment to bring the prisoner back for trial. Although Will thought it to be unnecessary, Greeley obviously thought it best to go "by the book." And that meant an extra man for backup plus a cook to feed the prisoner and deputies on the trip. With a wagon along, it was going to be a long trip, and it was going to seem longer if Greeley continued to assert his authority. At least Horace appeared to be a cheerful sort. Will supposed he could have turned the job down, but he could always use the extra money.

They left Fort Smith a little after seven o'clock, following the Poteau River toward the Winding Stair Mountains on a trek that would take them more than twice as long as it would have had they not taken the wagon. For a man accustomed to working alone, it was a tiresome trip of a full week for Will before the party reached the dusty station called Durant. For reasons that Will never could figure out, Alvin Greeley never warmed up toward him at all and seemed to strive especially hard to maintain an air of command.

Will wondered why Alvin had even considered working with him had not Dan Stone so ordered it. At least Horace Watson provided some sense of sociability.

Jim Little Eagle, Choctaw policeman, had said in his wire to Fort Smith that the prisoner, Jim Dockery, was being held in a smokehouse behind Dixon Durant's general store. That was the only place available and served quite often as Jim's unofficial jail. So the posse rode directly to the store, where they found Little Eagle drinking coffee with Durant's clerk, Leon Shipley. Jim's face lit up with a wide smile when he saw his tall friend astride the big buckskin gelding, riding beside the wagon. "Hi-yo, Will Tanner," Jim called out in greeting. "They didn't tell me who was coming down to get this man."

The Choctaw's friendly greeting to Will seemed to irritate Alvin Greeley and he was quick to inform Jim who was in charge of the arrest. "Jim," he acknowledged, "I've come down here to take your prisoner in custody. Tanner, here, came along to help out."

"How you doing, Alvin?" Jim Little Eagle replied. "Ain't seen you in a while." He nodded to Horace, who came in the door then. Back to Will then, he said, "I reckon you brought enough men to take your prisoner."

"Where *is* my prisoner?" Greeley pressed.

"He's back of the store in the smokehouse,"

Leon Shipley answered him. "And I wish you'd get him the hell outta there before he spoils the meat hanging in there. I had to leave the door open when I went back there just now."

His remark captured the attention of both deputies. "You left the door open?" Greeley responded. "Whaddaya mean? . . ." he stammered. "Is he tied up?"

Jim shrugged. "There ain't no worry about him going anywhere. You fellows might as well have some coffee and warm up a little."

"I don't think so," Greeley insisted, already impatient with the lax attitude of the Choctaw policeman and the store clerk. "We'd better take him into custody right now, before he decides to walk out of the place." He started toward the door, pausing only a brief second to motion to Will. "Come on, Tanner."

"Oh, he ain't gonna walk nowhere," Leon said as they all went out after Greeley, who was already hurrying around the side of the store. He stopped abruptly when he rounded the rear corner of the building to find the smokehouse with the door open wide. He instinctively drew the .44 he wore and proceeded with caution, unsure of what foolishness had prompted the Indian policeman to be so careless.

Like Greeley, Will was inclined to be cautious, too. He dropped his hand to the weapon on his hip, but a glance at Jim Little Eagle prompted him

55

to hesitate. Jim seemed unconcerned and walked casually in the door of the smokehouse behind Greeley, who stopped so suddenly that Jim almost bumped into him. "What the—" Greeley blurted upon finding his prisoner hanging from the center beam of the roof. He turned to face Little Eagle and demanded, "You hung him?" Openly appalled, he exclaimed, "You have no authority to hang a man!"

Jim shrugged. "I didn't hang him. He hanged himself. I reckon he didn't wanna wait for Judge Parker to hang him. And I reckon he was right in figuring a noose was waiting for him, 'cause there wasn't much doubt that he killed his wife. I expect he just decided to have his own trial and found himself guilty. That woman must have meant something to him. He did the hanging night before last. I left him there so you could see him like I found him yesterday morning."

"And now that you've had a chance to see him, how about gettin' him to hell outta my smokehouse?" Leon complained. "He dropped four hams on the floor to just lay in the dirt."

"He used the cords the hams were hanging on to make him a rope," Jim explained to Will.

"So we made a long trip down here for nothin'," Greeley grumbled, thinking about the money it cost him. There was no mileage compensation for the trip back to Fort Smith with no prisoner. In addition, it would be the deputy's job to take care of the burial of the prisoner. He looked quickly at Will, thinking it to his advantage to count him as a partner on the assignment at this stage.

Will was a step ahead of him. "Well now, Alvin, that's a helluva thing, ain't it? Come all the way down here and find your prisoner swingin' from the smokehouse ridgepole. I reckon, since this little job is all yours, you bein' the man in charge, ol' Jim Dockery cost you a helluva lot of compensation."

"That's one way of lookin' at it," Greeley said. He had planned to collect all the mileage pay from Fort Smith and back, and only pay Will the daily rate for possemen. Maybe, he was now thinking, he could soften his coolness toward the man on the long trip back, and Will might volunteer to share expenses. "We'll see how things work out on the way home," he said.

Will couldn't help smiling. He felt that he could see the wheels turning in Greeley's mind, and he was not inclined to put up with him all the way back when there was no prisoner to guard. He had been thinking about the proximity of Durant to his ranch in Texas, and the fact that he had not been back for quite a spell. He saw this as an opportunity to make a quick visit to see how Shorty and the boys on the J-Bar-J were getting along. He could make the ranch in a day and a half from here. "I'll be leavin' you and Horace here, since there ain't no job to do, anymore," he informed Greeley. "I've got other business to tend to down in this part of the territory."

"What the hell are you talkin' about?" Greeley responded, confused. "You can't quit on me."

"Sure I can," Will said. "I came along to help you transport a prisoner. You don't need any help to bury your man, and you oughta be able to find your way home without me. I'll wire Dan Stone and let him know where I am." Done with it, he walked out of the smokehouse and left Alvin Greeley standing there flustered.

"Well, I'll be . . ." Horace started, then as Will walked past him, said, "It was nice ridin' with you, Will." He had heard tales that Will Tanner was a hard man to figure out. Now he had evidence of it firsthand.

"Same here," Will replied. "Have a good trip back."

Jim Little Eagle walked out beside him. "What's up, Will? You need my help on something? I can hang around for a while if you want me to."

Will appreciated the offer. Jim had always been a good man to work with. "No, thanks, Jim, I'm just gonna take a ride down to Texas to visit my ranch while I've got a chance."

Jim nodded. "Greeley looks like he ain't too happy about you leaving. You think he might cause you trouble with Dan Stone?"

"Nah," Will replied. "And what if he does? I might decide to go back to ranchin' all the time."

He smiled and added, "And quit ridin' all over hell and back to arrest dead men."

Slim Rogers and Cal Perkins finished loading the wagon, then exchanged grins. "Reckon we've got time for a drink before we start back to the ranch?" Cal asked. The question was posed solely to razz his partner because he knew what the answer would be.

"You dern tootin'," Slim came back at once. "That's the only reason I rode into town to help you load supplies."

"Is that so?" Cal joked. "You sure fooled me. I've never known you to take a drink."

"Just climb up here and let's drive up to The Cattleman's," Slim charged. "I'm gettin' thirstier and thirstier while you're standin' there jawin'."

Cal chuckled as he climbed up on the wagon, barely able to settle in the seat before Slim slapped the reins across the horses' rumps and the wagon lurched off toward the saloon at the north end of town. There was another saloon in Sulphur Springs on the south end of the street, but The Cattleman's was the rowdiest. It also offered the opportunity to talk to a couple of women, and do more than talk if a man was so inclined and had the money to spare. With Slim and Cal, talking was more likely the prospect.

Slim pulled the horses to a stop beside the saloon where the wagon would be out of the way of the hitching rail, which already seemed to be crowded, even this early in the afternoon. "Looks like Moe's doin' a lotta business today," Cal commented as they walked into the noisy saloon. It *was* unusually busy for this time of year. The fall roundup was over, and the fat cows had been separated from the herd and driven to the railroad for shipment. That's why it was surprising to see so many idle cowhands still hanging around town. Most of them were no doubt riding the grub line, out of a job until spring.

A loud report of raucous laughter suddenly rose above the general buzz of the saloon, causing the two J-Bar-J hands to look toward a table against the back wall. "Cheneys," Slim pronounced, his tone heavy with disgust. Two of Ike Cheney's sons were sitting at the table, amusing themselves at the expense of Belle McClure, the younger of the two prostitutes who worked the saloon. It was typical behavior for all four of Cheney's sons, so it came as no surprise to Slim and Cal. Slim looked around the room to see if all the brothers were there, but he saw no one but Levi and Buck. "Those coyotes usually hunt in a pack," he said to Cal. "I reckon the rest of 'em are out stealin' somebody's cattle." It was not an idle comment. Not only the J-Bar-J, but a couple of the other ranches close by had all complained of missing cattle recently. Maybe it was purely coincidence that the reports started soon after Ike Cheney and his family moved into the territory. Maybe not.

"Hell," Cal said, "forget about those buzzards. Let's get us a drink and get on back to the ranch before Shorty sends Billy to look for us."

"Howdy, boys," Moe Garvin greeted them when they sidled up to the bar. "What'll it be?"

"We need a little drink of whiskey to keep us warm on the ride back to the ranch," Cal replied.

"Well, I can take care of that for you," Moe said, and set two glasses on the bar. "Ain't seen none of your crew lately. You been busy?"

"Nothin' special," Slim said. "Just tryin' to keep J-Bar-J cattle on our own range." He didn't elaborate on the trouble they had been having with missing numbers of cattle since the fall roundup ended. They were still trying to build up their herd, and it wasn't easy with the small crew of men they worked. Shorty had hired two additional men, Mutt Samson and Billy Wilson, to help after Will Tanner had signed on with the Marshals Service in Fort Smith. Ordinarily, that was crew enough to manage the cattle. But since the recent tendency for the cows to stray, especially along the eastern boundary of their range, Shorty was convinced they were dealing with some rustling. Since Ike Cheney had started grazing cattle close to that side of their range, it was easy to suspect that that had something to do with their missing cattle. Shorty was reluctant to make any accusations, however, until catching the Cheneys in the act. So far, that hadn't happened.

Ike's sons were well known around the little town of Sulphur Springs, Texas, even in the short time since they had shown up in the area. Most law-abiding citizens steered well clear of them whenever possible, and this was Slim and Cal's intent on this day as well. As a rule, all four brothers usually hit town together, but on this occasion there seemed to be only two, the youngest of the four, Levi and Buck. From the loud, boisterous conversation coming from the back table, however, they seemed to be creating enough noise to compensate for the absence of Rubin and Luke. Slim and Cal tossed their whiskey back, waited a few moments for the burn to die down, then ordered another. "This is gonna do it for me," Cal said. "We'd best get started back home." Slim was about to concur, but before he could say so, a loud scream pierced the noisy atmosphere of the smoky saloon. It was followed by an angry tirade from Belle McClure.

"You sick son of a bitch," she fumed as she tried to pull her arm from the grasp of Buck Cheney. Buck laughed at her efforts to free herself and clamped down harder on her wrist. "Let me go!" she demanded, frantically struggling to keep him from burning her forearm again with his cigarette. Levi, the youngest Cheney son at sixteen, laughed, enjoying his brother's methods of amusing himself.

Although reluctant to say anything to the feared Cheney sons, Moe decided he should do something. Already, sensing trouble to come, several of his paying customers were heading for the door, perhaps to find a more peaceful environment at his competitor's establishment. Moe walked back to the table. "Take it easy, boys," he said. "There ain't no call to hurt the lady."

"The lady?" Buck responded. "I don't see no lady in here. You ain't talkin' 'bout this ol' whore, are you?" He yanked even harder on Belle's wrist, causing her to fall against the edge of the table, almost knocking the bottle of whiskey over.

"We ain't payin' for no bottle of whiskey this ol' whore spills," Levi said.

"Come on, fellers," Moe pleaded. "There ain't no use to get rowdy. Why don't you let Belle go?"

" 'Cause she's supposed to be in here to entertain the customers," Buck replied. "And I aim to be entertained." Belle made another attempt to escape his grasp and was slammed down hard in the chair for her effort, an act that seemed to tickle Buck's younger brother.

"I swear," Levi said, chuckling, "you do have a way with women, brother Buck."

"That's a fact," Buck said, then turned to Moe. "Now, you can drag your sorry ass back over behind that bar and mind your own business. This business is between me and the whore."

Belle protested again at this point. "There ain't gonna be no business between me and you," she complained. "Now let me go."

"I'll let you go when I'm done with you," Buck blurted, and tightened down again on her already bruised wrist.

"There ain't no call to hurt her," Moe said in one last feeble attempt before retreating to the bar.

Witnessing the disgusting display of bullying was too much for Slim to ignore. "That just ain't right," he muttered to Cal. "Ain't no reason Belle should have to put up with them two bastards." Determined to come to the woman's assistance, he started toward the table. Cal caught him by the arm before he could take more than a step, but not in time to escape Levi's notice.

"Well, now, mister, you got somethin' to say?" He turned to his brother. "Look here, Buck, we got us a genuine hero who's fixin' to save this whore's honor." He rose slowly to his feet, his hand hovering close over the .44 he wore.

"It sure looks like he's thinkin' about it," Buck answered. A grin spread wide across his unshaven face as he released Belle's wrist and got up from the table. "All right, mister, you called the game." Those customers who had not already cleared out, backed away from the center of the room to get out of the anticipated line of fire. It was not the first time one of the Cheney boys had called out an unwitting cowhand in what amounted to a simple execution. Forgotten now by her antagonist, Belle moved quickly behind the bar to take cover behind Moe.

Slim found himself caught between his sense of honor and the stark awareness that he might be facing certain suicide if he did not turn tail and run. Cal, realizing that Slim was no match for either of the two gunmen, and neither was he, knew that he was a player in this deadly game as well. "Just hold on a minute," he implored. "There ain't no reason to let this get outta hand. And there sure ain't no call for anybody to get shot over a little argument. Slim wasn't callin' anybody out. Slim don't do things like that."

Unfortunately, Cal's attempt to reason with the two gunmen only intensified Buck's and Levi's desire to spill blood, especially since it was apparent the two facing them were not experienced gunhands. "Well, now," Buck said, "I'm callin' him out. Everybody heard him call me a dirty name. You heard him, didn't you, Levi?"

"I did," Levi said. "He called you a low-down dirty name."

"So I reckon you're gonna have to back it up," Buck said to Slim.

"I never called you no name," Slim said.

"Now you're callin' me a liar," Buck said. "So I'm fixin' to step out in the street and wait for you to come on out, and we'll see who's lyin' and who ain't." He waited for Slim to accept the challenge, but Slim was frozen in a state of panic. "If you don't come outside," Buck taunted, "I'll shoot you down right where you stand, you no-good son of a bitch. You're wearin' a gun, so you'd best be drawin' it, or crawlin' outta here like the cowardly dog you are. What's it gonna be?"

Cal could not let it go any further without trying to reason with the smug bully. "Look here, Cheney, there ain't no sense in this. Slim ain't never drew that pistol for any reason except to maybe shoot a snake or somethin'. Why don't we just forget this little disagreement and get on about our business?"

"That sounds like the sensible thing to do," Moe piped up, anxious to defuse the issue.

"The hell it is," Levi Cheney snarled, his gaze locked on Cal. "This is between Buck and this other feller, and anybody else butts in is gonna answer to me." His warning was enough to cause Cal to hesitate. There was little doubt that Levi hoped he would make a move to help Slim.

Buck grinned when Cal stepped back to the

66

bar. His full attention back to Slim again, he said, "You called me a dirty name and a liar to boot. I don't let a man get away with that. So go for that gun you're wearin' or I'll shoot you down where you stand."

Left with no choice, Slim tried to steady his hand, but he seemed to be paralyzed with fear as he stared helplessly into the sneering face of Buck Cheney. The single-action .44 resting on his hip suddenly seemed unusually heavy, when before he had barely noticed it. He wanted desperately to run, but he knew to do so would brand him a coward. His life was over, no matter which choice he made, so he stood frozen, knowing he was about to die. There was a long moment of total silence in the saloon until broken by the lethal sound of the cocking of a Winchester 73. It was followed immediately by a simple warning. "Pull that weapon and I'll cut you down before it clears the holster."

No one had noticed the arrival of the man in the doorway until that moment. "Will Tanner!" Cal gasped in surprise when he turned to discover the rangy, sandy-haired rifleman who had suddenly appeared. Hearing the name, Slim came close to fainting, but managed to turn to see that Cal had not seen an illusion. It was in fact Will Tanner, and had he appeared with wings on his back, he could not have looked more like an angel, even with a Winchester rifle in his hand.

The tense situation having been changed in an instant, the two Cheney brothers found themselves in an uncertain position. They were too recent to the little Texas town to know who they were now facing. At any rate, whoever he was, he had a definite advantage with a rifle cocked and aimed before they had a chance to reach for their weapons. Judging by the intense gaze he fixed upon them, it seemed likely that his warning was no idle boast. When he spoke, it was in a calm and even tone. "Like the man said, there's no call for gunplay. So I reckon it's best for you two to clear outta here now before somebody gets hurt."

Emboldened by the fact that the stranger seemed intent upon a peaceful solution to the face-off with the cowhands from the J-Bar-J, Buck was reluctant to back down completely. "Looks like you got the jump on us with that rifle," he scoffed. "I wonder how tough you'd be in a fair fight."

"You ain't likely to get a chance to find that out," Will replied. "Now, I'm startin' to lose my patience with you two. If you're so damned anxious to see who can draw those pistols and kill somebody the fastest, why don't you go out in the street and face off against each other? Maybe some of this crowd will go outside to watch the show. Maybe it'll be a draw and the town will get rid of both of you. So get movin' before I decide to do that little favor for the town, myself." He might have considered putting them in jail for disturbing the peace, but he was in Texas, not Oklahoma. He had no authority here. Aside from that, the last time he was in Sulphur Springs they didn't have a sheriff, much less a jail.

"Mister," Levi said when his brother seemed stumped for a response, "you don't know who you're messin' with. You ain't seen the last of us, and next time we'll see who gets the jump on who."

"Get movin'," Will replied.

Moe Garvin spoke up then. "They ain't paid for that last bottle they drank."

Will nodded. "Pay the man." He directed the command toward Buck.

Still sulking over losing face before the customers in the saloon, Buck reluctantly dug into his vest pocket for the money and slammed it down on the bar. When Slim and Cal both stepped aside to give him room, Levi saw it as the opportunity he had been waiting for. Confident with the knowledge that he was faster than any of his brothers, he reached for the .44 riding on his hip when everyone looked toward the bar—everyone but Will Tanner. Levi *was* fast, fast enough to raise his pistol almost to the point where the barrel would clear the leather holster before he doubled over with the impact of the rifle slug that tore into his abdomen.

Once again the barroom was struck dumb as everyone recoiled from the sudden report of the Winchester. Buck, as surprised as everyone else, turned to see his brother sink slowly to the floor, grasping feebly at the bar for support. His first reaction was to reach for his gun, but he got only as far as dropping his hand on the handle when he locked eyes with Will. "Do it and you're a dead man," Will calmly said.

Buck realized then that in the instant Will had fired the fatal shot, he had already cranked a new cartridge in the chamber and was poised to squeeze the trigger again. "Hold on!" he bellowed, and immediately raised his hands. Will directed Cal to lift the gun from Buck's holster, in case he decided to make the same foolish move that Levi had. Frantic then, Buck looked at his brother lying on the floor, a scarlet pool of blood spreading rapidly under his body. "Levi!" he cried out helplessly, seeing blood coming from Levi's stomach and mouth from the wound high in his midsection. Levi tried to speak but could not form the words until finally he quit trying and they knew he was dead. When Buck saw that his brother was gone, he looked up at Will and said, "You're as good as dead when my pa and my brothers find out you killed Levi. You ain't gonna get away with this."

"He had a choice," Will said, "and he picked the wrong one." He motioned toward the door with his rifle. "A couple of you fellows help him carry his brother outside to his horse and lay him across the saddle." To Buck, he said, "I expect you'd best be goin' about takin' care of buryin' him." He walked along behind them with his rifle trained on Buck. Once Buck was in the saddle, Will took his pistol from Cal and put it in one of the saddlebags on Levi's horse. "Now you get along home and tell your pa the straight of it."

"You're a dead man," Buck blurted as he kicked his horse hard and headed out of town, leading his dead brother's horse behind him.

The gathering of spectators stood behind Will, watching until Buck disappeared past the end of the ridge below the town. Only when they were sure he was gone, did Cal and Slim descend upon the man who was once their boss and still half owner of the J-Bar-J. "Will Tanner," Slim exclaimed. "I ain't never been so glad to see someone in my whole life! I thought you was one of them whatcha-call-its. You know when you think you're seein' somethin' that ain't really there."

"Like a ghost or spirit," Cal supplied for him. "What the hell are you doin' here, Will? Shorty ain't said nothin' about you comin' home."

"Shorty doesn't know," Will said. "I was sent down to Durant to pick up a prisoner to transport back to Fort Smith. Choctaw Lighthorse had him locked up in an old smokehouse. I guess the fellow didn't like it much 'cause when I got there I found out he'd hanged himself. Since I had no prisoner to transport back, I wired my boss and told him I was gonna take a few days to tend to some business. I didn't have any idea when I'd be back down that close to the Red River, so I thought I'd slip on over the line and pay you boys a visit. It's been a while since I've been back."

"It has been a while," Cal agreed. "And I'd say you picked a mighty fortunate time to visit."

Will grinned and said, "I reckon. Looks to me like you boys need somebody to keep you from gettin' into gunfights." He paused to give Moe a friendly nod when the owner of the saloon walked over to say howdy. "Who were those two?" Will asked.

"Good to see you again, Will," Moe said. "They was two of the Cheney bunch that moved onto that range between here and the Red. I'm sorry they were in town, but it's damn lucky for Slim and Cal that you showed up. I'm afraid you mighta stirred up some big trouble for yourself when you tangled with those bastards, though."

"I didn't see that I had much choice," Will said. "Looked to me like the big one was fixin' to shoot ol' Slim, here." He winked at Cal and joked, " 'Course, Shorty might notta even noticed he was gone." He turned serious then. "I don't like havin' to shoot anybody, but like I said, I couldn't see any way to avoid it."

"I ain't sure we weren't bound to have some trouble with that bunch, anyway," Cal said. "Ever since they showed up in this part of the country a couple of months ago, a few of the ranches have been missin' some cows. And it seems like the J-Bar-J has lost more'n our share."

"How many of 'em are there?" Will asked.

"It's all one family," Slim said. "I ain't sure if they've got anybody else on their payroll. But all we know about is the old man, Ike Cheney, and his four boys."

"Three now," Cal reminded him.

"And there ain't a meaner bunch of coyotes in all of Texas," Slim went on. "I heard they moved into an old line shack on Kettle Creek. Their mama's livin', but ain't nobody in town ever seen her. There's a daughter, too. She's been in town a couple of times. Moe says she ain't a helluva lot different from her brothers."

"That's a fact," Moe interjected. "She came in here one time and ordered herself a drink of whiskey, pretty as you please. Stood right there at the bar and knocked it back just like a man would."

"Where'd they come from?" Will asked.

"Don't know for sure," Moe said. "They ain't ever said, at least not to me."

It was certainly not the best of situations to have ridden into. And if that prisoner in Durant had not hanged himself, Will would have been on his way back to Fort Smith instead of speculating about the possibility of more trouble with the Cheneys. That was, of course, idle thought because, had that happened, Slim, and possibly Cal, would be lying dead instead of Levi Cheney. It's just the way things worked out. Will wasn't the only one thinking, what if? Both Slim and Cal were considering what a craving for a drink of whiskey had almost cost them. They were more than ready to drive the wagon back to the J-Bar-J, and grateful to have Will riding along beside them.

Like Cal and Slim had been, Shorty Watts was profoundly surprised to see the familiar sight of the tall rider on the big buckskin horse walking beside the wagon, as it ambled back into the yard. His first thought upon seeing Will was to hope his partner had decided to quit the Marshals Service and was coming back to raise cattle. He soon found out that it was not the case, however, with Cal and Slim both eager to relate the confrontation in The Cattleman's. "I don't know if I've caused you any trouble or not," Will said. "Maybe that fellow is all talk, but he was sure aimin' to shoot Slim down. At any rate, I think I'll hang around for a while in case they plan to come lookin' for revenge." After hearing about the incident in town, Shorty was relieved to hear Will was planning to stick around.

After the trouble with Ike Cheney and his sons was discussed, Shorty filled Will in on the status of the ranch. Will was frankly impressed, because he had no high expectations for Shorty when he had left him to run the J-Bar-J, after Jim Hightower had been killed and Miss Jean moved to Arkansas. At the time, his hope was that Shorty, with Slim and Cal's help, could manage to maintain a small operation, enough to keep them off the grub line. Now he was surprised to find that they had increased the size of the herd considerably and Shorty had hired on two more men. "Not only that," Slim informed him, "we got us a cook, too. She ain't the cook Sally Evenin' Star was, but it sure beats what we were doin' for ourselves."

"She can sure bake good biscuits, though," Cal added, "and that's one place where she outshines Sally."

"Well, that's the main thing, all right," Will said with a grin.

"You boys drive the wagon on up to the house and unload it," Shorty said to Cal and Slim. He turned to Will then. "I expect you're wantin' to take care of your horses. I'll go with you to the barn." They walked together toward the corral as Will led Buster and his packhorse behind him. "I see you're still ridin' ol' Buster," Shorty commented.

"Yep," Will said. "I ain't found no other horse that can stand up to him."

Something else occurred to Shorty then. "Me and Cal and Slim have been bunkin' in the house ever since you left. We'd best make some room for you to bed down. Cal and Slim can double up, or one of 'em can go down to the bunkhouse. I opened up the bunkhouse when I hired Mutt and Billy on. We're all eatin' at the kitchen table, though. I figured that was easier on Anna."

"No need to do that," Will insisted. "The bunkhouse will be just fine for me. I don't figure to be here but a few days, anyway. Ain't no use in movin' everybody around. Hell, I always stayed in the bunkhouse when Boss and Miss Jean were still here."

"You sure you're all right with that?" Shorty asked. "Don't seem right, I mean, for the owner of the ranch to have to sleep in the bunkhouse."

"Half owner," Will reminded him, "and a non-workin' one at that."

"All right," Shorty said with a chuckle, "if you're sure you don't mind."

After Will's horses were taken care of, they went to the house and sat down to talk over a cup of coffee. It was served by Shorty's cook, Anna Sanchez, a Mexican woman whose husband had been killed when he came off a bucking horse headfirst and broke his neck. A pleasant woman of uncertain age, Anna offered to fix them something to go with the coffee, but Will declined, saying he could wait until supper. He couldn't help noting the irony of the circumstances that brought her to the J-Bar-J, since it had been a bucking horse that widowed Miss Jean as well. The thought must have entered Shorty's mind, too, for he asked if Will had had any opportunity to visit the widow of the original owner, Jim Hightower.

"As a matter of fact," Will answered, "I do have occasion to see Miss Jean once in a while. I pick up extra horses from time to time, and Miss Jean's brother lets me pasture 'em on his farm about a half-day's ride from Fort Smith. I just came from there before ridin' down to Durant. She's gettin' along just fine livin' there with her brother's family. Her father, Mr. Ward, died last winter."

"I'm right sorry to hear that," Shorty said.

"From what they told me, they were expectin' him to go before long. He'd been ailin' for quite a spell. I think Miss Jean took it pretty well. I believe she was glad that she had a chance to visit with him for a little while before he died."

"Well, that's good. You say you're pickin' up some horses?" Shorty asked.

"I've got about twenty good horses now, fifteen of 'em with Miss Jean up in Arkansas. When I make an arrest, there's almost always some extra horses involved, and sometimes it's about the only profit I can show, so I keep 'em for myself. I figure that sometime in the slow part of the year, one or two of you boys could ride up to Fort Smith and help me drive those horses back here. Now that you've hired on some extra help, you can spare one of them."

"I could at that," Shorty said. "I've got two pretty good men, Mutt Samson and a young boy named Billy Wilson. You'll meet 'em tonight when they come in for supper. Me and Slim and Cal were doin' all right before we started missin' cows. That was the main reason we took on two extra hands to keep an eye on all the cattle, mainly those in that section to the east, next to the north ridge."

"You pretty sure they're the ones rustlin' the cattle?" Will asked.

"I'm damn sure," Shorty said. "I'll put it this way, we weren't missin' cattle before they turned up in this territory. Trouble is, we ain't been able to catch 'em at it. What I think they're doin' is cuttin' out some of our cows and some of Thompson's and Williamson's, too, all on the same night, and drivin' 'em over to the stockyards in Fort Worth to sell. There's buyers over there that ain't too particular about the brands, as long as the price is right."

"Maybe we can put a stop to it," Will said.

"We've all been ridin' night herd for the past week, tryin' to catch the bastards in the act, but we ain't had no luck so far," Shorty lamented. "They're pretty slick about it. Makes me think they've had a lot of experience at it. I don't know where they came here from when they drove that first herd over on Kettle Creek. It wasn't much of a herd, no more'n about forty or fifty head. I told the boys to keep an eye on 'em, make sure their cows didn't start mixin' in with ours. We ain't never caught 'em over on this side of the ridge, but that little herd they started with sure grew in a short time."

"Maybe we can ride over that way and get a look at the brands on some of their cows," Will suggested.

"Well, we mighta could have," Shorty said. "But they ain't got no herd right now. They just drove 'em to market. We've all been ridin' night herd to try to keep the bastards from buildin' up another herd to sell."

"I reckon I can help you with that while I'm here," Will said, disappointed to hear it was too late to check the brands.

CHAPTER 4

"Damn you!" Ike Cheney roared. "You come ridin' back here with your brother's body over his saddle and tellin' me the man who shot him ain't dead?" Buck Cheney cringed before his father's wrath, his face tinged red, a result of the vicious backhand delivered by the angry man.

"I couldn't do nothin' about it, Pa," Buck whimpered. "We didn't even know he was there, holdin' a rifle on us. Levi shouldn'ta tried it. He cut him down before he could clear leather."

"You sorry excuse for a man," Ike ranted on, his anger rising with each utterance out of Buck's mouth. "At least Levi didn't shame me and his brothers by backin' down." The rest of the family stood silently watching the old man expend his fury upon the unfortunate son. None dared speak in his defense, not his mother, nor his two brothers, nor his sister. "What's this man's name?" Ike demanded.

"I heard one of them J-Bar-J fellers call him Will Tanner," Buck answered. "I ain't never seen him before, but they acted like they knew him."

"Is he still in town?" Ike pressed.

"I don't know," Buck replied.

"You don't know?" Ike railed, his temper rising again. "You didn't even go back to look for him, just ran home with your tail between your legs, weren't man enough to avenge your poor brave brother." He looked away from the cowering brute at his feet as if he couldn't stand to look at him anymore, and cast his accusing gaze on his other two sons. "How many other cowards have I wasted my life raisin'?" No one dared to answer, except one.

"Why don't we just go find the son of a bitch and kill him?" Ike's daughter, Hannah, asked. "An eye for an eye."

"An eye for an eye!" Ike echoed, raising his voice in righteous anger. "Maybe I better send my daughter to find this murderer." He looked at his wife, Lorena, sitting on the floor, with Levi's head propped on her lap. She moaned softly as she rocked slowly back and forth. There were no tears in her eyes for her youngest. The years living with Ike Cheney had long ago drained any tears she might have saved to shed upon her children.

"Hell, I'll go to town and find him," Hannah said.

Ike's angry countenance momentarily took on a look of pride and his voice calmed slightly. "I know you would, darlin', but you'd best help your mama clean Levi up and get him ready for buryin'. Rubin and the boys can go look for this jasper and settle up for your brother." He paused then and turned to glare at his sons. "Well," he demanded, "what are you standin' around for? He ain't gonna come lookin' for you."

"We're goin', Pa," Rubin answered at once. "I didn't know if you meant right now, or after supper."

"After supper?" Ike echoed, furious. "You ain't got no more brains than Buck. The man killed your brother. Who knows where he'll be while you set around eatin' supper? Get saddled up and find that murderin' dog."

"Yes, sir," Rubin said. "We'll get goin'. Come on, Luke." He hesitated a moment more. "Whaddaya want us to do with him?"

Ike looked as if about to explode again, bewildered by the asinine question from his eldest. It took him a moment to find words before replying. "Why, buy him a drink and tell him it was a fine shot that killed poor Levi." When Rubin seemed confused, not recognizing the sarcasm in his father's retort, Ike roared, "Shoot him down like the dog he is, you damn fool! Now get outta here and go find the son of a bitch!" He stood clenching his teeth as he watched his three surviving sons file quickly through the kitchen doorway.

When the door closed behind them, he turned to look at his dead son, who had shared his favoritism with his daughter, Hannah. He had considered Levi to be more like him when he was sixteen, fearless and brash, more so than his other sons. Rubin was heartless and cruel, but he was decidedly slow-witted, and had to be told what to do. He was respected by his brothers, however, solely because he was the eldest. Luke seemed to have inherited many of his mother's tendencies, silently obeying orders with the same display of emotions whether it was to kill a man, or kill a chicken for supper. Ike nodded in silent approval. Then he thought of Buck, and his anger began to flair again. Buck was a bully, a trait that Ike was not critical of. But this time, it was Buck's bullying that got Levi killed. It should have been Buck lying dead on his kitchen floor instead of his younger brother. "Let's get him on the bed, so you can clean him up," Ike said to his wife. He reached down, took Levi's arm, and pulled him up to let his body fall onto his shoulder. Despite his years, he was still powerful enough to carry his son into the room the boys shared and lay him on the bed. "Get some water and a cloth," he ordered Lorena. When Hannah followed them into the room, he said, "You go ahead and get some supper started, sister. I'm gettin' hungry."

"Oh hell," Moe Garvin muttered when he saw them come in the door of the saloon. Buck Cheney was back and two of his brothers were with him. He was not at all surprised to see them, knowing full well the purpose of their visit. But he had hoped they would take their business directly to the J-Bar-J. He moved down toward the end of the bar, closer to the shotgun he kept underneath, praying that he would have no occasion to use it. As usually happened, the barroom suddenly grew quiet when the Cheney brothers walked in. They paused just inside the door to look over the small crowd of customers before coming directly to the bar, openly pleased by the cautious silence their entrance caused.

"You see him?" Rubin asked.

"Nope," Buck replied. So they moved down the bar to confront Moe.

"Evenin', boys," Moe greeted them as cautiously as he could affect.

"I'm lookin' for the bastard that shot my brother," Rubin announced. "Where is he?"

"I ain't got no idea," Moe said, and nodded toward Buck. "He left here right after you did."

Rubin turned to Buck then. "What did you say his name was?" When Buck replied, Rubin turned back to Moe. "Will Tanner," he repeated. "Is he stayin' here in town somewhere?"

"I don't know," Moe said. "I don't think so." He knew perfectly well where Will Tanner most likely had gone. He was out at the ranch he owned with Shorty Watts. There were a few others in the saloon who knew who Will was, but like Moe, they were reluctant to tell the Cheneys for fear it would mean a death warrant for him.

Luke Cheney stood with his back to the bar,

studying the faces of Moe's customers, now silent while every ear was tuned to the conversation at the bar. He was accustomed to the way a saloon quieted down when he and his brothers walked in. But this crowd seemed especially tense. It occurred to him that maybe everybody in town, except him and his brothers, knew who Will Tanner was. "You know what?" he said to Rubin. "I think these jaspers are playin' us for fools. I think they all know this feller, and they're coverin' up for him."

Rubin turned to study the crowd then. "By God, you might be right," he said. Turning back to face Moe, he ordered, "You'd better start talkin' and I mean right now, or me and my brothers are gonna start takin' this saloon apart, piece by piece, and skull by skull." He reached over, grabbed Moe's shirt, and pulled him halfway across the bar. "You're wastin' my time."

"I don't know where he is," Moe insisted frantically. "I swear, he rode outta town right after your brother did. He didn't say where he was headin'."

Several men decided it was time to leave when Rubin snatched Moe across the counter, causing Luke and Buck to draw their weapons. "Ain't nobody leavin' this saloon until we find out where Will Tanner is," Buck threatened. Then, to Moe, he said, "You'd better start talkin' right

85

now." When Moe still hesitated, Buck whipped his .44 up and fired it, shattering a large mirror hanging behind the bar. He then drew a bead on a large lamp on a stand near the end of the bar.

"Wait! Wait!" Moe cried out. "Will don't live around here no more. He was just passin' through."

"Is that so?" Rubin responded. "Well, I'm thinkin' you know where he was headed when he left here, and I'm tired of wastin' my cartridges on mirrors and lamps." He stuck the muzzle of his pistol against Moe's forehead. "If I don't get some straight answers, I'm fixin' to start bustin' some heads, and yours is the first."

"Hold on," Sam Harvey spoke up. He had been sitting, a silent witness to the altercation up to this point. Like Moe, he was reluctant to give the Cheney brothers any help in their hunt for Will Tanner. But the situation had progressed to a dangerous point and he feared someone was going to have to step in before Moe lost his life. "Will Tanner is a U.S. Deputy Marshal," he said, hoping that would serve to discourage them from going forward.

"Who the hell are you?" Luke demanded.

"I'm the town's undertaker, and I own the barbershop," Sam answered.

"What are you talkin' about? Whaddaya mean he's a U.S. Marshal?" Rubin responded.

"I mean he's an official U.S. Deputy Marshal," Sam replied. "So it's a lawman you and your brothers would be goin' after." When he saw Rubin and Luke hesitate and exchange uncertain glances, he continued. "You fellows don't wanna cause the Texas Rangers to come lookin' for you, do ya?"

Although his question obviously created some cause for second thoughts, it was for only a moment. "I don't give a damn if he's a lawman or not," Luke blurted. "I don't care if he's the president of the United States. He killed my brother, and he's gonna pay for that." He turned to face the undertaker. "And anybody protectin' him is gonna pay, too. I'm gonna start shootin' if one of you bastards don't tell me where this Tanner feller stays when he comes to town." He aimed his pistol directly at Sam's head. "I'll kill everybody in this whole town if I have to."

"The J-Bar-J!" A shrill voice from the kitchen door called out. They all turned to see Ellie Garvin standing in the doorway. "For God's sake, take your quarrel where it belongs," she screeched. "Nobody here had anything to do with killing your brother."

Like everyone else in the saloon, Rubin stood speechless for a few moments after the unexpected outcry from the kitchen. Then a slow smile spread across his face. "Well, now, looks like the lady's got more sense than the lot of you. The J-Bar-J, huh? Is that where he stays, ma'am?"

Moe answered for his wife. "Ever'body knows Will Tanner ran the J-Bar-J before Jim Hightower died."

"How come you didn't tell us that when my brother asked you where he was?" Buck challenged. "You said you didn't know where he was."

"I didn't know where he was headin'," Moe quickly replied. "Hell, I didn't know he was in town till he walked in the door today. And I didn't have no idea if he was goin' out to the J-Bar-J when he left here. Still don't. He mighta just been passin' through here on his way back to Fort Smith. That's where he stays."

"Why, you lyin' son of a bitch," Rubin growled. "I oughta shoot you, anyway, for wastin' my time." He pointed his pistol at the bartender and cocked the hammer back, causing Moe's wife to cry out again.

"You pull that trigger and I'll shoot you down, myself," Ellie threatened and produced a double-barrel shotgun that had been propped just inside the kitchen door.

"I believe you would," Rubin said, laughing again at the woman's spunk. He released the hammer on his .44 and slid it back in his holster. "Come on, boys, let's take a little ride out to the J-Bar-J."

"Wait a minute," Luke said, looking directly at Moe Garvin. "What was that you said about Tanner stayin' in Fort Smith?" Moe shrugged, but didn't answer. "If he's a marshal ridin' outta Fort Smith," Luke continued, "he ain't got no business in Texas. He's just another drifter when he's on this side of the Red." His assumption captured his brothers' attention right away.

"I swear . . ." Rubin muttered. "That is a fact, ain't it?"

"That's right," Luke said. "Them Oklahoma lawmen ain't nothin' but dead meat when they come into Texas. Let's get goin'."

Convinced that the three of them were no longer about to murder everyone in the saloon, Moe was encouraged to mention the destruction of his property. "You fellers oughta pay me for that mirror you shattered. That mirror cost me seventy-five dollars."

His request caused the three brothers to pause before reaching the door. "You'd best count yourself lucky it wasn't nothin' but that mirror that got shot," Luke said. Then when the fancy lamp sitting on the stand near the end of the bar caught his eye, he drew his .44 and shattered it with one shot. "There," he crowed, "ain't that better? Now everythin' matches." His action drew a chorus of rough guffaws from Rubin and Buck. They filed out of the saloon, leaving

89

a collective sigh of relief from Moe, Sam, Ellie, and the rest of the customers.

Outside, the three Cheney brothers climbed on their horses. "That oughta tickle Pa when he finds out it's been Tanner's cattle we've been stealin' all along," Buck said as he threw his leg over and settled down in the saddle.

"Maybe we ought not kill him right off," Luke joked, "just burn a new brand on his behind, like we do with his cows."

A little before dark, Mutt Samson and Billy Wilson had ridden into the barnyard at the J-Bar-J just as Will and Shorty were coming from the stables. "Any sign of those rustlers?" Shorty asked as the two men dismounted.

"Nope," Mutt answered. "Didn't look like they paid us a visit, at least not along the north ridge where me and Billy checked today." He eyed Will with curiosity, waiting for Shorty to introduce the solemn stranger. "Musta been Thompson's or Williamson's turn last night," he said, referring to the two closest ranchers to the J-Bar-J.

"Musta been," Shorty agreed. "This here's Will Tanner," he said then, nodding toward him. "Mutt Samson," Shorty announced to Will. "This scruffy-lookin' young feller with him is Billy Wilson."

"Will Tanner," Mutt echoed, and took the hand Will offered. "I've sure heard a-plenty about you.

I thought you was somebody Shorty made up. I'm glad to meet you."

"You can't believe half of what Shorty says," Will replied. "I thought everybody knew that."

Will and Shorty went on up to the house then to eat supper while Mutt and Billy took care of their horses before joining them. Will was pleased to find out that Slim had not exaggerated when he praised Anna's ability to bake biscuits. They were on equal footing with Ruth Bennett's biscuits back at the boardinghouse in Fort Smith. The comparison caused his thoughts to wander momentarily to Ruth's daughter, Sophie, and her upcoming wedding to Garth Pearson. He was happy to be distracted right away by a question from Mutt Samson.

"You aimin' to ride night herd with us, Will?" Mutt asked.

"I don't know. I thought I would," Will replied. "That would let us cover a little more of our range, but I ain't sure they'll be out rustlin' tonight after what happened in the saloon." He looked over at Shorty. "I ain't sure what would be the best thing for me to do, since I mighta brought some trouble down on us in town."

"I've been thinkin' about that," Shorty said. "The old man is gonna have more on his mind than rustlin' a few cows. You think they might be payin' us a visit here at the house?"

"I don't know," Will answered. "If they're as

mean a bunch of snakes as you say, they might try something like that. And if they do, I'd like to be wherever they show up. They might be more apt to try to catch me off by myself, watchin' the cattle, instead of takin' their chances in an open gunfight. I'm hopin' they don't connect me to the J-Bar-J, so you boys won't have to deal with 'em at all."

Puzzled by the conversation, Mutt glanced back and forth between Shorty and Will before interrupting. "Somebody tell me what you fellers are talkin' about. Who's liable to try what?" Slim told him about the incident in The Cattleman's. "I swear . . ." Mutt drew out, trying to picture which brother was called Levi.

"Levi was the youngest," Cal said. "And the old man ain't gonna be too happy when he finds out about it."

"Cal's right," Shorty said. "The old man ain't gonna set still for this. He's gonna be lookin' to settle the score with you." He turned back to Cal. "Does he know who Will is? Did anybody call Will by name?"

"I don't think so," Cal said. "Nobody had time to do much talkin' about anything when Will suddenly showed up." He looked to Slim for confirmation.

"That's right," Slim said, trying to recall the exact moment when Will had appeared at the saloon door, a moment when he thought he was facing sudden death at the hand of Buck Cheney. It was hard for him to remember anything but the sneering face taunting him. "Everything happened so fast, when Levi went for his gun and Will cut him down. They didn't know who he was. And Buck didn't ask his name. He was too busy worryin' about his brother. I don't think he had time to think about anybody's name before he rode outta town." Neither Cal nor Slim recalled everything about that fateful moment, most importantly the fact that Cal had blurted out Will's name the moment he walked in.

"Sounds to me like the other Cheney boy don't know who shot his brother," Shorty said. "But the only place they'd go to look for Will would be back in town. Somebody might tell 'em who he is and where to find him."

"There weren't nobody in there that mighta claimed knowin' Will but Moe Garvin and Sam Harvey," Slim said. "And they ain't likely to tell."

"You're probably right," Shorty said. "Moe wouldn't set 'em onto Will if he could help it. Sam wouldn't, either. And I don't reckon there's any reason for all of us to ride night herd again tonight. If it is the Cheneys that have been raidin' our cattle, they're gonna be busy havin' a funeral tonight."

It was settled then—only one man would ride night herd that night, and the unlucky one who drew the low card was Mutt. The rest of the crew were looking forward to a welcome break from a routine that they had been following for most of a month, when they first started missing cows. Instead of cutting out a fresh horse to ride night herd, Will left his saddle in the barn and stowed his saddlebags and his war bag of personal items in the bunkhouse with Billy Wilson. Since only Billy and Mutt were sleeping in the bunkhouse now, Will had a difficult time finding one of the rolled-up straw ticks that wasn't infested with bugs. He finally settled for his own bedroll on the wooden bunk. After another talk with Shorty regarding the general progress of the ranch, Will returned to the bunkhouse, where Billy was already snoring. He crawled into his bedroll and tried to get comfortable on the boards, but soon concluded that this might be a long night. Still, he preferred the hard planks to being eaten alive by what appeared to be a healthy colony of bugs in the old straw ticks. The fire in the little stove had long since died out when finally he succumbed to his need for sleep.

It was well past midnight when Luke Cheney rode his horse up beside the house and threw a flaming torch crashing through the window of the parlor. He then galloped back to join Buck and Rubin at the corner of the corral where they waited with rifles ready. Always the reckless one, Luke had volunteered to make the bold dash across the open barnyard to set what they hoped would be a blaze big enough to burn the ranch house down. Whether it succeeded in destroying the house or not, they figured they could count on it to bring the occupants running outside, where they would be easy targets. Although it was Will Tanner who had actually killed Levi, the three brothers decided that the rest of the J-Bar-J hands should share the blame. Having no knowledge of the recent hiring of Mutt Samson and Billy Wilson, they anticipated dealing with only three men in addition to Tanner. It seemed the opportunity to clean out the J-Bar-J and take possession of the ranch and cattle. There was no one to stop them from taking what they wanted, no law in the territory beyond that occasionally seen from the Texas Rangers, who were too far away to worry about.

After having watched the place for a good while, it had appeared that any activity at the ranch was concentrated in the house. There was a building below the barn that looked to be a bunkhouse, but it appeared to be deserted. At least there was no smoke coming from the one stovepipe extending from the side of it. The three brothers had concluded that Will Tanner and the others would most likely be sleeping in the house, anyway, so that was where they concentrated their attack.

"Good work," Rubin said when Luke reined his horse to a sliding stop beside the corral and hurried over to join his brothers.

"See anybody?" Luke asked anxiously as he fell in between them and brought his rifle to bear on the door of the house.

"Not yet," Rubin replied, "but there ain't hardly been time."

"What if it went out?" Buck wondered, referring to the crude torch Luke had fashioned using a tree limb, rags, and gunpowder he emptied out of some cartridges.

"Even if it did," Rubin answered him, "the noise from that broke window oughta wake somebody up. Hell, I could hear it from here." He was hoping for better results from the burning torch, however, for the idea of burning the house down had been his. And he felt sure his father would be proud of him for thinking of it. A few minutes later an excited exclamation from Buck brought him satisfaction.

"Look yonder!" Buck blurted, and pointed toward the house when a glow of flame suddenly bloomed in the window.

"Hot damn!" Luke exclaimed. "Won't be long now!" All three got set to aim their rifles.

Inside the unsuspecting house, the only person to have heard the window breaking was Anna Sanchez, who was sleeping in the bedroom next to the parlor. Not sure if she had heard something or not when first awakened, she lay there for a few minutes, listening. Then smelling smoke, she got out of her bed and opened the door to discover flames consuming the sheer curtains Miss Jean Hightower had hung when her husband built the house. Screaming an alarm, she ran to the back of the house and banged on Shorty's door, awakening him as well as Slim and Cal in the other bedroom. They ran to the parlor while she ran to the kitchen to get the bucket of water she had drawn to cook with in the morning in case the pump was frozen.

By the time she returned to the parlor with the water, the fire in the curtains had caught one corner of the carpet on fire. "Throw that water on the curtain!" Shorty yelled to Anna while he and Cal rolled the carpet up over the part that was on fire and smothered the flames. He looked around the room, but there was no other sign of fire. It was then that he saw the broken glass and the remains of the torch lying under the window. He yelled to Slim to stop when he reached for the front doorknob. "Don't open that door!" Shorty exclaimed, realizing that the fire had been deliberately started. "Somebody's waitin' for us to come out that door! Grab your rifles!" he called after them. "And bring mine with you." He remained behind to try to get a look at what might be awaiting them outside.

On his hands and knees, he crawled under the front window, then raised up just far enough on the other side to peer out into the yard. "Stay down till we find out what's goin' on," he told Cal when he handed him his rifle. "Anna, you stay away from the windows."

"See anything?" Cal asked.

"No," Shorty answered. "Too damn dark." He thought a moment before saying, "I don't know if Will and Billy know we've got company, so I think I'll make sure." He levered a cartridge into the chamber of his rifle and fired a shot through the broken window. "That oughta wake 'em up, if they ain't awake already."

"What the hell?" Buck Cheney blurted when he heard the rifle shot. "Whadda they shootin' at? They can't see us."

They waited, watching the house for someone to come outside. When it became obvious that their plan to burn them out had failed, Luke said, "They put the fire out. They ain't comin' outta there." Although coming to him after the fact, it occurred to Rubin that it might be a good thing that the house failed to burn down, since his father might have been planning to move in after they killed everybody. He didn't choose to confess his revelation to his brothers.

"Whaddaya reckon they shot at?" Buck still wanted to know.

"Most likely just fired a shot to let us know they was ready," Rubin answered him. "Damn it," he cursed, disappointed that his ploy had failed to provide the easy targets he had envisioned. But he was also relieved when he thought about the hell he might have caught from his father for the stupid plan to burn the house down. "Ain't nothin' left to do but make it hot for 'em, and maybe we'll get lucky and hit one of 'em." He pulled his rifle up to his shoulder and aimed at the front window. "Let's give 'em a dose of lead," he said.

For the next five minutes, they set off a steady hail of .44 slugs, peppering the front of the house, splitting out chunks of wood and shattering the windows, but to no effect beyond that. The besieged crew of the J-Bar-J was not only secure in the sturdy ranch house Jim Hightower had built, they were now returning fire from a couple of the broken windows. At this point, it appeared to be a standoff as the Cheneys continued to use up their ammunition. "This ain't no good," Luke finally announced. "I'm gonna be outta cartridges pretty soon if we keep this up. We gotta figure a way to get 'em to come outta the house."

"What if we go back to the barn and run their horses off?" Buck suggested. "They might have to come out to try to stop us."

"Good idea," Rubin said. "You and Luke go back and open the stalls and the corral and run the stock out. I'll stay here and wait for 'em to come outta the house."

The two younger brothers moved back from their positions at the corner of the corral. Hunkered over to keep a low profile, they ran along the back rails of the corral to the back door of the barn. Inside the darkened interior of the barn, they were met with a sudden eruption of gunfire that dropped both men to the ground, dead. "Careful," Will cautioned, and both he and Billy dropped to one knee, watching the barn door to see if anyone followed the two lying on the floor. When they had been awakened a few minutes before by the single shot fired by Shorty, Will guessed they might be under attack. A few minutes later, they heard the barrage of gunfire on the house, so he and Billy slipped out a back window of the bunkhouse. It didn't take long to determine where the snipers were positioned, and they moved quickly toward the barn to get behind them.

Not sure how many were in the attacking party, they waited in the barn for a few moments longer, listening to see if the shots upon the house continued. When they did not, Will figured the two just shot were the only shooters, or there was possibly one more and he was running. Chambering another round in his Winchester, he moved cautiously through the barn door toward the corral, arriving at the back corner too late to stop the lone figure galloping away in the dark. He threw one shot after him, knowing it was wasted. "There were three of 'em," he said to Billy. "Go light a lantern and we'll take a look at those two in the barn." Billy went at once to get a lantern, and Will called out to the men in the house. "Come on out, Shorty! It's all over. Anybody hit?" In a few moments, everyone but Anna was gathered around the two bodies in the barn.

Will had naturally assumed from the first that their attackers were Cheneys, and a moment later his suspicions were confirmed. In the light of the lantern, he recognized Buck as the instigator of the trouble in The Cattleman's that took the life of one of the Cheney brothers. "I know who the ugly one is," he said. "He was with the fellow I shot in the saloon." Cal informed him that the other body was Luke, leaving only one of Ike Cheney's sons alive.

"That would be Rubin that rode off. And there's gonna be hell to pay when he gets back and tells his pa that two more of his sons have been killed," Shorty predicted. "It's hard to say what he'll do about it, but I guarantee you he ain't gonna let it pass without doin' something." He looked at Will and shook his head, concerned. "So I'm tellin' everybody to keep your eyes open, especially those in the back of your head."

"I think you're right, Shorty," Will said. "And

I reckon I'm the cause of this trouble, so I think it's up to me to take care of it."

"I reckon you could say I'm the cause of it," Slim said. "You just showed up in time to save my bacon."

"That's right, Will" Cal said. "We'da been a whole lot better off if you had just let Buck Cheney shoot ol' Slim." He could not resist making a joke, even in circumstances so dire. No one laughed.

"I'm the one they want," Will continued. "And so I think it's best if I make it easier for them to find me. If I don't, none of us will be safe away from the ranch for fear of gettin' shot in the back."

"Whaddaya thinkin' about doin'?" Shorty asked.

"Well, I reckon I'll set up some bait to draw 'em out, and away from the J-Bar-J," Will said. "We'll load these two up and I'll take 'em into town. I'll have Sam Harvey nail a couple of coffins together and we'll set 'em up in front of The Cattleman's, stick a sign on 'em sayin' this is what happens to rustlers in Sulphur Springs." He thought about that for a moment, then added, "I'll sign it, 'Will Tanner, Sheriff.' "

Shorty didn't say anything for a second or two, then commented, "Yeah, I reckon that'd do it, all right, or you could just stick that Winchester up under your chin and pull the trigger."

"I'm gonna have to draw them out, or some of you are gonna get a bullet in the back," Will insisted, ignoring Shorty's sarcasm. "Now, tell me what I'm up against with Rubin and the old man."

They all participated in painting a picture of the fierce old man who headed the Cheney clan. And by the time they had all made their comments, Will had a pretty good idea that Ike might be harder to fight than all of his sons. Shorty, Cal, and Slim all agreed that Ike Cheney would keep coming after Will until one of them was dead. He would have to deal with Rubin as well, but it was Ike who posed the greatest threat. "Well, I reckon we'll see what'll happen when we put his two sons up for everybody to gawk at," Will said. "I figure he'll come through town on his way here, so I'll have to be in town early to give Sam Harvey time to nail a couple of coffins together. If Ike Cheney is as crazy as you're tellin' me, though, we might still have a visit from him tonight."

"That shack they're stayin' in is about twenty miles from here," Shorty said. "By the time Rubin gets there it's gonna be pretty close to daylight. There ain't likely to be enough time for Ike to get back here before mornin'."

"Yeah," Will said when he thought about it. "You're right, but we'd better stay alert for the rest of the night, just in case Rubin decides to come back for another try instead of riding back to tell his daddy." It seemed unlikely, since he had run the first time. "And I'd best get into town early in the mornin'," he repeated.

With no way to know if Rubin would return that night seeking vengeance, there was no choice but to remain in a state of readiness for another raid. No one was in a mood to go back to bed, anyway, so Anna built the fire up again in the kitchen stove. The temperature had not dropped to the point where the pump was frozen, so she was able to start a pot of coffee. It was not quite ready when Mutt rode back into the yard, having heard all the shooting that had taken place. "It sounded like a war had broke out over here," he exclaimed when he saw Billy coming out of the back of the barn. "I heard it from the other side of the north ridge." When he heard what had happened, he went in the barn to gawk at the bodies with Billy, who gave him an excited description of his and Will's reception for Luke and Buck Cheney. "Well, I'm sorry I missed all the fuss," Mutt said.

"Yes, sir," Billy said. "There was a lot of shootin', all right, but it's all over now. Will said we'd best be watchin' for that one that ran to come back, just in case."

When they went to the house to join the others, Shorty told them to help Slim and Cal carry some boards from the stack of lumber in the back of the barn. "Pick up a couple of hammers and some nails and cover those windows. Maybe that'll keep some of the wind out." He was calculating that it would probably take several weeks to get replacement sashes for the broken windows. "Then I reckon you can come on in the house and get some coffee. Ain't nobody gonna be sleepin' no more tonight."

CHAPTER 5

It was still dark when Rubin rode a weary horse splashing across Kettle Creek to approach the rustic cabin on the west bank. Without taking the time to tend to his horse, Rubin stumbled over the low threshold in his haste to get inside. He found his father sitting in the lone rocking chair before the fire where he had remained all night, awaiting his sons' return. "Pa!" Rubin cried out, dreading to tell him of his failure. "It was an ambush! They was waitin' for us!"

"Where are your brothers?" Ike asked, his voice deadly and calm, having already suspected the reason for Luke and Buck's absence, his eyes seeming to glow red from the reflection of the fire.

"There was too many of 'em," Rubin pleaded. "They musta hired on a bunch of men. It weren't just them three that we've been watchin', they've hired on a lot more that was waitin' in the bunkhouse, I reckon."

"Where are your brothers?" Ike repeated, his gaze burning into Rubin's soul.

"There was more of 'em set up in the barn, waitin' for Buck and Luke, and they never had a chance. They shot 'em down."

"But you got away," Ike said.

"I had to fight my way out," Rubin lied. "And I was about outta cartridges. I had to run for it. There weren't nothin' I could do to help Luke and Buck—they was already dead."

Ike said nothing for a long moment while he continued to study his eldest son's face, trying to decide if he was telling the truth about an ambush. The way Rubin was cowering before him as he told his version of what had happened at the J-Bar-J served only to raise the angry fire in Ike's veins. In a few seconds, his overpowering frustration spawned a rage that screamed for vengeance, and the only object to vent his passion upon was his sniveling son kneeling before him. Suddenly he struck out at him with his fist, the blow landing flush against Rubin's jaw, knocking him to the floor. After a few more moments passed, with Rubin afraid to move, Ike snarled, "Get up from there and get outta my sight, before I take a gun to you." Rubin wasted no time in obeying. Already resigned to the beating he had expected, he rolled over out of his father's reach before scrambling to his feet and heading for the kitchen. He almost collided with his sister, who had been awakened by his arrival and was on her way to the front room, where her father was seated.

Stopped by the sight of the lump already growing on the side of Rubin's jaw, she asked, "What happened to you?" Then before he could answer, she asked, "Where's Buck and Luke?" When he told her the same story he had just told their father, she showed the same sympathy as Ike had. "He oughta shot you," Hannah said. "You're lucky he didn't have a gun handy." When Rubin tried to excuse his actions, she cut him off. "Get your sorry behind outta here before he decides he wants his gun, because if he does, I'll sure as hell fetch it for him." Rubin knew it would be to no avail to try to plead his case to her, so he continued on through the kitchen to the tiny addition built onto the back of the cabin. Until this night, it had been the bedroom for him and his brothers. He was hungry, but decided it best not to mention it at this point.

Hannah went into the front room to find her father still sitting by the fireplace, staring, unseeing, at the front door. She didn't speak at once, but seeing that the fire was dying out, she picked up an iron bar they used for a poker and stirred up the coals before placing a couple more pieces of firewood on them. Only after there was a healthy flame again, did she turn to face her father. "I shoulda been the one that went over there to find that son of a bitch," she said. "They didn't get him, did they?"

He looked up to meet her gaze, the fury in his eyes turning now to pure frustration. But all he said was, "Rubin didn't say."

Like her father, Hannah did not have to be told

that Will Tanner was still alive. Rubin's whipped-dog demeanor when he slinked back to the cabin was announcement enough that they had failed. "It ain't over," she said. "Not as long as I can ride a horse and shoot a gun. I guarantee you, I'll see that he pays for the mistake he made when he decided to take on this family."

Ike looked up at her, wishing as he had many times before, that she had been born a man, for he believed that, of all his offspring, her veins alone were filled with 100 percent Cheney blood. Her brothers had been born with too much Mashburn blood from their mother's side. His eyes softened just a hair when he spoke to her. "I'll see to the rightin' of this wrong, myself," he said. "It ain't for you to do. I shoulda knowed your brothers couldn't take care of it. Now I ain't got nobody but Rubin to help me provide for this family." Although three of his sons had been killed, his sense of loss was more deeply seated in the knowledge that they would no longer be available to help rustle cattle. Their mother would do enough mourning for their deaths. "I'll take care of Mr. Tanner," he said to his daughter. "I need you to help your mama. When she finds out about Buck and Luke, she'll be moanin' like a sick cow." He paused to give Hannah a reassuring nod, then said, "You might as well wake her up, I'm gettin' hungry." Then he remembered something else. "Your mama was wantin' one of the boys to ride into town this mornin' to pick up some supplies, flour, and lard, and such. Maybe you'd better do that. I'd send Rubin after 'em, but I want him here right now. I ain't through with him yet."

"Whatever you say, Pa," Hannah said. "But I'd just as soon ride over to the J-Bar-J with you."

"I ain't ready for that yet," Ike said. "First, I need to find out how many guns I'll have to face. If there's as many as Rubin says, I don't wanna ride into no damn ambush like him and his brothers rode into."

"Is that a fact?" Sam Harvey asked when he read the crude sign Will had printed with a small paintbrush from Sam's workbench. "I mean, I thought you were a deputy marshal over in Indian Territory. Are you taking on the job of sheriff here in Sulphur Springs?" It seemed an obvious question to ask, considering the size of the town. There was only the one general store, Sam's barbershop, the stables, a blacksmith, one church, and two saloons. There was no sheriff's office or jail, and certainly no one willing to pay a sheriff's salary.

"Not permanently," Will said. "Just for a day or two. What do I owe you for these two boxes you call coffins?" Billy had offered to stay and give Will a hand, but Will sent him back to the ranch in case Cheney and his surviving son showed up there again. He figured it wouldn't hurt for Shorty and the boys to have another gun available.

"Two dollars," Sam replied, aware of the sarcastic tone of Will's question. "You said you didn't want anything fancy," he added in defense of the hasty construction. "And you didn't give me much time to make 'em. What are you gonna do with 'em now?" He stepped back as if to take another look at his presentation of the bodies in the open coffins. "You sure you don't want me to clean 'em up a little? Ol' Ike Cheney ain't gonna be too tickled when he sees 'em like this."

"Nope. They'll be just fine just like they are." Will peeled off two dollars and handed them to Sam. "Now you can give me a hand to tote these two over to that tree next to The Cattleman's," he said, taking hold of one end of Buck Cheney's coffin. The cottonwood he referred to was the only tree close to the road at the north end of the town. Close to the saloon, it offered the only place where the coffins could be propped up where they wouldn't be missed by anyone passing that way.

"Whaddaya taking 'em to the saloon for?" Sam asked as he picked up the other end.

"So everybody in town can have a chance to say good-bye before they're buried," Will said.

Knowing that the deputy was obviously joking, Sam walked the coffin out the door with him. "You're fixin' to set 'em up so everybody can

111

gawk at 'em, ain'tcha? Ol' Ike ain't gonna like that very much. The fact that they're dead is gonna rile him enough without putting his sons on public display. He's liable to come lookin' for you."

"You reckon?" Will replied facetiously. "Set your end down. We'll prop him up against the trunk. We can set his brother up right beside him." With Buck in place, they went back to get Luke. By the time they returned with the second body, a few people had already discovered the gruesome display. Fred Morris walked out of his store to ask Will if he was really going to be the sheriff. "Maybe," Will answered, "but not for long." His answer left Fred confused, but Will thought it best not to let anyone in on the ruse. He had been obliged to tell Moe Garvin what he had in mind, since he was setting his bait up so close to his saloon. Moe wasn't too enthusiastic about the plan, but agreed to it as long as Will stationed himself there to face any trouble it caused.

Once his bait was in place, Will took Buster down to the stable and told Caleb Smith to water and feed him. Then he walked back to the saloon. He was not at all sure if his plan would work, but he was hoping it would draw Ike Cheney's attention away from the J-Bar-J. The best solution to the problem would be if Cheney decided to take what was left of his family and move on to someplace else, but Will knew there

112

was little chance of that. Based on what he had learned about the old man, he expected that he would be satisfied with nothing short of complete revenge. The possible flaw in his plan was the likelihood that Cheney wouldn't find out that his sons' bodies were on display. He might not come through town on his way to the ranch. *Maybe,* Will thought, *I should have just gone out to Kettle Creek to find Rubin and hold him somewhere until the Texas Rangers could be contacted to come and get him.* After all, Ike Cheney had actually done nothing to be arrested for, unless it could be proved he was stealing cattle. "Hell," he muttered to himself, as he stepped up on the porch of the saloon, "we'll just wait a little while and see if anything happens."

"I was beginning to wonder where you were," Moe said when Will walked into The Cattleman's. "I thought you said you were gonna stay right here as long as those bodies are damn near on my front porch. I'm settin' myself up for a whole passel of trouble if Ike Cheney thinks I had anything to do with settin' those damn corpses so close to my saloon."

"I am gonna stay here," Will replied, "and right now I need something to eat. I ain't had my breakfast yet. Is your wife cookin' this mornin'?"

"Same as always," Moe said, and called his wife. "Ellie, you got a customer wantin' some breakfast."

In a minute, Ellie came to the kitchen door. "Oh, it's you," she grunted, apparently not pleased by the bait Will had set up so close to the saloon. "Whaddaya want, some eggs and ham? I've got some biscuits. I already threw the grits to the hogs."

"Eggs and ham and a couple of biscuits will do just fine, if you've got some coffee to go with it," Will said. She turned and went back into the kitchen.

When she returned with his breakfast, she set the plate before him and said, "You never said how you wanted 'em, so you're gettin' 'em over easy."

"I'll take 'em any way you fix 'em," he said, "just as long as they're cooked."

"Pay Moe for 'em," she said, and returned to the kitchen.

"I don't think your wife likes me very much," Will said to Moe when he sat down at the table to talk while Will ate.

"She likes you all right," Moe said. "She just don't like it too much when you hang around. That killin' in here yesterday got her to thinkin' bad things happen when you're around." Will took a gulp of coffee to wash a bite of biscuit down before reminding Moe that there was going to be a shooting in his saloon whether he had showed up or not, only it would have been Slim Rogers dead instead of Levi Cheney. "I tried to tell her that," Moe insisted. "But you know women."

"I don't reckon I do," Will said truthfully, thinking of the brief experience he'd had with the opposite sex.

With no one to feed now but the four of them, Hannah was thinking she might need to revise her list. She wasn't in the mood to go to buy supplies. She was more of a mind to take some restitution on the man who had destroyed her family, but they had to eat. Like her father, she didn't expect to miss her brothers, but she was damn mad that their livelihood would be shorthanded. They weren't getting rich in the cattle business as it was and now there were only Pa and Rubin to carry on the family business. They had a little money on hand since they had just sold some cattle, but it was going to be hard to get more with just her and Rubin to help her pa.

Damn useless boys, she thought. *First time they come up against a gunhand like Will Tanner, and all three of them got killed.* It didn't help that her father was getting long in the tooth, either. *Well, I reckon it's up to me now, and I know damn well I can handle it.* Her thoughts were interrupted then when she spotted the two odd-shaped boxes leaning up against the big cottonwood just north of The Cattleman's. She'd never seen them there before, so she kept a curious eye on them as she closed the distance between her and the tree. There were two young boys standing before them, looking at the boxes.

The road took a wide curve around the cottonwood, and as she drove the wagon around it, she could see that the boxes had no lids. *They look like coffins,* the thought occurred. A few yards farther brought her to a spot where she could see the contents. She hauled back hard on the reins, almost causing the horses to rear up when she saw the remains of her two brothers. Stunned by the lifeless eyes that stared, unseeing, at her, she was frozen for a long moment before she was able to force her brain to function again. She was at once furious that someone had seen fit to put her brothers on display. There had been no attempt to make the bodies more presentable. Their eyes were still open, their clothes disheveled and stained from the great loss of blood from several wounds on each one. This was no doubt the work of Sam Harvey. He was the undertaker, and surely the maker of the coffins. Her shock rapidly gave way to rage, and she vowed to repay the man for his disrespect.

When she climbed down from the wagon, the two boys decided it better to leave, judging by the look of fury they saw in her face. "Wait," she commanded, stopping them in their tracks. "What does it say?" she demanded, pointing to the sign someone had lettered and leaned against Buck's coffin. None of her family had been to school, so none could read. When the boys hesitated, she commanded, "Read it to me."

There was something about the woman's face that told the boys it might be unwise to ignore her and run away. She looked to be a woman, with her long hair, but she carried herself more like a man. Dressed in men's clothes, she even wore a gun belt with a pistol on one hip and a long skinning knife on the other. One of the boys, who appeared to be the older, read the sign for her, pronouncing the words slowly and distinctly, "This is what happens to cattle rustlers in Sulphur Springs, Will Tanner, Sheriff."

"Sheriff?" she exclaimed, surprised. "Will Tanner." She spat the name out as if it were a foul thing on her tongue. "He's a dead man." She stood, transfixed in her fury for a moment before seeming to remember the boys' presence. "Get the hell outta here before I put a bullet in your head," she hissed. "No, wait!" she ordered, stopping them before they could flee the scene. "Pick up the end of that coffin." She tilted the top of Luke's coffin over and caught it in her hands and waited while the two boys strained to pick up the other end from the ground. Amazed by the woman's strength, the boys managed to lift their end of the coffin and hold it up until Hannah could slide it into the wagon. Then they repeated their efforts and guided the other coffin in beside the first one.

Figuring it worth a try for their efforts, the older boy, the one who had read the sign for her, risked offering a suggestion. "Mr. Morris, down at the general store, would give me and Raymond a penny apiece for helpin' load supplies."

Never one to suffer children or pets, Hannah drew the skinning knife from her belt and retorted, "Get your sorry little asses outta here before I cut your ears off." One step toward them was enough to send them running.

Her one thought after the bodies of her brothers were removed from public humiliation was to seek out the man who was responsible for their death. No longer concerned about the supplies she had come to town to buy, she climbed back on the wagon and drove it straight to Sam Harvey's barbershop, where she found him in the process of giving the Reverend Edward Garrett a haircut. Even though the times when she had been to town were few, Hannah Cheney was easy to recognize and was often the topic of amused comments whispered behind her back. One look at her face told Sam that this was not a friendly visit. She had obviously seen the coffins, and since she was a formidable threat, he stepped around behind the chair to position the preacher between himself and the obviously infuriated woman. "Is there something I can do for you,

Miss Cheney?" he asked politely, knowing full well the reason for her visit.

"Yeah, you son of a bitch, there's something you can do for me. Who told you you could stick my brothers at the edge of town like a damned circus sideshow?"

"Now, don't blame me," Sam replied at once. "It wasn't my idea at all. I never had anything to do with it, anyway. I just sold him the coffins. He did the rest, I swear. He wouldn't let me clean 'em up or nothin'."

"Him bein' Will Tanner," Hannah charged in contempt. "Damn Oklahoma marshal, callin' hisself the sheriff, is he? He ain't no damn sheriff in Texas. Where is he?"

Stunned to that point by the blunt language of the woman, Reverend Garrett had been struck wide-eyed and speechless. Finally finding it difficult to listen to her profanity without reprimanding her, he found his voice. "Look here, young lady," he blurted, "that's no language for a respectable woman to use. You should be ashamed of yourself."

Hannah recoiled as if just noticing him. "Who the hell are you?" she demanded.

"He's the preacher of our new church," Sam answered for him.

"The preacher?" Hannah responded, staring hard into Garrett's eyes. "Well, let me tell you something, Preacher," she said, and drew her skinning knife from her belt. "You set there with your mouth shut, or I'll geld you, so you can sing like an angel when you get to heaven."

Shocked, Garrett started, "Why, I never . . ." but could not finish when Hannah drew the .44 she wore on her hip and aimed it at his nose. He sat there in terrified silence until she turned her attention back to Sam again.

"Where is Will Tanner?" she demanded.

"I swear, I don't know where he is," Sam replied. "He mighta took a room over The Cattleman's, but I don't know that for sure."

Without holstering her pistol, she turned abruptly and marched out of the saloon. "Hell hath no fury . . ." the preacher mumbled to himself, still in shock.

Sam wiped the beads of sweat away that had suddenly appeared on his forehead. "That's the maddest I've ever seen a woman in my entire life," he said. "I don't know where Will is right now, but he'd best be ready for a heap of trouble."

Will had not taken a room at The Cattleman's as Sam Harvey had speculated, preferring to sleep in Caleb Smith's stable with his horse while he remained in town. Much to Ellie Garvin's distress, however, he did declare Moe's back corner table to be the temporary Sulphur Springs sheriff's office. "Whaddaya gonna use for a jail?" Moe wanted to know.

"I ain't sure right now if I need one," Will replied. "But if I do, I'm thinkin' about that storeroom on the back of your saloon. You ain't usin' it for anything, are you?"

"Well, no, not right now." Moe hesitated, almost as uncomfortable with Will's presence as his wife was. "But I might need it before long."

"Well, I don't expect to be needin' it, or your table here, for very long," Will tried to reassure him. He figured to see Ike Cheney and his son Rubin in town as soon as word got to them that Luke and Buck were in boxes at the north end of town. His official plan was to attempt to arrest them. Realistically, however, he antici-pated a gunfight, and hoped that he would still be standing when it was all over. Practically thinking, he knew as long as there were two of the Cheney family alive, the town of Sulphur Springs and the surrounding ranches would be in danger of rustling and murder. Apparently, it had become his lot to take care of the problem. The one dilemma he had failed to consider was Hannah Cheney, and the first hint of it came in the next minute.

"Uh-oh," Moe muttered, standing at the front window of the saloon. He turned toward Will, who was sitting in the unofficial sheriff's office drinking a cup of coffee. "Here comes your first official business, and it ain't gonna be no picnic."

"Cheneys?" Will asked, getting up from his chair.

"The daughter," Moe answered. "She's comin' this way, and she don't look like she's comin' to get a drink. I don't see no sign of Rubin or the old man, but it looks like she's got those two coffins in the back of her wagon."

That was disappointing news to Will, for he was anxious to get the issue settled with the Cheney men, so he could get back to Fort Smith. He had no choice but to listen to the daughter's complaints about having her brothers on display, he supposed. But at least she should take the news back to her father, and that was all he had planned for. This would turn out to be his first exposure to Hannah Cheney's method of complaining.

He remained standing by the back table, waiting until she appeared in the doorway. Expecting to hear the irate complaints of a grieving woman, he was taken completely by surprise when she pushed through the door, her .44 revolver still in hand, and upon spotting him, immediately started shooting. As soon as she raised the weapon, his reactions had been automatic. Consequently, he had been quick enough to turn the table over and dive for cover behind it while bullets were flying all around him, gouging the heavy tabletop and ripping splinters from the wall behind him. The only thing that saved him, however, was the woman's rage, causing her to empty her gun in her haste to punish him. She seemed startled when she heard the click of the hammer on an empty cylinder. Well aware of his good fortune, Will was quick to take advantage. He charged toward her before she could even think about reloading, so she threw the empty weapon at him, which he easily dodged. He reached her as she was pulling her knife from her belt, and lowered his shoulder, driving her back through the door to land on the porch. The impact of her body against the boards knocked the wind out of her as she fought frantically to retain possession of her knife.

He wrenched the skinning knife from her hand and stood back while she struggled to her hands and knees and tried to get breath back in her lungs. She had not even asked if he was Will Tanner, just assumed as much and opened fire. He glanced at the wagon behind her and saw the coffins in the back. His bait was gone, but his message would be sent. When she started showing signs of recovering, he gave her warning. "If you get up from there, I'm gonna knock you flat. I'm gonna let you get by with tryin' to shoot me. I'll give you that for losing your worthless brothers. So get on your wagon, take your brothers back, and bury them. There's been enough killin' over this trouble, and there will be no more cattle stolen from the J-Bar-J and Williamson's and Thompson's range. Take that message back to your pa, then you and your family can move on outta this territory. If I find you still in that cabin on Kettle Creek tomorrow, I'll clean you out like I would any other pack of coyotes. You understand?"

Knowing she had been whipped, she said nothing for a long moment while still struggling to get her wind back. Her voice seemingly subdued, she spoke then. "I'll have my gun back, and my knife."

"Sorry," he replied. "I've got a rule that says anytime women try to kill me, they don't get their weapons back. Get on your wagon now, and get on back home. And the lot of you be gone tomorrow. I might not be in such a forgivin' mood like I am today." She made no move to resist, got to her feet, and with his rifle aimed at her back, walked outside. Consumed by sullen anger, she climbed up on her wagon, moving slowly as she favored the soreness in her muscles, a result of his tackle.

A hell of a note, he thought as he stood watching her until the wagon was out of sight. *I come back here for a visit, and I end up destroying a whole family.* It was not something that would weigh heavily on his conscience, however, no more than the destruction of a nest of rattlesnakes might. He reminded himself that the J-Bar-J and the town of Sulphur Springs were in danger as long as Ike

Cheney and his kin were in the vicinity. The next step would be to wait for Ike's move. He and Rubin would either show up here in town, or they would figure their losses great enough and move on. Will hoped they would move on. At any rate, he knew his job was to wait them out and ride out to Kettle Creek in the morning if they didn't show up in town tonight. His thoughts were interrupted then by a question from Moe Garvin.

In the midst of the sudden assault by the irate woman, Will had forgotten the owner of the saloon. "What the hell am I gonna do if Ike Cheney and his son come back here and shoot the place up? I've already lost a mirror and two lamps, and look at that table that woman shot to pieces." He came out from behind the bar, where he had taken cover during the shooting, in time to meet his wife coming from the kitchen.

"I thought we were all gonna die!" Ellie exclaimed, still holding the shotgun she kept in the kitchen. She calmed down a little when she saw that her husband was all right, then turned her attention to Will. "Will Tanner, I've always found you to be a fair and reasonable man. But if you stay in Sulphur Springs much longer, I'm afraid we're all gonna be dead. I know Moe won't say it, but I will. We'd appreciate it if you'd take your temporary sheriff's office someplace else. Maybe the Dixie House has a table for you down the street."

Will knew she was deadly serious in her request, and he felt bad for her, but he tried to explain that to leave The Cattleman's now would leave them on their own when Ike showed up. "I'm really sorry, Ellie, but I can't leave Moe to face Ike Cheney by himself. If he's gonna come lookin' for me, this will be the first place he'll look. And if he does decide to come after me, he won't take long to do it. If he doesn't show up today, I'll ride out to his place in the mornin', and I hope we'll settle it out there."

She knew he was right, but at a loss for a reply, she turned abruptly and returned to her kitchen. *Ain't nothing as enjoyable as a visit to the old home place,* Will thought facetiously.

CHAPTER 6

Ike Cheney was standing outside the cabin when Hannah drove the wagon across the shallow creek and pulled up before the door. Hearing her arrive, Rubin came from the cabin to stand behind his father, although not too close. He was still wary of a sudden fit of rage from the old man. Without a word, Hannah stepped down from the wagon seat, walked around to the back, and dropped the tailgate. Then she stood back for them to see. Expecting to find supplies to be carried into the cabin, both father and son were stunned to discover the wagon's gruesome cargo. "How did you? . . ." Ike stammered, but he couldn't finish, unable to understand how she could have gotten the bodies. "They was shot at the J-Bar-J," he said, and turned at once to confront Rubin, who was as baffled as his father. "Leastways, that's what you told me."

"They was," Rubin insisted. "They shot 'em in the barn." He continued to gawk at his two brothers.

"You went to the J-Bar-J?" Ike turned back to Hannah. "I sent you to town."

"I went to town," Hannah said, speaking calmly. "That's where I found 'em, stood up against that big tree near The Cattleman's, propped up for ever'body to see. There was a sign that said this is what happens to cattle rustlers and murderers in Sulphur Springs. It was signed by Will Tanner, and it said he was the sheriff." She waited then to see her father's reaction, knowing it would be as she imagined.

"That son of a bitch," Ike growled through teeth clinched in overpowering anger. "He's got the whole town stirred up against us now." The knuckles of his hand were turning white from the tightness of his grip on the side of the wagon as he gazed down at his two dead sons. "Did you see Tanner?" he asked after a moment.

"Yeah, I saw him," Hannah answered, then told them about her confrontation with the deputy marshal.

"Damn," Ike cursed softly when she had finished. "How many men did he have with him?" he asked, thinking of Rubin's accounting of the gunfight at the ranch.

"He was by hisself when I saw him," Hannah said. "He mighta had some men upstairs, but nobody came down when the shootin' started."

"By hisself, huh?" Ike pondered that for a moment. He turned to Rubin. "Are you sure there was all them extra men waitin' for you and your brothers when you rode out to that ranch?"

"Sure I'm sure," Rubin replied. "That was the reason I had to run for it, that and the fact that my cartridges was running out." That was the story he was sticking to. He could not tell his father that he didn't know if there were extra men there or not because he had run as soon as he had heard the shooting. "I couldn't count all of 'em in the dark, but there was a-plenty of 'em. I reckon I coulda stayed till my cartridges was gone, but I thought you needed to know what happened."

Ike considered that for a few more moments, wanting to believe Rubin was telling the truth. "Maybe," he allowed, "Tanner had men from Thompson's and Williamson's spreads." That seemed a reasonable assumption since all three ranches had been victims of their rustling.

"Maybe he got up a posse in town," Hannah speculated, "since he's gone and made himself sheriff."

"Maybe," Ike allowed. The many possibilities were beginning to sound like the vigilante activity that had forced him to leave Montana a few years back. It might be the sensible thing to do to heed Tanner's warning and get out while there were still some members of his family left. Still, there was the gnawing worm of vengeance eating away at his innards. It would be difficult to live with the knowledge that Will Tanner had killed three of his sons, and no Cheney had settled the debt. To make sure he had heard Hannah right, he asked, "And he told you he was comin' out here tomorrow to make sure we were gone?"

"That's what he said," Hannah replied. "I figured we'll be waitin' for him to show up, if he didn't have no better sense than to come."

"I don't reckon he's plannin' to come out here by hisself," Ike said, still thinking about the possibility of vigilante activity. "I don't think this Tanner feller is that big a fool. We'll pack our stuff up and move on outta here tonight before him and his posse show up in the mornin'. That'll keep him off our tails till I can get a chance to settle his bacon once and for all. He ain't gettin' away with killin' my sons." He paused to look at his wife, who had come out when she heard them talking outside the cabin. She was sobbing dry tears over the pitiful sight of her dead sons. "We've got graves to dig before we do anything else," Ike said.

"It's a mighty poor time of year to set off to find another place to stay," Hannah said, still in favor of waiting for Tanner and his posse to show up.

"I know it," Ike said. "And it's a mighty poor time to get hemmed up in a half-rotted little line shack by a posse, too. They'd shoot this little cabin to pieces and we wouldn't stand a chance. We'll worry about findin' us a new camp somewhere else, and then I can settle with Will Tanner when he ain't surrounded by a posse. So you go on and help your mama get everything packed up. Me and Rubin will dig a couple of graves for your brothers." She did not respond right away, the frown on her face giving evidence of her reluctance to run. "Don't worry, honey," he said, "I'll see to Mr. Will Tanner, but I want him to know who's killin' him, and I wanna take my time doin' it. He's a dead man. It's just a matter of when, so go along now."

She could understand that, and she knew that when her father promised something, he wouldn't stop until it was done. It was in line with her feelings for revenge. "Why don't you let me help Rubin dig the graves, Pa? There ain't no call for you to do it." She was concerned about his tendency to think he was as good as any man, in spite of his age.

Knowing what she was thinking, he couldn't help a faint grin. "I ain't as old as you think. I'll most likely wear your brother out tryin' to keep up with me." He turned to his wife then. "Get done with your good-byes and help Hannah pack up our possibles. I wanna find a place to camp while it's still daylight."

Rubin got a pick and shovel from beside the door of the cabin, where they had been left after digging Levi's grave. He followed his father to a rise near the creek bank and the mound of fresh dirt that marked Levi's final resting place. "We'll lay 'em beside their brother," Ike said.

"You gonna dig two graves?" Rubin asked, remembering the hard-packed ground he had labored in before. "Looks like it'd be easier to put 'em in one hole."

"We'll dig two graves," Ike answered him emphatically. "They're your brothers, and they'll each have their own graves. That way, Levi won't be no more important than Buck and Luke. I'd do it the same if it was you we was fixin' to bury." When Rubin's expression revealed his obvious disagreement, Ike said, "Here, gimme that pick. You can do the shovelin'. That's the easy part." He snatched the pickax from Rubin's hand and set in to work on the hard ground, attacking the tree roots he encountered with a vengeance, intent upon setting an example for his son.

After a few minutes, when the old man was already breathing heavily, Rubin felt compelled to comment. "You'd best slow down a little before you bust a gut."

"You just be ready to get that shovel workin' on this part I'm breakin' up," Ike told him. "I can go at this pace all day long, and half the night, if I have to." To emphasize, he sank the pick deep in the ground and pulled a large chunk of dirt back.

As he had boasted, the old man maintained the demanding pace until he had broken up enough of the bank for Rubin to dig out a suitable grave, resting only long enough to catch his breath. "That'll be wide enough," he told Rubin. "There ain't no reason to bury 'em in them coffins. Levi ain't in no coffin. We can put the wood in them coffins to better use, even if we was to use 'em for nothin' but firewood." He spat on his hands, rubbed them together, then grabbed his pick again and started in on the third grave, attacking the ground with the same tenacity he had shown before. And as before, the hard ground was no match for the big man's resolve, until he encountered a large root that was as defiant as he was determined.

"Damn you!" Ike cursed, and strained in an effort to pull the root loose from the ground. It seemed a standoff for a time, causing Rubin to pause to watch the contest. That was enough to inspire Ike to reach down deeper inside. A grin slowly began to form on his grizzled face when the root gradually began to give way—until he was struck in the chest by a blow so strong that he was sure he had been shot. Suddenly, he could not breathe. He dropped the pick handle and sank to his knees, clutching at his shirt collar, trying to loosen it to help him gasp for air.

All the while, Rubin stared wide-eyed, astonished by his father's bizarre actions. Standing knee-deep in the grave he was digging, he was stunned by what he was witnessing. Finally the dumbstruck son realized that something was dreadfully wrong. "Pa!" Rubin bellowed, and scrambled out of the grave. He crawled over to his stricken father's side. "Pa!" he pleaded. "What's the matter?" When Ike did not respond, instead clutching his chest, Rubin yelled for Hannah and his mother. They both rushed out of the shack, alarmed by the panic in his cries.

"What is it?" Hannah demanded, then saw her father keel over to lie on his side, still clutching for his heart. She and her mother reached him at the same time. "Papa," Hannah pleaded. "What happened?" But Ike could not answer. She knew then that it was his heart and turned an accusing eye in Rubin's direction. "Why did you let him work so hard? You know he's gettin' too old to work like that." Rubin could only respond with a helpless look. "Damn fool," Hannah muttered, and returned her attention to her father.

"He's still breathin'," Lorena said. "Help me carry him in the house." The three of them carried him inside and put him on the bed, then Lorena covered him with a heavy quilt. She stood wringing her hands, watching him for some sign of recovery, at a loss as to what she could do to help him. "I knew it was gonna happen," she murmured over and over, then looked at Hannah and said, "He ain't no young man no more. I tried to tell him that."

As much at a loss as her mother, Hannah could only reply, "Ain't your fault. Can't nobody tell him nothin'."

After what seemed a long time, Ike's eyelids fluttered and opened halfway, and he seemed to relax under the quilt. In a few more minutes, he opened his eyes fully and cursed. "Damn." He looked up at the anxious eyes staring down at him. "Damn," he repeated. "That felt like the devil hisself reached up and grabbed me round the chest."

"You're all right now, ain'tcha?" Rubin asked hopefully.

"I reckon," Ike said, "as all right as a man can be after gettin' kicked in the chest by a mule."

"You had a heart attack," Hannah said. "Sure as hell."

"Maybe that's what it was, and maybe it wasn't," Ike replied, feeling better now. "Whatever it was, it's over and I'm still here." He started to get off the bed, but Hannah stopped him with a hand on his shoulder.

"You'd best take it easy for a spell," she said. "The Lord don't give too many warnings before he says 'To hell with you.' "

"It'll take more'n that to put me under," he blustered, although a little weakly. In fact, the pain had been so intense it had scared him plenty. And he couldn't help thinking how disastrous it could have been if it had happened while under attack by a posse. "We've got to get back to work, so we can get outta here before Tanner and his men show up."

"How do you know you ain't gonna have another one of them attacks?" Lorena asked, worried to have seen a sign of weakness in the

135

strongest man she had ever known. "I think Hannah's right, you need some rest."

"Damn it, Mother!" he stormed, "It's gonna be damn hard to rest while fifteen or twenty men are circled around this shack shootin' it to pieces. Don't argue with me. Pack up our stuff and get ready to roll. Rubin, finish diggin' those graves. I want them boys to have a fittin' burial." Although he made a show of throwing off the quilt and sitting up on the side of the bed, he was aware of a feeling of weakness, and it worried him. One thing for sure, he knew that he wanted to get away to someplace safe where he could get his strength back. And then he would track Will Tanner down and settle up his debt. No sooner did that thought occur than he experienced another sharp pain in his chest. It was nowhere near the crushing blow he had experienced before, so it gave him hope that he was getting over the attack. He decided, however, that he was past the time in his life when he should be thinking about what he wanted done if anything happened to him. Although Rubin was the eldest, and his son, Ike felt that Hannah was the strongest, so it was his daughter he motioned to come to him.

"It's time I talked to you about what I want you to do if anything ever happens to me," Ike said. "Just in case," he added when she reacted with surprise.

"All right," she said. "You want me to go get Rubin?"

"Nah," Ike said. "Let him finish diggin' them graves. You're the one with the most backbone, so it's you that oughta run things if I ain't here."

"Whadda you talkin' like that for, Papa?" she replied. "You ain't goin' anywhere." She clearly didn't want to have any such discussion.

"Yeah, but in case I do, you most likely wouldn't know what's best. It's your mama I'd be worried about. Rubin, I ain't worried about him. He can just figure out how to make it on his own, without nobody to tell him when it's time to squat and empty his bowels. I keep waitin' for him to start actin' like he's his own man, but so far I ain't seen no sign of it. So here's what you need to do. Take your mama back to her sister's place up on Blue River in Injun Territory. They'll take her in, as long as I ain't with her. Then you can stay there, too, if you want. If you don't, it's up to you." When he was finished, he paused to test her reaction. "Will you do that?" he asked.

"Yeah," she answered. "I'll take Mama there, but I doubt I'll stay there at Uncle Albert's place."

He grinned. "I didn't expect you would. Ol' Albert and your aunt might have you goin' to church on Sundays."

"That'll be the day," Hannah said, and grinned

137

back at him. "Where do you think we oughta be headin' right now?"

"I'm thinkin' the best place to go is straight north, back to Injun Territory to that little camp we had at the fork of Clear Boggy and Muddy Boggy."

"Injun Territory?" Hannah replied, surprised. "Hell, that's Oklahoma. That's where they say Will Tanner's a deputy marshal. He could arrest us up there."

"That's the reason he ain't gonna think we headed up that way. I expect that's the last place he'd look for us. We'll start out from here, due west, leave him an easy trail to follow till we hit the river. Then we'll lose him there and head straight north."

"Ain't it gonna be kinda hard to cover our trail drivin' a wagon?" Hannah asked.

"We ain't takin' the wagon," Ike said. "It'll slow us down too much. We can tote ever'thin' we need on the horses. The only thing we can't haul on the horses is this broken-down old bedsprings, and we can do without that easy enough." She nodded her understanding. "Now," he continued, "let me get up from here and let's get ready to ride." He got to his feet, although a little unsteady, and went outside to supervise the digging of the graves.

Sweating heavily in spite of the cold wind that ruffled the cottonwood leaves over his head,

Rubin climbed up out of the second grave when Ike walked up. "You all right?" he asked. Ike said that he was, so Rubin said, "I'm done. We can put 'em in the ground."

"You need to shave some off the side of that one," Ike said, indicating the grave Rubin had just stepped out of.

"Why?" Rubin replied. "Luke oughta fit in there all right."

"Ain't wide enough for the coffin," his father said.

"You said we was gonna keep the coffins," Rubin reminded him.

"I changed my mind. We ain't takin' the wagon, so we can't haul the coffins."

"Ah hell, Pa," Rubin protested, "I'm tired of diggin' in this damn hard ground. I'm done with it. Like you said, Levi ain't got no coffin, so Luke and Buck don't need one, neither. To hell with the coffins." He threw the shovel to land on the pile of dirt between the two graves and picked up the pickax as if ready to defend himself with it. Although he couldn't really understand it at the moment, his defiant reaction to his father's orders had exposed a new vulnerability in his father. All he realized was that he was tired of the fearful obedience he had always shown.

Ike paused to stare at his eldest, standing poised with the pick in his hands, his outright expression of defiance undisguised. Instead of igniting what would have been a typical storm of fury, Ike welcomed a sign he had waited for in vain up to now. It was the first hint of real backbone in Rubin and came with a sense of relief for Ike. After a long moment, Ike simply said, "All right, then, let's put 'em in the ground, and we'll get Hannah and your ma to say a few words over 'em."

Surprised by his father's lack of anger, Rubin hurried to help him drag the coffins off the wagon. They laid the bodies in the freshly dug graves, and Rubin called out for the women to come to the burial. It was a solemn funeral for the two departed brothers, with no tears shed, even from their mother, who rocked from side to side in silent grief. When Hannah finally pulled the grieving woman away, Ike and Rubin hurriedly filled in the graves, anxious to put some distance between themselves and the posse they felt certain would be on the way in the morning, and possibly sooner.

In spite of the frightening attack he had suffered earlier, Ike was feeling pretty much back to normal by the time the four of them reached the Sulphur River, a ride of no more than ten miles. They paused there to rest the horses and eat something before starting out to follow the river. Riding in the shallow water for over two miles until finding a flat rock next to a grassy bank, Ike decided it was the best place to exit the river. Carefully leading the horses onto the rock, they spread them out and walked them across the grassy bank, trying to leave as little evidence as possible. "They're gonna have to be pretty doggone good to find these tracks," Rubin declared when they were ready to climb in the saddle again.

Just in case Tanner and his posse were that good, Ike led them west again, skirting a long bank of berry bushes and heading toward a low ridge of pine trees not far away. Riding up through the pines, they crossed over the top of the ridge before turning back north and heading for Oklahoma. "They might trail us," Ike said, "but it ain't gonna be easy. It's less than a two-day ride from here to the Red River. And if they don't start out till tomorrow mornin', we'll have too good a start on 'em for them to catch us. If that posse does cut our trail after we turned north, they ain't gonna wanna keep ridin' across the Red into Oklahoma." That made sense to Hannah and Rubin. If what they suspected, that the posse was made up of cowhands from the ranches around Sulphur Springs, then they wouldn't likely want to be gone from their work too long. So Ike Cheney and what was left of his family just concerned themselves with making as good time as possible.

It was already getting dark when Ike picked

a spot to camp by a tiny stream. He and Rubin took care of the horses while Hannah and her mother got a fire started and prepared to cook something for supper. "We'll be startin' out early in the mornin'," Ike told them, "so don't set around drinkin' coffee too long." Feeling a bit weary from the day's ride, he climbed under his blankets while the others were still finishing up their supper.

"Best get some more wood for this fire," Hannah said to Rubin, speaking softly so as not to disturb their father, who was already snoring. "It's gonna be cold as hell tonight, from the feel of that wind. I just hope it don't snow." If it did, there would be no point in trying to hide their trail.

Without protest, Rubin did her bidding, then rolled up in his blankets close to the fire and was soon asleep. Hannah helped get her mother settled up against her father's back before climbing into her bedroll. Lorena Mashburn Cheney had borne four sons and one daughter for Ike Cheney. She had always imagined that someday she would watch them all grow old and start families of their own. It had not happened, and now she lay awake grieving over the loss of three of those children. She found herself praying that maybe this was enough to persuade her husband that it was time to find a place to build a proper home and abandon his lawless ways. Even as she prayed, she knew it was a hopeless endeavor. The man had lived on the wrong side of the law for too long to change his ways now. After a while, she succumbed to her weariness, pressed up close against her sleeping husband, and finally drifted off to sleep. In the wee hours of the morning, she did not feel him suddenly jerk violently when his heart suffered the attack that carried him away.

Hannah was awakened the next morning by her mother's sudden outburst of agonized wailing. Thinking they were under attack, Hannah bolted upright, her pistol in hand, to discover Rubin already on his feet, having thought the same. After looking frantically all around them to discover no threat, they hurried to their mother's side. They saw immediately the cause of her beastlike howling, like that of a coyote, as she bent over her husband's cold body. Hannah was immediately shocked. Somehow she had thought it impossible that her father should succumb without a fierce battle with death. For him to have passed on while he was sleeping peacefully seemed to her to be a cowardly act by the grim reaper.

Rubin had yet another grave to dig for the men of Ike Cheney's family, the only one that Hannah admired. Like her brothers, her father's death was surely by the hand of Will Tanner. They buried Ike near the bank of the rocky stream, and Hannah looked for a sizable rock to use as a headstone. When she found one that would do, she also noticed an unusually smooth pebble lying next to it in the water. She picked it up and turned it over and over in her hand. It felt cold to her touch, like her father now. She dropped it in her coat pocket, resolved to let it remind her of her promise to avenge his death.

Will walked the big buckskin gelding slowly through the band of cottonwoods that lined Kettle Creek. Scanning the trees before him, as well as those on the other bank, alert for any sign of a reception, he continued until he got the first glimpse of the line shack. He dismounted then and drew the Winchester from the saddle sling. After looping Buster's reins loosely around the branches of a laurel, he made his way cautiously along the creek bank until he could reach a clear view of the cabin. He dropped to one knee to look the place over. For all appearances, the shack looked deserted. There were no horses in the small corral, and no smoke from the chimney. The wagon Hannah Cheney had driven into town was in front of the shack, but there was no sign of anyone about. His gaze fell upon the three freshly dug graves on the other side of the creek, under a large cottonwood. The coffins Luke and Buck had occupied had been discarded and lay not far away from the graves. Back to the cabin again, he watched it for a long spell until there was no doubt Cheney was gone, so he got to his feet and went back for his horse.

It didn't take long to confirm his first impression. They had vacated the cabin, all right, leaving nothing behind but the wagon and an old bedspring. From the cold ashes in the fireplace, Will figured they had been gone since the day before. This suited him just fine. He was glad they had decided to depart instead of making a fight of it. He had to admit that it surprised him, though. He might have misjudged old Ike Cheney. *I reckon he figured he'd lost enough of his family,* Will thought. Left to determine now was which way they had gone. He scouted around the cabin and the corral looking for their tracks. It didn't take much of a search, for there seemed to be no effort to hide them. They led straight west. Thinking he'd like to know if they held to that trail, he guided Buster along after them. He followed the tracks until he struck the Sulphur River and the first place they had attempted to lose anyone coming after them. There were no tracks on the other side of the river, so he followed the river north, looking for a good place to come out of the water. He found what he was searching for a couple of miles above the spot they had entered. It would have been the spot he might have picked, had he been the one being followed, so he dismounted by a large flat rock at the water's edge. As he suspected, there were still traces of the horses' passage over the short grass beyond the rock. Still on foot, he followed the tracks for a short distance. They never varied from a straight course west, and seemed to be heading toward a low ridge of pines a mile or so distant.

Will stood gazing at the ridge for a while before deciding that Cheney intended to continue toward the west, probably to Fort Worth, the town where Shorty figured Cheney had been selling his stolen cattle. It would appear that the J-Bar-J had seen the last of Ike Cheney, a fact that Will still had difficulty accepting. He had evidently misjudged the depth of the old outlaw's desire for vengeance. Ike and what was left of his family could now be a problem for the Texas Rangers, as far as Will was concerned, and they were welcome to them. *My business is in Oklahoma Territory,* he thought, *and I'd best get back to Fort Smith to see if I've still got a job.*

Back in the saddle, he returned to the shack on Kettle Creek and stopped there to rest Buster and make himself some coffee. Figuring to get back to the J-Bar-J by nightfall, he planned to spend one more night at the ranch before starting back to Fort Smith. There was no further need for him at the ranch, but it had been fortunate that he had happened to come when he did. He could still see Slim's face, wide-eyed and white as a sheet, as he stood facing Buck Cheney. Things work out like they're supposed to, he thought, and Slim Rogers damn sure wasn't supposed to die at the hands of a no-good killer like Buck Cheney. For no particular reason, a stray thought of Sophie Bennett crossed his mind suddenly. *How long is it until Christmas?* he wondered. She had said that Christmas was when she and Garth Pearson were to be married. Somehow, that didn't seem to be the way things were meant to be for Sophie. She and the young law clerk just didn't strike him as a good fit. It always seemed to trouble him whenever he thought about Sophie, so he wondered why she popped into his mind so often. *Maybe,* he thought, *after she finally marries that law clerk, I won't be thinking about her at all.*

As he had anticipated, he got back to the J-Bar-J in time to get some supper. He heard Anna banging on the angle iron just as he rode into the barnyard. Cal Perkins walked out of the barn on his way to the supper table and paused when he saw Will ride in. Anxious to find out what had happened in town, Cal hurried to meet him. "Did you see 'em?" he asked, referring to the old man and Rubin. "Billy came back and said you told him you didn't want no help. Shorty already said a couple of us oughta get ready to ride in if you didn't show up back here by tonight. He said you mighta had more'n you could handle. Did you get 'em?"

When Cal finally paused to take a breath, Will answered him. "No, I didn't. I rode out to Kettle Creek this mornin' and they had cleared out. I expect they decided to practice their brand of mischief somewhere else."

Cal helped him take care of Buster, then they walked up to the house to find the rest of the crew already around the table. Will couldn't help noticing a look of relief in Shorty's face when they walked in.

While polishing off a plate of Anna's beef stew, Will told them about his introduction to Hannah Cheney and the trip out to the line shack at Kettle Creek. "They left a wagon out there," he said. "I didn't see anything wrong with it, so you might wanna take a couple of horses out there and pick it up."

"Maybe they figured they owed us somethin' for all the cows they stole," Slim said.

"Then I reckon they shoulda left it full of money," Shorty said. "You didn't see any money in it, did you, Will?"

"Yeah," Will answered. "I put that in my pocket."

The mood was obviously light and easy,

decidedly different from what Will had met when he had first ridden in. All hands were looking forward to returning to a normal work schedule, with only one unlucky soul riding night herd.

CHAPTER 7

A light snow began to fall in the early evening of the fourth full day of riding since he left the J-Bar-J. Will had been expecting it to start, because the skies had been threatening for the past couple of hours. Now as he rode along beside the Poteau River just short of its confluence with the Arkansas at Belle Point, the weather was no longer a concern. His horses were tired, but they would soon be resting in the stable at Fort Smith. However, he would not make it back to the boardinghouse in time for supper, and he felt he could really enjoy a good meal right about now. That thought was enough to cause him to ask Buster to increase his pace to a fast walk. The big buckskin willingly obliged and maintained the pace until reaching the stables on the south end of Fort Smith.

"Hey-yo, Will," Vern Tuttle called out when he saw Will ride in and dismount. "I was wonderin' when you'd be showin' up again."

"Howdy, Vern," Will returned. "Looks like I just beat the weather in."

"Yeah, it's been wantin' to snow for the last two days," Vern said. "I reckon it was just waitin' for Christmas."

"Maybe so," Will allowed, but had to stop and

think about it. He had lost track of the days while he was down in Texas.

"They're both gonna need a ration of oats." He pulled his saddlebags off and drew his rifle from the saddle before carrying it to the tack room. After packing away what supplies he had left in the small room he rented for that purpose, he bade Vern a good night and started toward Bennett House. Had it been a little earlier in the day, he would have reported to Dan Stone, but the marshal had most likely gone home by now. He would see him in the morning.

There was a horse and buggy tied up in front of Ruth Bennett's boardinghouse, one of Vern Tuttle's fancy rigs, Will figured. He heard a lively conversation coming from the parlor even before he stepped up on the porch. So he paused for a moment, about to decide to walk around the house and use the kitchen door, when the front door opened and Garth Pearson came out. "Oops," Garth uttered. "I almost ran right into you, Will. I was just going to get something from the buggy."

Oops? Will repeated silently to himself sarcastically, then turned to leave the porch. "Sorry. Looks like I was about to walk in on a party."

"Oh no," Garth replied. "There's no party. Please come on in. I'd like you to meet my folks. They got in yesterday from Little Rock, and I know they'd like to meet you."

What for? Will thought. To Garth, he said, "I

ain't in too good a shape to be meetin' anybody. I need to wash up and shave, else I might frighten your folks."

"Nonsense," Garth protested. "They know what kind of man you are. Sophie has told them about your being a deputy and all. I know the judge, my father, would like to meet you."

Will held back. He just hadn't been able to bring himself to the point where he could stand Garth Pearson. And he really had no reason for it. Maybe it was because Garth worked as a clerk for Judge Parker, and couldn't saddle a horse if his life depended on it. If he was honest about it, he could admit that he resented Garth simply because Sophie wanted to marry him. There was no other reason. "Maybe later, when I'm a little more respectable," Will said.

"I insist," Garth said, and opened the door again. "Hey, everybody, Will's back."

Sophie looked up immediately. "Well, what's he standing out there for? Both of you come in and close that door. You're letting all the cold air in." To keep from looking totally foolish, Will decided he had no choice but to go on inside. It didn't help when Sophie gave him a critical looking-over and remarked, "My goodness, you look like you've been living in a briar patch somewhere. Where were you? We thought you were only going to be gone for a few days. I see you lost your razor."

"I was in Texas," Will answered, rubbing his scraggly beard. "I was on my way to clean up when Garth grabbed me." It seemed that she was going out of her way to embarrass him, and yet there was a wide smile on her face as if beaming with pride. He looked around the room at the small group gathered there. The distinguished-looking gentleman seated beside the lady on the settee was Garth's father. There was no mistaking the resemblance. Ruth Bennett sat on a straight-backed chair in the corner, smiling warmly at Will. One of her longtime boarders, old Leonard Dickens, sat enjoying the party in the corner opposite her.

Ruth got up from her chair and took Will by the arm. "I want you to meet Garth's parents, Will. Judge Pearson, this is Will Tanner, one of our regular guests."

"Glad to meet you, Will," Judge Pearson said as he got up and extended his hand. "We've heard a lot about you in Little Rock. This is my wife, Anne, Garth's mother."

Will shifted his Winchester to his other hand and grasped Pearson's, wondering how they could have heard of him in Little Rock. "Pleased to meet you, sir," he said, then nodded to the judge's wife. "Ma'am." She said nothing, but favored him with a polite smile. He turned to Ruth and apologized for his appearance. "I'd best go and get myself cleaned up." He nodded once more to Judge Pearson, then started for the stairs.

Ruth caught his arm again. "I'll bet you haven't had any supper," she said. "There's still some biscuits and cold ham left. I'll fix you some while you clean up."

"No, ma'am," Will said. "You stay with your company. I was plannin' to walk over to the Mornin' Glory and have a couple of drinks of whiskey. I'll just have Mammy rustle me up something to eat over there."

Ruth had a pretty good idea why he really refused her offer. He felt out of place in the company of Judge and Mrs. Pearson and the talk about the upcoming wedding. Will Tanner was a good and decent man, but she would be relieved to be free of the worry that Sophie's attraction to him had caused her. Each time he was sent out to apprehend an outlaw there was the chance that he wouldn't make it back home safely. And one of these days he wouldn't. Ruth was certain of that from her own experience. At least Sophie would be spared that pain. "You go along, then," she said to him. "I'll put some water on the stove for you while you go up and get some clean clothes to put on."

" 'Preciate it," he said, and headed for the stairs.

Things were pretty quiet in the Morning Glory Saloon when Will, freshly scrubbed and shaved, walked in. It was the way Will preferred it, although he was certain Clyde Bradley would have liked to see it a little busier in his establishment. Gus Johnson was tending bar as usual and he greeted Will as soon as he saw him at the door. "Hello, stranger. I thought you musta started doin' your drinkin' at one of them fancy saloons over by the courthouse. Either that, or you got religion and turned into a teetotaler."

Will laughed. "Even if I got religion, I reckon I'd still need a drink on a night cold as this." He watched while Gus produced a glass from under the counter and poured from a bottle of whiskey. "I just rode in about an hour ago, and I didn't have any supper. Reckon Mammy's got anything left in the kitchen she could throw on a plate for me?"

"I expect so," Gus said. "I'll ask her." He walked to the kitchen door and was back in a few moments. He looked back over his shoulder to make sure she wasn't following him, then lowered his voice and chuckled when he said, "I used to just holler for her, but the other day she told me not to holler for her no more." He laughed again and took another glance toward the kitchen door. "She said it sounded like I was callin' hogs or somethin', said if I yelled at her like that again, I'd be lookin' for a new cook." He was about to continue, but she came out of the kitchen at that moment. "Will, here, asked me if he could get somethin' to eat," he said to her.

155

The skinny little woman walked toward the end of the bar, stopping a few feet in front of Will. She reached up to brush a stray wisp of thin gray hair away from her forehead. Then with hands on her bony hips, she looked Will up and down, as if never having seen him before. "You're wantin' to eat?" she asked.

"Yes, ma'am," Will answered. "I surely could use somethin' if there's anything left."

"You're lucky you didn't show up here five minutes later," Mammy said. "I've got a little bit of stew left. I was just fixin' to throw it to the hogs. There's still coffee in the pot that ain't got really strong yet. I'm drinkin' it. Think that'll do ya?"

"Yes, ma'am," Will said. "That would do just fine."

"Sit down at a table and I'll get you a plate." Before she turned to leave, she frowned at Gus and said, "It does sound like you're callin' hogs when you go to hollerin' for me. And I weren't japin' you when I said I'd quit." With that said, she spun on her heel and headed for the kitchen.

Will couldn't help grinning at Gus, whose face flushed slightly in embarrassment. He shrugged as Will continued to smile. "Damned if she ain't the feistiest woman I've ever seen, and ears like an antelope," Gus said, his voice barely above a whisper.

Will walked over to a table not far from the

kitchen door just as Lucy Tyler came down the stairs on the opposite wall. Seeing Will, she went directly to join him. "Hey, darlin', where have you been? You haven't been in to see us in I don't know how long."

"Yeah," Will replied. "I've been outta town for a spell. Just got back tonight."

"And you came here first thing to see us," she said, smiling sweetly.

"Well, not exactly first thing. I went home first, but I was too late for supper, so I came here to get somethin' to eat." As if to confirm that, Mammy came from the kitchen at that moment and set a plate piled high with stew in front of him.

"Let the man eat," Mammy said to Lucy, then to Will she said, "I'll get your coffee." Back to Lucy, she asked, "You want a cup, too?"

"I'd appreciate it, Mammy," Lucy said. "It's been a slow evenin' so far and I've got a headache. Maybe some coffee will help. Want me to get it?"

"I'll bring it," Mammy said, and went back to the kitchen.

Lucy remained at the table, talking to Will while he ate his supper, complaining about her headache and the fact that she couldn't afford to take time to herself to pamper it. "I don't know what it is about Christmastime. Some of the rowdiest men I entertain all year seem to get religion around Christmas. Hell, I'd like to have a little Christmas, too." She had given up on trying to entice Will to follow her upstairs to her room. For a long time, she found it frustrating that he never seemed to be in the mood to succumb to her charms, but after a while, she found that he was a friend. And a girl in her profession seldom had any true male friends. She suspected he might be true-loving some girl in town. But if that was the case, he never gave the slightest hint to support it.

He finished his supper and remained at the table, drinking the last of the coffee. Lucy sat with him, but didn't finish the one cup that Mammy had brought her, complaining that it was a little too stout for her taste. "She must have made that pot yesterday," she joked. In a little while, three of the Morning Glory's regulars wandered in, planning to play cards and drink up some of Gus's supply of whiskey. Recognizing Will, one of them invited him to sit in on the poker game, but he declined, saying he was going home to catch up on his sleep. So they started a three-handed poker game, knowing someone would come in later to sit in. When Will got up to leave, Lucy drifted over to the poker game to watch.

With a full stomach and a couple of drinks under his belt, it felt good to be back outside in the cold night air. As he walked back to the boardinghouse, a soft flurry of snowflakes was still falling, but he decided they weren't going to amount to much after all. There was no sign that they were accumulating on the shoulder of the road he walked along. When he got back to the house, the buggy was still parked out front, so he walked around to the kitchen and went up the back stairs.

"What time did you come in last night?" Ruth Bennett asked Will when he came down to breakfast. "It must have been late. I thought you might have gotten back before the Pearsons went back to the hotel."

"They were still here," Will said as she filled his coffee cup. "I went up the back steps."

"Arthur and Anne Pearson seem like nice people," Ruth said. "And Garth is absolutely taken with Sophie. I'm so happy for her. I know I can stop worrying about her. She will be very happy married to Garth." Her comments were solely for his ears, hoping to discourage him in case he might have had thoughts of something developing between Sophie and him. Even though he had never given any real evidence of any interest in her daughter, she always knew Sophie was attracted to him. She thought surely he must have realized it as well.

"I reckon so," Will said, not really enthusiastic about speculating on how happy Sophie was going to be with Garth Pearson. In fact, the discussion was enough to cause him to cut his breakfast short. "Well, I'd best be gettin' on over to the courthouse. I've got to report to my boss this mornin'." He stood up from the table and paused while he gulped down the rest of his coffee, snared another biscuit from the plate in the center of the table, and headed for the door.

Only a few minutes after he had gone, Sophie walked in the dining room. After saying good morning to her mother, she asked, "Has Will come down yet? I thought he'd be early for breakfast as usual."

"He was," Ruth said. "Come and gone. Why? Was there something you wanted?" *Damn it,* she thought, always fearful that Sophie might wreck her wedding plans by doing something stupid, like asking Will if he knew any reason she shouldn't marry Garth. *That girl is going to drive me out of my mind before she is legally hitched.*

"No," Sophie answered. "We just didn't see much of him since he got back last night." She went to the cupboard to get a cup for herself. "I hope we didn't embarrass him too much last night. Sorry I'm so late getting up this morning. Garth came back after dropping his parents off at the hotel and I didn't get to bed until after midnight."

"I suspected as much," Ruth said. "Margaret and I didn't need you, anyway. Your head's too full of wedding plans. Right, Margaret?"

"That's right," Margaret answered. A big-boned woman of middle age, Margaret Thatcher, although a recent hire to replace Sophie in the kitchen, had rapidly settled into the family. She couldn't help being aware of Ruth's concern for her headstrong daughter.

Unaware of the worry he caused his landlady, Will walked through the streets leading to the courthouse. Thinking Sophie would probably insist upon his presence at her wedding, he decided he would tell her that he had to go to Ward's Corner. He could say that Henry Ward sent a wire to the marshal's office about some trouble with his horses. That should be excuse enough. They all knew that he kept some horses at Henry's farm. Satisfied with that, he put it out of his mind as he went up the steps to U.S. Marshal Daniel Stone's office over the jail.

Stone's office door was open and the marshal seemed absorbed in a paper on his desk, so much so that he wasn't aware of Will's presence until Will tapped lightly on the doorjamb. Stone looked up, frowning, until he saw who it was. "Well, well," he remarked, "so you ain't dead after all."

"I was meanin' to wire you from Sulphur Springs, but I got too busy to ride to the telegraph office," Will said. "I didn't count on runnin' into

161

trouble down in Texas, else I'da been back a week ago."

"Is that a fact?" Stone replied. "Well, if you'da took the time to wire me, I coulda told you I had a job for you back up near Tishomingo. And you wouldn't have had to ride all the way back here, just to turn around and go back. Mileage you won't get any pay for," he added. "What kinda trouble did you run into down in Texas?"

Will told him of the cattle rustling that led to three men getting shot, and how it affected him personally. "I figured I didn't have any choice. I had to take care of it, since they were trying to kill my people on the J-Bar-J," he concluded.

Stone could really not find fault with Will's actions. He would have done the same in his shoes. Will Tanner was his most effective deputy, but Stone thought it best that the young cougar not find out he held him in such high regard. He paused then to change the subject. "What the hell did you do to get Alvin Greeley so riled at you? He came back complaining that you ran off and left before the job was finished."

"I figured there wasn't any reason to ride back with him and Horace when I was so close to the J-Bar-J. I told you that in the wire I sent."

"Yeah, you did," Stone allowed. "It sure set ol' Alvin off, though. He told me he didn't especially wanna work with you in the future."

"Is that a fact?" Will replied. "Well, I certainly respect the man's wishes. I don't like to cramp anybody's style." He didn't say more, but he was more than happy to know it would be unlikely he'd have to put up with Alvin Greeley's sour disposition.

Back to the issue at hand, Stone said, "Well, I reckon if the Texas Rangers can excuse you for doin' their jobs for a little while, maybe you can do some work for the people of Arkansas, who pay your salary."

Will shrugged. "I reckon."

"Course, with Christmas comin' up," Stone went on, "you might suddenly become hard to find, like some of my other deputies." He didn't say so, but he had been laboring over a difficult decision when Will suddenly showed up, and it had to do with a telegram he had received that morning. There was a bad situation that could possibly be developing in the Chickasaw Nation and he had no one to send to take care of it other than Ed Pine. He hesitated to send Ed because he had been wounded pretty seriously a while back and was still not fully recovered, in spite of his insistence that he was ready to ride. Stone had begun to think Will had met with disaster when he didn't show up for so long, but here he was, right when the marshal needed him. "How soon can you be ready to ride?" Stone suddenly asked.

"Not before this afternoon," Will replied, "dependin' on where you want me to go. If it's back in the Nations, I need to get my horses shod and back up my supplies."

"This might take a little time," Stone said. "I know you mighta been thinkin' about doing something special for Christmas."

Will interrupted before Stone went any further. "I ain't got no special plans for Christmas. Where you want me to go?" An assignment couldn't have come at a better time, giving him a legitimate excuse for not having to witness Sophie Bennett's wedding.

This was what Stone wanted to hear. "I got word while you were gone that we might have some real trouble outta Kansas headed our way. A gang of outlaws that have been operating in Colorado Territory, holding up mine shipments, stagecoaches, banks, and about everything else, have moved into Kansas. Their leader is a man the law has been trying to track down for a couple of years. His name's Jack Lynch. At one time, he was operating in Arkansas, but that was a while back. He left there after he killed a deputy marshal. He's got a nickname. They call him Scorpion Jack."

"Why do they call him that?" Will asked.

"Hell, I don't know," Stone said. "Maybe he hides somewhere and you don't even know he's there till you turn over a board or something and get stung. Anyway, things were getting too hot for Jack and his gang in Colorado, I reckon, so they decided to get out and lay low for a while. But they robbed a bank in Wichita. So if they had planned to stay in Kansas, they musta changed their minds and decided to hightail it to Indian Territory. A posse of deputy marshals out of Wichita cut their trail before they reached Oklahoma, but lost 'em again. Best they could figure was they were headed down through Osage country. I got word this morning from Tom Spotted Horse that some of his people reported seeing four strangers hanging around a trading post near Tishomingo. Spotted Horse said he hadn't seen 'em himself, but they might be Jack Lynch and his boys, and they're figuring on holing up in Indian Territory."

"I expect I'd best get ready to ride, then," Will said. "Like I said, my buckskin and my bay packhorse both need new shoes. I reckon I can get that done this afternoon and head into the Nations first thing in the mornin'."

Stone hesitated, knowing he could expect the usual argument from Will about working alone. According to law, a deputy marshal going after a felon was required to take at least one posse-man and a cook if he would be transporting prisoners back to court. Stone had to remind Will of this law every time, and every time Will talked him out of it. On this occasion, however, there was no one else available but Ed Pine, and he had already ruled Ed out. So the argument this time amounted to no more than a precaution to Will that he had no notion of the number of men riding with Jack Lynch. Consequently, his job might be to simply find him and keep an eye on him until more deputies could be called in to make the arrest. "We can get some help from Tom Spotted Horse and Jim Little Eagle, maybe some of the other Indian policemen," Stone said. "So don't go getting yourself in a spot trying to arrest any of those outlaws by yourself."

"You don't have to worry about that," Will assured him. "I'll take care of my horses today and head out in the mornin'." He started to leave, but paused at the door. "It's a good four days' ride down to Tishomingo. There ain't no tellin' if Jack Lynch will be there when I get there. He mighta just kept on ridin' on down into Texas."

"I hope to hell he has," Stone said. Even though he said it, he was thinking how good it would look on his record to have his deputies put the noose on Scorpion Jack Lynch. And he couldn't think of a better man to go after him than Will Tanner. "And Will, let me know what's going on," he called after him. "There's telegraph offices up and down the railroad over there." The tall, intense young deputy had a way of disappearing for long periods of time.

"I will, boss," Will said. He paused before going out the door. "Say, did you ever find out who that horse thief I shot was?"

"Not yet," Stone answered. "I wired Little Rock and told 'em about the fellow wearing those marked boots. So far, they haven't responded. Christmastime and all that, I reckon."

The rest of the day was spent taking care of his horses and restocking his supplies and ammunition. He returned to Bennett House for the noon meal while Fred Waits shoed his horses. Fred's shop was right next to the stables, so he said he would take them back for him. With everything taken care of, there was time left for Will to while away an hour before suppertime. He took the time to voluntarily split some firewood for the kitchen stove and some for the stove in the parlor as well. He gave a thought toward sitting in one of the rocking chairs on the front porch, but it was a little cold for that. So he stoked up the parlor stove and made himself comfortable on the settee where Judge and Mrs. Pearson had sat the night before. In no time at all, the little iron stove took the chill out of the parlor. He stretched his long legs out in front of him, enjoying the efforts of the little stove. Before he realized he was headed that way, he dozed off to sleep.

"Well, if that isn't a pretty picture, I don't know

what is." He woke up immediately upon hearing her voice. Always a light sleeper, he was jolted awake, even though she had made an effort to speak softly so as not to awaken him. "Sorry," Sophie said. "I didn't mean to disturb your little nap."

"That's all right," he stammered, "I wasn't really asleep."

"You weren't?" she teased. "Liar, you were sleeping like a baby."

"No, I wasn't," he insisted, somehow embarrassed to have been caught sleeping by her.

She laughed, delighted to see his embarrassment, but became serious then. "Mama said you told her you were leaving in the morning."

"That's right," he said.

"Where are you going?"

"Tishomingo."

"Tishomingo," she echoed, at once alarmed. "That's way over in Indian Territory. What about my wedding?"

"I figured you'd still go ahead with it, anyway," he said, trying to make a joke of it.

She didn't appreciate his attempt at humor. "I thought you would be sure to be at my wedding. Can't Tishomingo wait until after?"

He was frankly surprised by her concern. "I'm afraid not. Dan Stone told me I needed to get down there just as fast as I can, to try to head off some trouble. I woulda headed down that way this afternoon if my horses didn't need shoein'." Still somewhat astonished by the deep frown on her face, he asked, "Why does it matter if I'm at the weddin'?"

She hesitated, suddenly realizing that she wasn't sure of the reason herself. "I don't know," she stammered. "Because you're my friend, I guess. I just thought you'd want to be there."

Well, I don't, he thought. "I ain't got much say in the matter," he said. "There ain't nobody else to go down there right now, and that's the job I signed on to do, to go where and when they tell me to." She made no response to his statement, but continued to gaze into his eyes for a few moments more before abruptly spinning on her heel and returning to the kitchen. "I wish you all the best," he called after her, still puzzling over her attitude.

"What's eatin' at you?" Margaret asked when Sophie came back in the kitchen, her face still wearing a deep frown.

"Not a thing," Sophie declared emphatically. "Why would you think something was?" She was having trouble, herself, trying to understand her feelings.

"Because that expression on your face looks like you smelled some rotten eggs or something," Margaret answered. "You're supposed to have a constant smile on your face, thinkin' about your weddin' night comin' up."

169

Overhearing, Sophie's mother playfully scolded her. "Hush your mouth, Margaret. She should be thinking about helping us fix supper instead of what'll happen between the sheets on her wedding night."

CHAPTER 8

Two days out of Fort Smith, Will guided Buster toward a gap in the middle of a long line of hills before the Sans Bois Mountains. The gap marked the end of a narrow passage that led through the hills to a small meadow and the cabin of Perley Gates. Will planned to camp with Perley that night before moving on in the morning. It had been some time since he had seen the elflike little man, and he was curious to see if he was still there. He knew that, if he was, he could count on some fresh meat for supper, for Perley was a hell of a hunter. And he also knew that Perley would be joyfully grateful for the sack of coffee Will had brought for him.

By the time he reached the gap, the sun was already settling low on the horizon. He followed the narrow pass that wound its way through the hills until finally coming out on the small meadow at the foot of a steep incline. The first time he had ridden into this meadow, he had to take a second look before he spotted the log structure built against the base of the mountain. Looking at it now, there was no sign of anyone about, but Perley's dark Morgan gelding was grazing in the meadow grass. Perley was probably watching him, so he thought it best to announce his presence. "Hello, Perley!" he called out, and waited. In a few seconds, he heard a reply.

"Hello, yourself." The response came from behind him. It was followed a moment later by another. "Will? Is that you? Well, I'll be go to hell!" Perley stepped out from behind a large pine tree at the edge of the clearing, his Henry rifle in his hand. "I swear, I watched you ride in, but the light's got so dim down in this gulch that I couldn't tell right off who was comin' to call." He waited for Will to dismount, then pumped his hand vigorously in welcome. "What brings you up this way? You chasin' somebody and thinkin' they mighta holed up in that cave up above here?"

"Perley," Will greeted him, "you old buzzard, I just wanted to see if you were still kickin'." Perley gave him a big grin in reply. "No," Will said, answering his question, "I ain't lookin' for nobody in that cave. I'm on my way to Tishomingo, and I figured I'd camp with you tonight, figured I'd best stop by because I know you're outta coffee."

"By damn, that is a fact," Perley said. "Been out for three or four weeks. How'd you know that?"

Will laughed. " 'Cause you're always out, and every time I meet up with you, I have to give you half of mine." He walked back to his packhorse and untied a sack from the pack saddle.

"Hot damn!" Perley exclaimed as he accepted the sack. "I can already taste it. You're always welcome, Will, but when you bring coffee, you're really welcome."

Will had to laugh at the little man's childish delight for the gift. "You mentioned the cave. Like I said, I ain't lookin' for nobody in the cave, but what about it? Anybody hidin' out up there now?" He asked the question only out of curiosity. It was really a stone passageway over forty feet long, near the top of a mountain, its existence known by few, but often used by outlaws on the run. Perley had led Will to it when he was tracking a vicious killer named Eli Stark. In fact, that little adventure was how Perley came by the dark Morgan in his corral. The horse had belonged to Stark. Will made him a gift of the horse for his help in finding the vicious outlaw.

"Last time I was huntin' up that way, couple of weeks back, there weren't nobody up there," Perley said. "Who you lookin' for now?" Will told him he was on his way to Tishomingo because Tom Spotted Horse had reported that some strangers had shown up near there that might possibly be an outlaw gang out of Colorado. "Fellow named Jack Lynch is supposed to be the leader. I don't reckon you've heard anything about him over this way, have you?"

"Jack Lynch," Perley repeated, and shook his head. "Can't say as I have. Course it's dang near

173

a three-day ride from here to Tishomingo. You think they might be over this far?" The thought was enough to cause concern.

"I doubt it," Will replied. "Like I said, they've been operatin' in Colorado. Probably never heard of Outlaw Cave."

Perley nodded his agreement. "A gang, you say. How many?"

"Don't know for sure," Will said. "Tom didn't say."

"And you came by yourself," Perley commented dryly. He shook his head as if exasperated. "I ain't never seen no other deputy marshal come over here in the territory without a posse and a wagon. And most times that was to arrest one man. You ever think you might need a little help?"

"I reckon not," Will replied, then grinned. "I figure if I need some help, I can just call on you."

"Huh," Perley snorted, and took Buster's reins. "Come on, let's put some meat on the fire and build us a pot of coffee."

Will unsaddled Buster and stripped the packs off the bay, then turned them out to graze with Perley's horse. While he was doing that, Perley built up the fire inside the cabin to roast some fresh venison he said he had killed that afternoon. Before putting the meat on to cook, however, he got his coffee grinder out and went to work on some of the beans Will had brought. Will decided it had been a good decision to visit Perley on his way to Tishomingo. Perley was happy to have some company for a change, and Will was able to enjoy some fresh-killed game instead of the salt pork he was packing. If things turned out like they usually did, it might be the only night he could relax with a friend and talk about things that weren't important.

"I'm right glad you got here this evenin'," Perley said, " 'Cause I'd halfway made up my mind that I need to move my camp to a better spot." This surprised Will because Perley had often boasted that there would always be enough game in the Sans Bois Mountains for him in his lifetime. He continued. "I was thinkin' about ridin' down toward the Jack Fork Mountains—in the mornin', as a matter of fact. I ran up on some deer down there about a week ago, and there's a heap of sign. And deer is gettin' kinda scarce around here lately. I ain't been able to get enough hides to even buy myself a little coffee now and then." He paused to chuckle. "Have to wait for you to come by."

"I expect if you're really thinkin' about movin' your camp, you'd best get it done before hard winter sets in," Will said. "You know deer as well as any man. Maybe they'll be back in these hills again if you ain't huntin' 'em for a while."

"That's kinda what I'm hopin'," Perley said. "I've got a pretty good camp here, been here for a long time. I'd like to come back." He shrugged. "Anyway, I'm gonna ride down to the Jack Forks for a spell, and if it's all right with you, I'll ride along with you in the mornin', at least that far."

"Sounds like a good idea," Will said. "I'd be glad to have the company."

Close to one hundred miles away, a man and woman sat on their horses, watching a log building beside the Blue River. They had been there for some time watching the place, trying to determine if it was deserted. They had been told by Albert Clinton that the cabin, barn, and outbuildings were once a trading post belonging to an evil old man named Lem Stark, who was now deceased. So far, they had seen no sign of anyone about, nor any sign that anyone had been there recently. "I reckon Uncle Albert was right," Hannah Cheney said to her brother. "There ain't been nobody livin' in this place for a long time. We might as well ride on in and see what the inside looks like."

"Looks all right to me," Rubin said. "It'll be dark pretty quick now. Let's get in there and get a fire goin', so we can fix somethin' to eat. I'm 'bout to starve to death."

"I'll take a look inside," Hannah said. "You put the horses in that little corral and see if there's anything left in the barn. Then bring the packhorse up and we'll unload it into the house.

176

I just hope to hell that when they left here they didn't tear the place up. Looks like a stack of firewood on the porch. That'll be right handy as long as they didn't mess up the fireplace."

Accustomed to taking orders from his sister, Rubin dutifully started out toward the barn, leading the horses while Hannah walked up on the porch of the cabin. She paused only a moment to draw the .44 out of her holster before pushing the door open. The handgun had belonged to her father. Hannah had lost hers in a confrontation with the deputy marshal in Texas. The memory of that face-off was still fresh enough to cause her to scowl. *Will Tanner,* she silently pronounced the name. *We ain't done yet, you and me,* she thought, *not by a long shot.*

She pushed the door halfway open and peered inside. The room was empty, so she went on in. The main room still had the look of a store, with a long counter running almost the length of one side of it. There were some shelves behind the counter, now empty, and one table with a broken leg and a couple of chairs. It was obvious that there had been more, but the rest had been removed. There was a fireplace on the wall opposite the counter and a scorched square in the middle of the floor where a stove had once stood. Looking up, she could see the hole where the stovepipe had gone through the roof. She stood there a moment and looked all around her. "This'll do," she announced to herself, even before checking to see what the door in the back led to. She was joined a moment later by Rubin.

"How's it look?" Rubin asked, standing as she had, looking around him at the empty room.

"It'll do us just fine," Hannah answered. "Go ahead and start unloadin' the packhorse. I'll help you in a minute. I just wanna see where that door leads."

The door led to a short hallway with two rooms off it, one a bedroom, the other the kitchen. Like the storefront, the kitchen had been gutted, stove and all. *Too bad,* she thought, but she had figured she'd be cooking in the fireplace, anyway, what little bit of cooking she planned to do. If her brother was hungry, he could cook for himself. She had never been one to play the part of the suffering pioneer woman like her mother did, and she sure as hell didn't intend to start now. Only she and Rubin were left of the Cheney gang, but she intended to carry on in the same fashion as before her father and three brothers were killed. And that was by living off the toils of honest folk.

As her father had requested, she had taken her mother several miles up the river above this abandoned trading post to her uncle Albert's farm. She and Rubin had buried her father at their first camp near the forks of Clear Boggy and Muddy Boggy creeks, after leaving Kettle Creek. They bade their mother good-bye and left the uncle's farm, much to the relief of Albert and Mae Clinton. Finding this trading post still abandoned was a stroke of good luck as far as Hannah was concerned. It saved her and Rubin from setting up in a makeshift tent or shack, what with winter already on its way. She found it odd, however, that no one had claimed it before now. Had she known the reason, she would have laughed. The closest people to the store were in a Choctaw village at Switchback Creek, and they were convinced that Lem Stark's evil spirit still inhabited the trading post. It would have made little difference to Hannah Cheney, because she feared no one, evil spirit or human. She went outside then to help Rubin.

"Let's get a fire goin'," Hannah said after their packs were brought inside. "I'll slice off some bacon and make some pan biscuits, but don't go thinkin' I'm gonna be takin' Ma's place. Damned if I'm gonna be doin' all the cookin' around here, so you might as well get used to doin' for yourself. You can start by primin' that pump in the kitchen to see if it works. If it don't, go fill the coffeepot at the river."

"Why, yessum," Rubin replied sarcastically, "I'll jump right to it. I didn't expect you'd try to take Ma's place, and I sure as hell didn't figure you'd try to take Pa's. Maybe I was wrong." He

179

picked up the coffeepot and left to do her bidding, anyway.

Dumb as a stump, she thought, *but I need him right now.* In spite of the near annihilation of Ike Cheney's gang, she had no thoughts of retiring from the family business of robbery and rustling. It was in her blood and she had never known any other way to survive. So she was confident that she and Rubin would be back in business as soon as she had the opportunity to see what potential the territory offered. There was one piece of business that she was determined to settle and that was Deputy Marshal Will Tanner. She made a vow to make sure he paid for the death of her father and her brothers. And to make sure she never let herself forget that vow, she reached in her pocket, as she often did, and felt the smooth round pebble she had found near her father's grave. The opportunity would come, she would see to it. She was smart enough to know it was foolish to make an attempt on him when he was riding with a posse. But he wasn't always going to have a posse to protect him. In the meantime, she and Rubin had to make a living.

After two nights and a day at their new hideout, Hannah and Rubin had settled in to make it a more permanent base. They had a small amount of money left from the stolen cattle they had sold at the Fort Worth market, enough to see them through the winter. With the coming of spring, however, they were going to have to decide where their best potential to find more might be. At this point, they sorely missed their father. Old Ike Cheney would know where best to target their next payday. At least Hannah knew it wasn't smart to strike targets close around Tishomingo. Her pa had always said it wasn't smart to do your business in the same place you had to sleep at night. When she thought about it, she wondered if he had broken that rule when they had moved into the cabin at Kettle Creek, and it contributed to the deaths of her father, Luke, Levi, and Buck. They were sure as hell rustling cattle right there where they camped. She and Rubin were discussing the problem of working too close to home late that afternoon when visitors rode in.

Rubin spotted them when they left the river trail and rode down the path to the cabin. "We got company!" he blurted as he was standing at the window. "Damn! Damn!" he cursed in alarm. "There's four of 'em, and they're comin' right toward the door."

"Where?" Hannah demanded, and came running with her rifle in hand.

"There!" Rubin said, and pointed. "Looks like a posse. How'd they know where we were?"

"Maybe a posse, maybe not," Hannah said, thinking it unlikely that the law knew they were there. *Unless,* she thought, *Uncle Albert told them.* She quickly discarded the thought. Albert clearly didn't care for his sister-in-law's family, but he wouldn't turn them in. She peered at the four riders for another few moments before deciding they didn't look like a posse. For one thing, they didn't seem to take any precautions, as they would have if they thought they might be riding into an ambush. "Let's just let them make the first play," she said. "Maybe they'll just ride out again when they find out this ain't a tradin' post no more. Get over behind the counter." Rubin followed her over to stand behind the counter to await their visitors, their rifles resting on the counter before them and aimed at the door.

"There's some horses in the corral," they heard one of the men yell outside. A short time after, the front door was slowly eased ajar, but no one came in.

After a moment, Hannah called out, "You comin' in or not?"

"Depends," the answer came back.

"On what?" Rubin asked.

"On whether or not I'm gonna walk into a shootin' gallery."

"Might be you should state your business here," Hannah said. "Are you a lawman? Who are you lookin' for?"

"If that's what you're worried about," the voice said, "then you ain't got nothin' to worry about. We sure as hell ain't lawmen. We was just lookin' for a place to set up camp, and we was told this place was empty. I was here three years ago when a feller by the name of Lem Stark had a store here. Bought some supplies from him."

"Lem Stark is dead," Hannah said. "This place belongs to us now and it ain't a store no more. We ain't sellin' nothin'."

"That a fact? Well, we ain't lookin' to buy nothin'." They could hear a discussion taking place on the porch among the four riders, but it was not loud enough to understand what was being said. In a few moments, the one doing all the talking came back. "Hey," he asked politely, "mind if we come inside? It's gettin' a mite chilly out here, and we've been in the saddle a long spell. We ain't lookin' to cause you no trouble, and we've got food and coffee to spare—be glad to share it with you folks."

"I don't like the sound of this," Rubin whispered. "We don't want them in here."

"I know it," Hannah whispered back. "But there's four of 'em. If they're thinkin' about doin' us some harm, they could burn us outta here and we couldn't stop 'em. Might be better to let 'em come in where we can keep our rifles trained on 'em."

"Whaddaya say?" the voice asked when there had been no response to his request after a long pause. "Can we come in and sit by the fire for a spell?"

"Come on in," Hannah answered. "But make it slow, and one at a time. There's a lotta bad people driftin' around this part of the territory. A body can't be too careful, and that's why I'm tellin' you there's a couple of Winchester rifles pointed at that door. But if you ain't got no mischief on your mind, come on in."

"Fair enough," the voice said. "You ain't got nothin' to worry about from us. I'm comin' in." Very slowly, the door opened wider and the man stepped inside. He stopped abruptly when he saw the two rifles leveled at him and raised his hands almost shoulder high to indicate he had no intention of drawing his weapon. "Easy does it, folks," he said. "We ain't here to do you no harm." He called back over his shoulder, "Come on in, Rafe, one at a time, like the lady said." He turned back to look at the man and woman standing behind the counter while one by one his three companions came inside. He felt as if he had seen the man behind the counter somewhere before, but he couldn't place him. "Rafe, here, has got a wound in his shoulder that don't seem to wanna heal up. All right with you folks if he sits down over there by the fire?" When Hannah nodded, Rafe went to the fireplace and sat down on the floor next to the fireplace. He was obviously in some discomfort. "These other two fine-lookin' gentlemen are Mace Weaver and Tater Smith."

"What's your name?" Hannah asked.

"Jack Lynch," the rangy man answered.

A smile spread slowly across Hannah's face, and she exchanged a quick glance with Rubin. "Scorpion Jack, ain't that what they call you?"

Jack looked genuinely surprised. "Some do, I reckon," he confessed. "My name is Jack Lynch. What's yourn?"

"I'm Hannah Cheney," she answered. "This is my brother, Rubin. My daddy was Ike Cheney. Maybe you remember him."

"Well, I'll be . . ." Jack started, clearly astonished. "The last time I saw Ike was two years ago, down in Texas. I swear, I thought there was somethin' familiar-lookin' about your brother. He was with your pa, if I recollect. Don't believe I ever saw you before, though." He shook his head and chuckled, then turned to the two men standing beside him. "You've heard me talk about Ike Cheney. Hell, we was in on a train holdup together. That's before I ran into that trouble in Arkansas." He turned back to Hannah then. "You said your daddy *was* Ike Cheney. Is Ike dead?"

"We buried him last Tuesday," Hannah said.

"Well, I'm right sorry to hear that. What put him under—lawman?"

"I reckon you could say that," she replied. "We were runnin' from a posse when Daddy's heart just gave out on him."

"There were other boys, what about them? They still down in Texas?"

"Yes, they are," Hannah said, "under the ground, shot dead by a deputy marshal ridin' outta Fort Smith."

"Well, now, that is sorry news," Jack said. "And I reckon you and Rubin are on the run. Is that right?" Hannah nodded, so Jack said, "Maybe we could join up. I lost a couple of good men in Colorado. This place looks like there's room for all of us if there ain't but the two of you. I believe we could help each other out." He favored her with a wide grin. "I'd admire havin' a woman around. Whaddaya say?"

The idea appealed to Hannah, but she wanted to get one thing straight before she agreed to anything. "That might work out pretty good, but don't go gettin' any notions about havin' a woman around to do the cookin', and waitin' on a bunch of lazy men, and I damn sure ain't interested in providin' any entertainment for the four of you. If you've got that straight, then we've got a deal."

"You're a feisty little woman, ain'tcha?" Mace Weaver spoke up then. "I'll bet you ain't even been saddle-broke yet."

"You wanna be the first one to try it?" Hannah responded as she pulled the long skinning knife from her belt. " 'Cause it'd be the last time you could sit in a saddle without cryin' like a baby."

Her threat brought a laugh from the three men with Mace. "You'd best mind your manners," Tater said. "That woman will whip your ass."

"He musta thought she was standin' on a box behind that counter," Rafe joined in the japing.

Soon they were all laughing at Mace's expense, even Rubin. "Mister, you'd do well to listen to your friends," he said. "She ain't standin' on no box back of this counter. I can tell you that. And most of the time she can back up what she says, but if she can't, then I lend a hand."

"Ain't no need to get your back up," Jack said to Rubin. "Mace's always japin' somebody. He don't mean nothin' by it. Ain't that right, Mace?" He cast a quick menacing glance in his direction.

"Why, sure," Mace replied at once, "I was just japin' you a little. You don't have to worry 'bout any trouble like that from me."

"As long as everybody understands that, then I reckon we can work together," Hannah said. "That all right with you, Rubin?" He responded with a shrug of his shoulders. The question was asked merely as a courtesy to her brother. She was confident that he wouldn't protest any decision she made on their behalf. Back to Jack and his friends, she continued. "I'll do some cookin' when it suits me, 'cause I know most men would starve to death if they had to depend on themselves. But I can handle a gun as good as any man, and I expect to carry my end of the load on any jobs we take on. Is that clear?"

Jack couldn't help being amused by the woman's brashness. "I reckon it's clear enough, all right, ain't it, boys?" Amused as well, they all grinned and nodded. "Like I said," he went on, "all we're lookin' for right now is a place to hole up till spring. Then I expect we'll be headin' back Colorado way. I figure we were awful lucky to find a place like this to winter in. Course we was told there weren't nobody in it, like I told you. But I'm tickled to find it's kin of Ike Cheney, an old friend of mine. We oughta get along just fine."

Hannah glanced at Rubin and grinned. "Brother, we're back in business." She was satisfied that it was a stroke of good luck that Jack had showed up at this point. There was strength in numbers and the possibility of planning bigger jobs. She had been fretting over the thought of no one but her and Rubin and, consequently, the necessity to work on a smaller scale. Looking back at Jack, she said, "Well, I reckon we've got us a deal. You fellers can put your horses in the barn and move yourselves in here. You can spread your bedrolls right here near the fireplace with Rubin. I sleep in the bedroom."

"You sure you don't want somebody to sleep in that room with you?" Mace Weaver asked, grinning mischievously. "In case there's some ghosts movin' around this place at night."

Hannah cocked a warning eye in his direction. "Mister, you're a slow learner, ain't you? Didn't your mama ever tell you you was a little slow in the head?" Her reply brought a few chuckles from Mace's companions.

"I expect you've found out what you need to know," Jack said to Mace. His tone was deadly serious. "So that'll be the end of it."

"Aw, I was just funnin' with her," Mace said.

With that settled, Jack turned back to Hannah. "There'll be one more of us showin' up here any day now. My son, Mike, was released from prison. I sent word to him to meet us here. When I sent the letter, I didn't know Lem Stark was dead and the place was empty. It's been a long time, but I knew Mike would remember where it is." He paused to reflect. "Ten years since I've seen my boy, and I can hardly wait till he gets here. I blame myself for him bein' in that stinkin' prison. I shoulda sat down hard on him when he wanted to go off with a couple of two-bit outlaws to steal cattle." He paused again, obviously thinking about his son. "Anyway," he concluded, "like I said, he'll be showin' up any day now."

That was all right with Hannah—the bigger the gang, the bigger jobs they could target. She was not blind to the potential for problems when it came to making decisions, however. Jack Lynch was without question the leader of the three

189

men following him, and that would be four men when his son showed up. Obviously, Lynch was accustomed to calling all the shots, and she was not prone to follow his orders blindly. It might cause trouble down the line, and if it did, they were two against five, not good odds. "We'll just have to wait and see how it goes," she told Rubin later that evening.

CHAPTER 9

Will and Perley rode out of the ravine that led into Perley's camp before the first rays of the morning sun had found their way through the narrow passages. They planned to stop to rest the horses and drink some coffee by a little creek that Perley said was about twelve miles from the foot of the Jack Fork Mountains. Perley figured he'd leave Will about eighteen miles beyond that and turn north. It was afternoon by the time they reached the point where Perley pulled up, reached out to shake Will's hand, and said so long. Then he turned the dark Morgan's nose due north. Both men planned to get another ten miles or more before making camp for the night.

With Perley's departure, Will turned his thoughts back to the purpose of his trip. He figured to stop at Jim Little Eagle's cabin near Atoka and see if he had any information about a new gang around that area. By the time he reached Tishomingo, Jack Lynch and his friends could be anywhere, if it was Jack Lynch that Tom Spotted Horse had reported. That thought caused him to consider the short, broad-shouldered Chickasaw policeman. He hadn't worked with Tom but once before. And for some reason, he had felt a sense of resentment on the

Indian's part, as if Will was trying to challenge his authority. *Maybe I just caught him at a bad time,* he thought, thinking Tom may have been having some personal trouble. He couldn't help thinking about Alvin Greeley then and the trouble he had with him. *Maybe it's me,* he thought. *Maybe I'm getting hard to deal with.* He didn't recall ever having the problem with anyone else. As far as Tom Spotted Horse was concerned, whatever his problem, Will was not planning to spend much time with him in any event.

After riding under cloudy skies during the past couple of days, it was nice to get a glimpse of the sun, even though it was setting when he approached the railroad in Atoka. He pushed on through the little town and took a trail that followed Muddy Boggy Creek, hoping to find Jim Little Eagle at his cabin a shade over a mile from town. If he did, then he could count on an invitation to supper, and Mary Light Walker, Jim's wife, was a damn good cook. While he was riding along beside the Muddy Boggy, he had to think hard to remember exactly what day it was. Was today Christmas, or is it tomorrow? Maybe Sophie Bennett is married by now. "Sophie Pearson," he said aloud. "That'd be her name tonight." It didn't sound right to him.

He was saved from further thoughts on the subject by the sight of Jim Little Eagle's cabin as he rode around a bend in the creek. Jim was outside splitting some firewood and stopped as soon as he saw Will approaching.

"Will Tanner!" Jim called out. *"Halito! Chim achukma?"*

"I'm fine," Will returned, *"Chisnato?* How 'bout you? And if we're gonna talk much more, we'd best do it in English, 'cause that's pretty near all the Choctaw I know."

Jim laughed. "All right, my friend. Did your trip down to your place in Texas go well? I thought maybe you would be riding with Alvin Greeley when I saw you again." He chuckled at his intentional joke. "What brings you out this way so soon?"

After he told him about the trouble he had run into in Texas, Will told him about the reports of some suspicious-looking riders in the Chickasaw Nation. "Over near Tishomingo," he said. "Tom Spotted Horse telegraphed the message in to Fort Smith almost a week ago now. I'm on my way there, but I thought I'd check with you to see if there's been any strangers showing up in your area that didn't look just right."

Jim shook his head. "I read the wire Dan Stone sent out, but I ain't seen anybody like that around here. The wire said they might be Jack Lynch and his men from over Colorado way."

"That's what Dan suspects," Will said, " 'Cause a deputy's posse up in Kansas was chasin' 'em, but they lost 'em. They figure they headed on down in the Nations. Then we got a wire from Tom Spotted Horse sayin' there's a bunch of strangers over his way that might be Lynch and his men. Dan sent me over to find out."

"Who is Jack Lynch?" Jim asked. "You ever hear of him?"

"Never heard of him, myself, but Dan says his gang's been raisin' a lot of hell all over Colorado Territory and part of Kansas," Will said.

"You want me to go with you?"

"No, I reckon not," Will replied. "I'm just gonna try to locate 'em. If it is Lynch, then I'll decide what to do about 'em. I ain't even sure how many men are ridin' with him. If it's more'n I can handle, I might call on you for some help."

"Good enough," Jim said. "Come now and we'll take care of your horses, then I'll tell Mary you'll have supper with us."

"She already knows," Will said, having noticed the Choctaw woman standing just inside the cabin door, watching them. "I 'preciate the invitation to supper. I hope I don't put her out too much. I thought she might be needin' some flour, so I brought her a sack of it on my packhorse."

" 'Preciate it, Will," Jim said. "Mary will be tickled." The gift was not totally unexpected. Will usually brought a little something in exchange for their hospitality.

As Jim had predicted, Mary was delighted to

194

get the extra flour. She used some of it to bake them some biscuits for their supper. They added to a pleasant evening with his friends before Will thanked her and bade them a good night. Then he retired to the small barn to sleep with his horses, saying that he had to make an early start in the morning, since he planned to make the trip to Tishomingo in one day. In spite of the fact that he insisted they should not worry about seeing him off in the morning, when he rolled out of his blankets there was coffee bubbling on Mary's iron stove, and Jim showed up in the barn to help him saddle up. When he was on his way, it was impossible not to contrast their hospitality with the sullen reception he could expect from Tom Spotted Horse.

Crossing the Blue River, where he had often crossed before, Will found a cabin where there had been none the last time he had ridden this trail. It appeared to be a trading post situated on the bank of the river. It was a sizable structure with a couple of smaller rooms built on the back of it, which Will assumed to be living quarters. The timbers of the tiny barn behind it were still green, evidently having been finished most recently. It was already in the middle of the afternoon and he had a few miles to travel before reaching Tishomingo. But he decided he might as well stop and see who the owner was, thinking it a good idea to rest his horses for a short while, even though they didn't really need it yet. There was a woman with a broom, sweeping the bare ground in front of the store. She stopped when she spotted him crossing the river.

"Somebody's comin'," Melva Sams called back toward the door. Then she stood there for a moment staring at the rider approaching. "One fellow leadin' a packhorse," she announced, turned about, and returned to the house.

In a few moments, a short bald man appeared in the doorway of the cabin, silently watching Will as he guided Buster to a hitching post several yards shy of the front door. "Evenin', neighbor," the man finally called out. "Welcome to my little store. My name's Dewey Sams and I'm happy to have you stop in."

"Howdy," Will returned. "Looks like you've been workin' mighty hard. It ain't been that long since I rode this trail to Tishomingo and there wasn't any cabin here then."

"It ain't been long, that's a fact," Dewey said. "Me and my brother finished the store last month and the barn about a week ago. Don't many folks know we're here yet, just a few riding that trail you just came in on, but I'm hopin' they'll find us before long." He watched while Will stepped down from the saddle. "If you're lookin' to buy some supplies, I've got a fair amount of trade goods, but I'll have a lot more things in stock as soon as my brother gets back from Fort Smith with a wagonload of goods. Is there somethin' I can help you with today?" While he talked, he gave Will's packhorse a quick going-over with his eyes, a little disappointed to see that the bay gelding was loaded fairly heavily.

"Sorry," Will said. "Right now, there ain't nothin' in particular I'm short of. Maybe some coffee, if you have some." He reminded himself of the sack he had left with Perley, and he could always use extra coffee. "I just stopped to see who was settin' up here. I'm a U.S. Deputy Marshal, and I'm on my way to Tishomingo. I was gonna ask you if you've seen any new faces in the territory in the last week or so, but since you're a new face yourself, I reckon you wouldn't know."

Dewey laughed. "Reckon you could say that, but I ain't new to the whole territory, just around this part. Me and my brother had us a little place down near Durant, but we couldn't make a livin' out of it. Dixon Durant's general store had too much of a head start on us, and there just wasn't enough business to go around. So me and my brother pulled up stakes and came up this way when we heard the tradin' post that was up here went outta business. Fellow's name that owned it was Lem Stark—got into some kinda trouble with the law. From what I've heard, this Stark fellow wasn't doin' much trade with folks around here. More into providin' a hideout for outlaws to hole up for a while. We thought about goin' up the river to take a look at the old store. But to tell you the truth, we didn't want to deal with any of his old friends that might show up thinkin' Stark was still there. Anyway, he's dead and the store's abandoned. Maybe you know somethin' about that."

"Yeah," Will said. "I know about that." He didn't bother to offer any details. He followed Dewey into the store then and paused to look around at the sparsely filled shelves.

"Like I said," Sams remarked, "not much stock right now, but my brother oughta be gettin' back here any day now with a load of merchandise." Remembering then, he said, "But I do have coffee, two sacks of coffee beans I got shipped from New Orleans."

"Let me have ten pounds of 'em," Will said.

"Yes, sir. You want me to grind 'em for you?"

"Nope," Will replied. "I'll just grind what I need when I want it." He always carried a small coffee grinder he had bought in Floyd Meeks's store in Fort Smith. "I might be needin' some other things if I'm down this way very long this time. Maybe I can give you some more business later on."

"I'd sure appreciate it," Dewey said as he scooped beans out onto a scale. "Sometimes it takes a good while for folks to find out about you, but me and Jake are gonna give folks their money's worth." Melva Sams came in from the back room at that point and offered a "Good evening" to Will. "This here's my missus," Dewey said. "Melva, this is . . ." He paused then. "I didn't catch your name, mister."

"Will Tanner," he said. "Glad to make your acquaintance, Mrs. Sams."

"Mr. Tanner," Melva replied politely. "I overheard you tell Dewey you were a deputy marshal. I had just made Dewey and myself a pot of fresh coffee when I saw you ride in. It oughta be done in a minute or two. Cold day like today, I thought you might could use a cup."

"Why, that's mighty nice of you, ma'am," Will said. "I surely could." For a moment he couldn't help thinking what a difference these folks brought to the territory when compared to the likes of Lem Stark and the outlaws that had frequented his store. Maybe Tishomingo might grow into a friendly little town if more people like this couple moved in around it. Then he remembered the reason he was sent down there. "I expect I'll have to drink it pretty quick and be on my way, though. Beggin' your pardon if I'm impolite, but I need to see if I can catch the Chickasaw policeman in Tishomingo tonight if I can."

"Tom Spotted Horse?" Dewey asked.

"So you know him already," Will said.

"Yeah, he introduced himself one mornin' when Jake and I were still workin' on the barn. I think he just wanted to make sure we weren't fixin' to sell whiskey in our store, especially to the Indians. I told him we weren't in that business. We're just a couple of honest storekeepers hoping to make a livin'. He said he was the law around here, and he was the man who watched out for that kind of business." He glanced at Melva again as if undecided whether or not he should say more. "He's stopped by a couple of times since, but he doesn't seem like a friendly sort of fellow."

Will nodded, understanding why Dewey would think so. "It ain't nothin' against you folks," he said. "He's just that way with everybody, myself included. The first time I worked with him, I thought I musta said something that insulted his people or something. I think when he was born he musta sucked on a sour—" He caught himself just in time. "I mean his mama's milk musta been sour." He realized he was digging the hole deeper and deeper the more he tried to recover. "Beggin' your pardon, ma'am. I think I'll roll my tongue up and wait till my brain starts workin' again."

Melva threw her head back and laughed at the deputy's embarrassment. She went at once to the stove and poured a cup of coffee for him. "Here," she said. "You can take enough time to try some of my coffee."

He had a couple of cups of Melva's coffee before he finally got under way, explaining again that if he didn't get to Tishomingo before sundown, he'd most likely miss Tom Spotted Horse. *Nice folks,* he thought as he turned Buster back on the trail leading southwest to the capitol of the Chickasaw Nation.

There was one horse in the corral next to the small cabin that had served as the headquarters for the Chickasaw Lighthorsemen. That was before the individual nations were consolidated under the Union Agency, headquartered in Muskogee. So now the cabin was used by Tom Spotted Horse only. As he passed Wilbur Greene's stable, he noticed a paint horse in the corral, like the one Tom rode. *Good,* Will thought, *looks like I caught him before he went home to that coyote bitch he's married to.* Unlike his visits to Jim Little Eagle's cabin, Will preferred not to ride out to Tom's house. Equally as gruff and inhospitable as Tom, his wife was openly hostile to visitors. This attitude was reserved for white men only, Will supposed. Whatever the reason, he felt that his onetime exposure to her hospitality was all he cared to experience.

Tom stepped out the door of the cabin as Will pulled up before it. He was carrying his saddle on his shoulder, obviously heading to the stable to saddle his horse. When he saw Will, he stopped, still holding the saddle. "Will Tanner," he stated soberly, in the same tone as if discovering a bug on the kitchen floor. He stood there, his face expressionless, staring dull-eyed at the deputy.

"Tom," Will returned, reflecting the Indian policeman's somber greeting. "Dan Stone sent me over here to find out about that bunch of strangers you spotted."

Tom shrugged, his expression never changing. "That was a week ago. I don't see them no more."

"Where did you see them?" Will asked, "And how many were there? You didn't say in your telegram."

"Hadn't seen 'em when I sent the telegram," he said. "Wilbur Greene told me they stopped at the stable. He said they were strangers and looked no good, so I sent telegram. I saw 'em next day. They had a small camp on the creek north of town," he said, referring to Pennington Creek, beside which Tishomingo was built. I count four white men I never see before. I watch them for a while, but they only stop to rest horses. Then they ride east, I don't follow them no more. I think maybe they headed to Choctaw Nation, so I ride to railroad and wire Marshal Stone again."

Will thought about that for a second. It wasn't a hell of a lot of information, but at least he knew that he was dealing with four men. Spotted Horse wouldn't know if the men he saw were Jack Lynch and his gang, and he obviously

202

didn't care as long as they bypassed Tishomingo. Maybe Will could pick up their trail, so his ride to Tishomingo wouldn't be a total waste of time. "Can you take me to the place you saw them?"

Tom turned and pointed to the creek that ran through the town. "Follow the creek, one and a half, maybe two, miles. Camp on west bank. They ride toward Atoka, I think."

Will couldn't help a feeling of irritation. He had just come from Atoka, and now if Tom was right, he had wasted his time riding all the way over to Tishomingo. "Maybe we coulda saved a little time if you had said they had headed toward Atoka in your wire," he said, forgetting that he had already left Fort Smith when Tom's second wire arrived.

Again, Tom shrugged, making no effort to disguise his lack of interest in the whereabouts of Jack Lynch and his gang. "Maybe they don't go to Atoka," he said. "I just told you which way they headed after they left here. I think maybe they long gone from Chickasaw Nation, maybe ride down to Texas."

"Maybe so," Will said, making an effort to hide his irritation, since Texas would be in the opposite direction from Atoka. He climbed back into the saddle and turned Buster toward Pennington Creek, thinking he might as well see if he could find the campsite Tom referred to. Possibly there might be a trail to follow. It might be a total waste of time, but there was nothing else to go on at this point. The men Tom had seen could be anywhere, and they might not even be Jack Lynch and his gang.

Will found the evidence of a campsite approximately where Tom Spotted Horse had told him. The remains of a sizable campfire bore testimony that there was a camp there, but nothing more than that. Tracks of horses he found between the fire and the riverbank told him there were at least three in the party, maybe four. A thorough scout along the bank was enough to discover the party's trail upon leaving, and as Tom had said, headed in the general direction of Atoka. Will experienced a slight feeling of irritation again when he considered that he had just come from Atoka on his way to Tishomingo. At this time, it would take him the rest of the day to ride to Atoka, especially since he was trying to follow a trail that might fork off in some other direction anywhere between the two towns. There was still the question of whether or not the tracks he intended to follow were left by Jack Lynch and his men. But that was all he had at the moment, so he quit deliberating over the matter and started out following the trail that led along the bank.

As he guided the big buckskin along beside the creek, he thought about a time not long before when he had ridden up the Blue River on a search for Eli Stark. Lem Stark's old trading post was no more than five or six miles from where he was now, but in the opposite direction from the trail he was following. The storekeeper, Dewey Sams, had said that Stark's old store was still empty. Will was not surprised. It was not in a good location to do business with the farmers and cattlemen around Tishomingo, and that was why it was a favorite with outlaws on the run. Had he not been following the one lead he had on the possible movements of Jack Lynch and his men, he might have been inclined to take a ride up the river to get a look at the old store.

At almost the same time Will's thoughts wandered momentarily to a time when he was pursuing Eli Stark, the present occupants of that infamous trading post were sitting down to devour a freshly butchered deer that Tater Smith had killed. Hannah Cheney had taken charge of the roasting of the meat in the huge fireplace, only after Tater proceeded to serve up slices of half-cooked venison. Although she was determined not to take on a woman's chores for the gang of men, she was averse to eating meat that was almost raw. Mace Weaver winked at Tater when Hannah took over. He had boasted to Rafe and Tater that he would saddle-break the defiant woman before winter really set in. "Then we'll get a lot more than cookin' outta that big ol' tough-talkin' woman," he promised.

"All right, you worthless bunch of coyotes," Hannah said when the meat was done. "If you want any of this, you'd best get up off your lazy behinds and come get it. I ain't gonna bring it to ya." The men seated around the table dutifully got up and filed by the fireplace to receive a slice of the meat. Hannah set aside a couple of choice portions for herself and her brother.

"How long do you think it's safe to hole up in this cabin before the law comes snoopin' around here lookin' for us?" Rafe Yeager asked. "They sure as hell know about this place."

"We lost that posse when we left Kansas," Jack Lynch answered. "And there ain't been no sign of any Oklahoma deputy marshals on our tail since we crossed the border. So that tells me they don't know which way we headed when we hit Injun Territory."

"This place is too close to Tishomingo and Atoka," Mace said. "And there's them Injun police in both of those towns."

"I thought they weren't supposed to bother with nobody but Injuns," Tater said. "Hell, if one of them shows up here, we'll just shoot him."

"And then the deputy marshals will be showin' up next," Lynch said. "Rafe's right, though, we probably ought'n hole up here all winter. Too many folks know about this place. I've been thinkin' maybe it would be a good idea to go up in those hills about a day and a half or two northwest of here. A few years ago, I spent a winter up there with a couple of ol' boys from Texas. There's a right sound little cabin up in those mountains, and there's a helluva lot less folks that know about it."

"Hell, if it ain't no farther away than that, why didn't we go on up there in the first place?" Tater asked.

"Because we're gonna wait here till my son gets here," Lynch said. "He knows about this place, and he oughta be showin' up any day now." He paused to think about it. "Matter of fact, he shoulda already showed up." He got up from the table and walked over to the fireplace to pour himself another cup of coffee. "As soon as Mike gets here, we'll take a ride up there and see if that cabin's still fit to live in." He watched the last little bit of coffee trickle out of the pot. "We're about outta coffee, and we could use some flour, too. I've got a hankerin' for some biscuits." He grinned at Hannah. "Reckon you could see your way to makin' some biscuits? I guarantee you, ain't none of us can make a biscuit fit to eat."

She couldn't help a chuckle. "I reckon I might, as long as you don't expect 'em every day."

" 'Preciate it," he said. "Somebody can ride downriver to that store we passed the other day."

"I'll go," Tater volunteered immediately. "I

need to see if that feller carries any tabacky. I ain't had a chew in a week."

"I'll go with you," Rubin Cheney said. No one else spoke up, since they had already found out that Dewey Sams had no whiskey to sell.

"Mornin', fellers," Dewey Sams greeted the two men when they walked into his store the following day. "What can I do for you this mornin'?"

"We'll be needin' some coffee and some flour," Rubin replied.

"And some tabacky, if you've got any," Tater said.

"You talkin' about chewin' tobacco?" Dewey asked. "Plugs? 'Cause if you are, I just got some in yesterday. My brother just got in with a wagonload of supplies last night, and I know for sure there was supposed to be some tobacco in it. Right, Jake?"

"There sure is," Jake answered, having heard the request just as he walked in from the back room. "Got some with some kinda wine mixed up in it, real fancy stuff."

"I'm mighty glad to hear it," Tater said. "I've had an awful cravin'." Naturally curious, he asked, "Where do you haul goods in from?"

"Well, sometimes down in Texas, Fort Worth, mostly, but sometimes we'll go over to Fort Smith," Jake said.

Impatient with Tater's tendency to make idle conversation, Rubin spoke up. "We're needin' coffee and flour for sure."

"Yeah, coffee and flour," Tater echoed. "What's the news from over that way? I ain't been to Fort Smith in I don't know when."

"Nothin' much, I reckon. That town's about as wild as ever, even with a U.S. Marshal and a hangin' judge right there." Jake said, then remembered what he'd heard. "Feller told me that a few days ago this lawman was bringin' a young feller to that jail under the courthouse when all of a sudden he musta tried to run for it or something. And, bam! The deputy shot him down, right there in the street."

"You don't say," Tater said.

"Yep," Jake said. "He said the feller's name was Lynch. I remember thinking it was a good name for him because he was most likely gonna get lynched if he went up before Judge Parker. But he got shot before they got the chance to lynch him." He grinned, then paused before continuing his story, stopped by the sudden blanching of Tater's face.

It was a few seconds before the color returned to the old outlaw's face. But his eyes were still staring wide when he asked, "You sure about that? Who told you the feller's name was Lynch?"

"I stopped for one last shot of whiskey at a saloon down by the ferry slips. I was askin' the feller that owns the place about the shootin' and he said he knew the young feller, and he said his name was Lynch. Can't remember his first name, mighta been Mike or Matt, somethin' like that. I just remember the part about lynchin'." Jake looked from Tater to Rubin, whose eyes were also wide open in shocked surprise. His next statement brought an involuntary grunt from one of the two men. "I've heard of that lawman that shot him. Folks around this part of the Nations say he works here all the time, feller name of Will Tanner."

"Now I'll tell you something you don't know," Dewey said, interrupting his brother. "Will Tanner stopped by here just yesterday. He said he was on his way to Tishomingo to talk to Tom Spotted Horse. Bought a big sack of coffee beans."

"You never said a thing about that," Jake said.

"I never thought about it," Dewey replied. "Didn't think you'd care, anyway."

Dewey exchanged glances of astonishment with his brother when their two customers seemed to suddenly be suspended in the grip of a speechless void. After an uncomfortable lapse lasting a long moment, Tater finally spoke, his seeming paralysis broken by a sense of urgency. "We'd best get on back to our camp," he stuttered, and took a step toward the door.

"What about your goods?" Dewey asked,

pointing to the sacks still sitting on the counter. "Did you change your mind?"

Just then remembering their purchases, Tater stopped and replied, "I reckon we're still gonna need that stuff, all right." He looked at Rubin. "Grab one of them sacks. Don't make much sense to go back without what we come for." Rubin did as he was told and picked up the flour and coffee beans, leaving the tobacco for Tater.

The two brothers walked outside and stood watching as Tater and Rubin hurriedly tied the sacks to their saddles. When their purchases were secure, they both climbed aboard and wheeled their horses away from the hitching rail. " 'Preciate the business," Dewey called after them as they hurried away at a fast lope. There was no response from either of the two.

"What the hell got into them?" Jake wondered. "They all of a sudden got tongue-tied when I told 'em about Will Tanner shootin' that outlaw."

"Most likely just you mentionin' Will Tanner," Dewey speculated. "Don't think I've ever seen those fellers before. Maybe they're wanted somewhere, and they're hidin' out here in the Nations like so many outlaws. They sure got in a hurry when I told you about Tanner bein' in here, though, didn't they?"

"At least they paid cash money for those supplies," Jake said, "instead of takin' 'em at gunpoint."

· · ·

Tater and Rubin did not spare their horses in their rush to get back to the cabin with the news. By the time they reached the path that led down over the bluffs to the river, the horses were heavily lathered in spite of the cold temperature. Tater started yelling for Lynch even before reaching the small barn behind the cabin. His cries of alarm were enough to bring Lynch and the others out of the house with weapons drawn. "What is it?" Jack demanded, seeing no one chasing after the two. Standing with him, Mace and Rafe, their pistols ready to fire, quickly scanned the bluffs behind the riders, back and forth, expecting to see a posse storm into view at any second.

"They shot your son!" Tater blurted. "They shot Mike!"

Stunned, Jack Lynch responded. "What are you talkin' about? Who shot my son?"

"A deputy marshal named Will Tanner!" Tater answered. "Shot him down dead, right in the middle of the street in broad daylight, right there in Fort Smith!"

"Who told you that?" Lynch demanded. "How do you know it was Mike?"

Tater related the story as Jake Sams had told it, including the reason Jake had no trouble remembering the victim's name was Lynch. Stunned, Jack Lynch held on to the porch post for a moment to steady himself, scarcely able to believe what he was hearing. By the time Tater had repeated every detail he could recall about the shooting, Lynch had recovered his usual stony demeanor, and his shock was replaced by anger and outrage. "And he's here, this Tanner son of a bitch, he's here in this territory?"

"That's what that feller at the store said," Tater replied. "Said he was on his way to Tishomingo to find the Indian policeman down there."

"I want him!" Lynch exclaimed. "I'll hang his guts on a fence post! Get ready to ride. We're goin' to Tishomingo and find the son of a bitch that killed my son. Rafe, saddle my horse." Rafe and Mace responded immediately, running for the corral, but Tater and Rubin were still there, hesitating, their lathered horses standing, still saddled by the barn. Lynch, his face twisted in a black rage, looked at the two and demanded, "What are you standin' here for? I told you to get ready to ride."

"Our horses ain't fit to ride, Jack," Tater explained. "We damn near foundered 'em on the way back from that store."

Tater's answer seemed to further infuriate the already-enraged man. "I don't give a damn if you run them into the ground," he at first responded. Then struggling to calm himself, he said, "Take the packhorses." Knowing neither of the two pack animals had ever been saddle-broken, he then glanced at Hannah Cheney, who had come out behind him. "Take her horse."

"You'll not take my horse," Hannah stepped forth and stated calmly. "I'll be goin' with you." She had stood silent during Tater's entire accounting of Mike Lynch's death, her eyes locked with Rubin's as they exchanged solemn glances at the mention of Will Tanner's name. Her hand had automatically found the small pebble she carried in her pocket to remind her of her vow for vengeance. And as she turned it over and over in her hand, feeling its smoothness, she recalled the crushing defeat and humiliation she had suffered in her first encounter with the hated lawman. She knew that this might be her chance to settle a debt she had vowed to pay.

Although Lynch had been amused by the young woman's aggressive manner in the short time since they had agreed to join forces, he was not inclined to be bothered with her at this critical moment. "I ain't got time for your foolishness right now," he snapped. "We need your horse, so you can stay here and try to act like a woman."

His remark served only to further inflame her. "Maybe we'd better get something straight right now," she shot back. "Not you, nor any other man, can tell me how to act. I'll act as I damn well please." For emphasis, she dropped her hand to rest on the handle of the .44 she wore on her hip. "I've got a claim on Will Tanner's life that came before you ever heard of him. And I ain't plannin' on lettin' you, or the sorry lot ridin' with you, stop me from doin' what I've got to do." She continued to glare at him, prepared to react to any move he might be inclined to make.

In spite of his anger, he was stunned by the woman's defiance. Thinking to call her bluff, he suddenly dropped his hand on the handle of his six-gun. Before he firmly gripped the pistol, her .44 had already cleared the holster and was aimed squarely at his midsection. "Whoa!" he blurted. "Hold on! There ain't no call for you to draw on me. I wasn't fixin' to pull on you." It was a lie, for he had intended to demonstrate how easily she could be facing sudden death, but he had never seen a weapon drawn that fast before, and it was he who was now facing death. Thoughts of Will Tanner were forgotten for that moment, replaced by the fear of losing his life. The woman was a little crazy, anyway, that was evident from the start. He realized now that she might just as easily pull the trigger on that .44 staring at his belly button. So he slowly raised his hand from the handle of his pistol. "Just take it easy with that pistol," he said in a voice as calm as he could manage. "You got the wrong idea. Hell, I thought we was partners. I wouldn't never draw on a partner. Ask any of the boys. Tell her, Tater." He glanced at the grizzled old man, who was standing with his mouth agape, just then noticing that Rubin was watching him with his gun drawn as well. It was plain to see that he would have gone down, even had he drawn quick enough to beat her, for her brother was obviously ready to back her. As for Tater, he was still standing there with his lower jaw hanging open, dumbfounded by the woman's speed with her handgun.

"I'll be goin' with you," Hannah repeated calmly.

"Yes, ma'am, you sure will," Lynch said, swallowing a large mouthful of humble pie. "I'll be glad to have you." He turned to Tater. "I don't reckon we'll need anybody else to go with us after one damn lawman. You and Rubin might as well stay here and look after our possibles while we're gone."

That suited Tater just fine. "Whatever you say, Jack." He turned toward the barn to help with the saddling.

"I'll saddle your horse for you," Rubin said to his sister. "Me and Tater will look after things here," he aimed at Lynch. His horse was spent, but that aside, it was just as well that he missed another encounter with the deputy marshal.

CHAPTER 10

Melva Sams paused after throwing out some potato peels for the two hogs to eat. She shielded her eyes against the rays of the afternoon sun as she tried to make out the riders approaching along the west bank of the river. There were four of them and they seemed to be in a hurry. That didn't always mean good news to the folks scattered around the small settlement, so she hurried in the kitchen door to alert Dewey and Jake. She found the two brothers in the store at the front of the cabin, standing by the window. "There's some riders comin' and they look like there's somebody chasin' 'em," she said.

"Yeah, I saw 'em when they came down the bluff," Dewey replied. "Looks like a bunch I saw ride through here a couple of days ago. At least three of 'em are. I don't recognize the other 'un."

"I thought them two that was in here a little while ago might be part of this bunch," Jake said, "but I don't see either one of 'em."

"They do look like they're in a big hurry to get here," Dewey said. "Somethin' about those men makes me think it wouldn't be a bad idea to be real careful when we're dealin' with 'em. Jake, why don't you get over there at the end of the

217

counter with that scattergun of yourn?" Dewey went back to the counter then and reached under it to get his gun belt and revolver. While he strapped it on, he said to Melva, "You go on back in the kitchen, hon, till we make sure these boys ain't lookin' to start no trouble." She nodded and returned to the kitchen. He often felt a little guilty to have brought his wife to this part of the territory. It was well known that there were a good number of outlaws in the Nations to escape the law. But it was also common thought that while in Indian Territory, most of them behaved themselves, not wishing to call marshals down upon them. Whether or not there was any basis to that thought, Dewey couldn't truthfully say, but he had counted on it when he moved his business from Durant to the remote riverbank near Tishomingo. Thinking they were about as prepared as they could get against the four, Dewey and Jake waited inside for their visitors to arrive.

When Lynch and the others pulled up in front of the store, the Sams brothers were mildly surprised and somewhat relieved when only Lynch dismounted and came inside. It was immediately obvious, however, that he was not there to buy anything. Before Dewey could greet him, he asked bluntly, "That deputy that was in here yesterday, did he come back this way?"

Astonished, Dewey replied, "Why, no, he

didn't, least not that I know of. I mean, we ain't seen him."

"You told my man that deputy said he was goin' to Tishomingo to see the Injun policeman. Is that right?" Dewey nodded. "Did he ask you about seein' us?"

Dewey hesitated, not certain he should tell him that the lawman did inquire about whether or not he had seen any strangers in the territory recently. At the same time, he was not sure it was a good idea to lie to the tall baleful outlaw. And at this point, he was certain he was an outlaw, else he wouldn't be concerned about Tanner asking about strangers. And the tone of his voice, combined with the cold squint of his eyes, seemed to indicate that he was accustomed to being obeyed. "Well," Dewey stammered, "not about you fellers. He just asked if we'd seen any strangers." Then he quickly added, "I told him no, we hadn't."

"I thought so," Lynch muttered to himself. He had a strong feeling that it wasn't mere coincidence that the deputy marshal who had shot his son down had suddenly shown up in Indian Territory right where he and his men were hiding. It was the only reason Lynch had taken the time to stop at the trading post on his way to look for Will Tanner. Now he felt his hunch was confirmed. *The son of a bitch is tracking me,* he thought. *He killed my son and now he's tracking me!* Lynch and his men had given the Kansas posse the slip. In all of Indian Territory, he wondered, how could the Oklahoma lawman have known that he would show up here, on Blue River? *Could he have gotten it out of his son before he shot him down?* As soon as he thought it, he scowled and cursed himself for even thinking it. Mike would never betray his father. Still, it was a possibility, and made it even more imperative that Will Tanner must pay with his life. The scowl on his face gradually turned to a smirk as he thought, *Now, Will Tanner, you ain't tracking me no more. I'm tracking you.*

He turned and marched out the door without another word to the two uneasy brothers, his mind working on several different possibilities. Maybe since Sams had not seen Tanner again, the deputy might still be in Tishomingo. If that was the case, he was as good as dead, because Lynch would find him and kill him. He knew he was counting on a long-shot possibility. Tanner would not necessarily have returned from Tishomingo on the same trail he rode down there on, but Lynch figured the odds were that he might. Even if he did, it was another long shot that he would have stopped at the little store again. But that was the only possibility that offered Lynch the opportunity to corner the lawman right now because he had no idea where else to look for him. He had to still be in Tishomingo—he had to, because his son's soul cried out for vengeance.

No longer in mortal fear of their lives, Dewey and Jake walked out on the porch after Lynch and stood there while he climbed back on his horse, wheeled the gray gelding, and charged up the path through the bluffs. His gang, having never dismounted, followed silently, causing Jake to comment, "That's a hangin' party, if I've ever seen one. I hope to hell Will Tanner ain't still in town."

Dewey didn't reply right away as he watched the last of the four ride up the path. "Damned if that last one ain't a woman," he finally decided. It was hard to tell at a glance, since Hannah was dressed in men's trousers and a heavy coat, her hair in one long ponytail down her back.

Tom Spotted Horse stepped out of the small shack he used as an office, preparing to go home to supper. He paused to squint at the riders just coming into view as they rounded the curve around the stables at the north end of the short street. When they passed the feed store, they spread out, four abreast, proceeding cautiously. He recognized them now as the men he had seen before and reported to the marshal in Fort Smith. *Damn white outlaws,* he thought. When he had seen them before at their campsite on the river, he had been satisfied that they were passing on through his territory. Now it looked like he was going to have to deal with them after all.

When they passed the post office and continued toward him, he stepped back inside his door, went to the rack that held his Spencer carbine and his double-barreled shotgun. He wasn't sure if he was about to have trouble or not, but in case he did, he figured the shotgun would give him the most firepower the quickest. After slipping a buckshot shell into each barrel, he put a handful of shells in his coat pocket, then returned to stand in the doorway to wait.

Spotting the short, broad-shouldered Chickasaw policeman standing in the door of the weathered shack, Jack Lynch wheeled his horse to face him. The others followed suit, forming a line to pull up before the door to sit facing him. "You the law here?" Lynch asked.

"I am," Tom answered. "What is your business here?"

"My business is a deputy marshal named Will Tanner," Lynch said. "He rode in here yesterday. Where is he now?"

Sullen as ever, even in the face of such odds, Tom answered gruffly, "How the hell would I know? I don't keep track of everybody that rides through town. He ain't here now, so maybe you just ride on out of here, too."

Not happy with Tom's answer, Lynch pressed further. "Did he say where he was headin' when he left here?"

"He don't say and I don't ask," Tom said. "I told you I don't know where he went, white man, and I don't care. Now, you got no more business in Tishomingo, so ride back the way you came."

Lynch was in no mood to put up with the sullen Indian's surly manner. "I don't take no orders from no damn Injun," he said. "Maybe I need to teach you some manners when you're talkin' to a white man." He possessed an overpowering desire to kill someone in payment for the death of his son. Although it was Tanner he wanted, he would settle for the Indian policeman's blood on his way to Tanner.

"Maybe you and your trash best get outta my town," Tom replied, and brought his shotgun up waist high. That was as far as he got before a .44 slug from Mace Weaver's Colt Peacemaker slammed into his right hip, causing him to go down on his backside in the doorway. He responded automatically by squeezing the trigger on his twelve-gauge shotgun, sending a wide pattern of buckshot to spray a deadly pattern over the outlaws closest to the door. Rafe Yeager, who was still wearing a sling on his wounded shoulder, caught the brunt of the shot in his chest. Mortally wounded, he fell backward off his horse to land in the street.

Stung by the wide pattern of flying buckshot in his shoulder and arm, Jack Lynch pulled his pistol and threw a series of quick shots at the lawman lying in the doorway, backing his horse away at the same time. Mace and Hannah followed suit, firing at the wounded Indian while trying to back their horses out of range of the shotgun. Tom Spotted Horse pulled the other trigger, his shot resulting in inflicting flesh wounds in two of the horses, but no further harm to the outlaws still backing away while firing wildly at the doorway. Because of the rearing and bucking of their wounded horses, it was impossible to shoot accurately. As a result, their shots tore hunks of wood from the doorjambs and the planks of the little porch, but found no purchase in the wounded Chickasaw policeman, who managed to drag himself inside and shut the door.

"We got the son of a bitch trapped in there now!" Lynch yelled, and pulled the rifle from his saddle sling while still fighting to settle his frightened horse. "Shoot that shack to pieces!" Mace and Hannah followed his lead, quickly guiding their horses to charge into the black-smith's shop across the street, where the three outlaws flushed the alarmed smithy from behind his forge. With nothing for a weapon but his tools, the blacksmith scurried out the back and ran for his life. Mace took a second to send a harmless pistol shot after him. The three outlaws then set in to fire a continuous barrage of lead upon the shabby building.

"What about ol' Rafe?" Mace asked during a pause to reload his rifle.

"What about him?" Lynch replied, taking aim at the front window. "Ain't nothing we can do for him. He's done for." They had no way of knowing that for sure, but he had not moved since being knocked from his horse.

"Why don't you go over there and see if he's all right?" Hannah suggested sarcastically. Equally as anxious to settle with Will Tanner as Lynch was, she was contemptuous of the mess he had made of the confrontation with the Indian policeman. With the right kind of persuasion, the Indian might have come out with more information as to the whereabouts of Tanner. She was distracted from those thoughts in the next second by a burst of return fire from the window of the shack. Tom Spotted Horse had managed to drag his wounded hip to the gun rack to get the Spencer carbine. She ducked down behind the anvil to avoid the .50 caliber slugs zipping over her head. "We're wastin' our time tryin' to smoke out this damn Indian," she shouted over the gunfire. "We scared hell outta the blacksmith. Now he's run off and he mighta been able to tell us which way Tanner went when he left town, but you're so damn anxious to shoot somebody. That Indian ain't gonna be any use to us if he's dead."

Her comments caused Lynch to pause and turn to stare at her, the fury and frustration still twisting his face in anger. In his rage, he was tempted to settle with the scornful female and be done with her sarcasm, especially since what she said was probably true. The blacksmith most likely saw all comings and goings at the policeman's office, since his forge was right across the street. And it might have been much easier to get the information out of him than the defiant Chickasaw.

"What are we aimin' to do?" Mace asked when he realized that both Hannah and Lynch had stopped shooting. He looked at Lynch, recognizing a deadly stare that he had seen on other occasions. Someone usually died soon after. Glancing at Hannah then, he saw the now-familiar smug expression of confident defiance. For a long moment, the two stared at each other, and it suddenly struck him that a showdown was threatening, even in the midst of the shoot-out going on. He could not help gaping in amazement. It seemed that even Tom Spotted Horse had become aware of the change of their intent, for he stopped shooting as well.

A wicked smile began to slowly form on Hannah's face and she asked, "Well, are you gonna try it?" The Winchester she had been firing was now leaning against the anvil, and she stood facing Lynch with her right hand hovering a few inches over the handle of her .44.

He didn't answer for a moment, remembering

the lightning-fast draw she had exhibited back at the cabin when he had sought to call her bluff. And looking into her eyes at this moment, it seemed that she was praying that he would try her. His rifle was in his hand while hers was not, but he had not ejected the spent cartridge from his last shot. And he felt sure that she knew it, and was confident that she could draw her pistol before he could chamber another round. Suddenly he relaxed. "You're crazy," he said. "What kinda crazy talk is that at a time like this?" He turned his back to her, focusing on the building across the street again. "You might be right, we might be doin' nothin' but wastin' cartridges, but I aim to kill that damn Injun before I leave here."

"Well, we ain't doin' so good so far," Mace said. "We've done shot that shack so full of holes it's a wonder it's still standin'. And it looks like he's got plenty of ammunition to keep us from gettin' in there to get him. Maybe we can get behind him. I'll circle around and get a look at the back of that shack. If there's a back window, we might could get at him that way."

"Might could," Lynch said. "It's worth a shot and it would sure beat settin' here behind this forge, shootin' up all our cartridges."

Mace gave Lynch a nod, then withdrew cautiously to the back of the shelter where their horses were tied. Climbing into the saddle, he rode out behind the shop and took a wide circle around behind the police shack. It didn't take but a glance to send him back to report. "There ain't no window in the back," he said. "There ain't nothin' but a little door at the top of the loft, right under the roof. It was open, but it ain't big enough to crawl through, even if you could get up that high."

"Damn," Lynch swore.

"I reckon we could burn him out," Hannah said. Ready a few moments before to shoot her new partner, she was now becoming impatient with his lust to shoot the Chickasaw policeman. She didn't care if Tom Spotted Horse lived or died, but she decided to help Lynch kill him if only to get on with a search for Will Tanner.

"How we gonna do that?" Mace wanted to know.

She pointed toward a can in the corner of the shop, well away from the forge. "That looks like the kinda can kerosene comes in," she said. "And we've got coals still burnin' hot in that forge. Looks like we've got everything we need to make some torches."

Lynch paused to give it some thought. "Maybe," he finally said. "But it ain't gonna be so easy to get close enough to set 'em without gettin' shot."

"Get a couple of torches made up," Hannah said, "and I'll get 'em inside that shack." Mace said there was a small loft door near the peak of the roof, and it was open. It was no doubt there to give the office ventilation, especially if it was heated by a stove. And a stovepipe protruding through the side wall of the office verified that. Seated on her horse, she felt sure she could reach high enough to shove a torch through the small opening.

"How you gonna get two torches inside without throwin' 'em through the door," Lynch asked, "or the window?"

She told him her plan. "He can't see anything behind that building," she concluded. "There ain't even a window. He couldn't see out of it if there was, draggin' himself around with that bullet in his hip. And he sure as hell can't see that little door up near the top of the roof. Just find something to make a torch out of. I'll get it in the shack."

"All right," Lynch quickly agreed, and started looking for materials to make a torch. It might work, he figured. There might be a shelf or full attic over the office, which would prevent a torch from falling down in the office, but if there was, the roof could still catch on fire. At any rate, he was willing to let Hannah try it. If it didn't work, then maybe the irritating woman might get shot in the process, and that wouldn't be bad. "Here's just the thing," he announced when he spotted a barrel containing a half-dozen ax handles. Mace took the cap off the kerosene can and confirmed that it indeed held the inflammable liquid. There were plenty of rags in another barrel in a corner of the shop, so Hannah and Lynch fashioned two torches while Mace kept Tom Spotted Horse occupied with his rifle.

When the torches were finished and soaked thoroughly with kerosene, it was obvious that they would be too difficult to handle if they were both lit from the coals still glowing in the forge, so only one was set aflame. Hannah got up on her horse, and Lynch handed her the two missiles. She gave Mace a threatening glance and said, "Make sure you don't shoot me." Confident in what she was undertaking, she rode out the back of the shop then, made a wide circle around an outhouse, and came up beside the back wall of the police building.

As she had figured, she was just able to reach up far enough to get an ax handle through the open loft door. So she lit her second torch with the first one, then shoved one after the other through the opening. As soon as the second one dropped inside, she wheeled her horse and galloped away to safety. She dismounted when she reached the shelter of the smithy's shop again and joined her two partners as they eagerly watched for the results of her assault. In what seemed an extra long few minutes, they stared at the shack, their rifles aimed at the door, waiting for some sign of smoke. Finally, a light wisp of smoke drifted out of the loft door. "It's caught onto somethin'," Mace said. There was a lull in the shots from the window of the office, causing them to wonder if maybe Spotted Horse was done for.

"There ain't enough smoke to run him outta there," Lynch said. "He might just be playin' possum, hopin' we'll come out in the open." They continued to watch the door.

Inside the police shack, Tom Spotted Horse was startled when an ax handle, wrapped in flaming rags dropped from the sleeping platform overhead. Forcing himself to move, he dragged himself over and grabbed the handle before any damage was done. Then he managed to open the door just enough to shove the torch outside. His actions were enough to draw a series of rifle shots from the blacksmith shop. He quickly closed the door again and dragged himself back to his position by the window. His wound was serious, but as long as he could remain alert, he knew they couldn't get to him. His options were to change, however, for he began to smell smoke from overhead, and guessed that the torch had caught the straw pallet on fire. He could only hope that the pallet would burn up, catching nothing else on fire, for because of his shattered hip, he was unable to climb the ladder up to the sleeping loft. There was nothing for him but to wait and see if it went out.

It wasn't long before he knew he might be in a more serious situation because the office began to fill up with smoke. Worse yet, looking up he could see flames lapping the edges of the pine boards of the sleeping loft. Helpless to stop the fire, he pulled himself up as close as he could to the front wall, hoping that the fire would burn itself out on the platform above him. He thought of the ammunition in the cabinet below the gun rack. He was not in a good spot if fire got to it.

In the blacksmith shop across the street, the three outlaws watched eagerly as the fire progressed. Having tied their horses at the rear of the open shelter covering most of the shop, Lynch and Rafe had joined Hannah behind the forge, that being the only real cover. From their vantage point, they could see that the roof was beginning to catch fire as flames leaped out the loft door. "He ain't gonna be able to stay in there much longer," Mace said. At this point, they knew the policeman was finished. He was either going to get shot if he tried to escape the burning building, or burn to death if he didn't. As if to add emphasis to that thought, there was a sudden explosion of fire inside the shack, throwing a sheet of flame across the interior of the building, breaking the glass in the front window, and blowing the door open. The center of the overhead platform, where the second torch still lay flaming, had collapsed onto the hot stove in the middle of the office, causing the explosion and startling the three observers. "Hot damn!" Mace blurted, caught up in the excitement of the moment.

Inside what was now a flaming furnace, Tom Spotted Horse could scarcely believe he was still alive. He had been thrown violently against the wall by the force of the explosion, losing his carbine in the process. He knew now that his time had run out, for it was difficult for him to breathe in the smoke-choked fiery oven as the flames were even then hovering over his body. It was a terrible choice to have to make, but he quickly decided he had rather be shot to death than suffer the alternative of burning. He looked around him for his carbine, but it had already been engulfed in the inferno. *It is a good day to die,* he tried to tell himself, but he did not want to end his life at the hands of a lawless gang of white men. There was no more time to think about it—he could stand it no longer, he had to escape the fire. So he steeled himself to his fate and dragged his broken body out the open door to meet his end.

"There he is!" Jack Lynch exclaimed. "Now, by God . . ." He jerked his rifle up to his shoulder. "Don't nobody shoot," he commanded, as the wounded man crawled out of his trap. "This is my shot." As he took deliberate aim at the helpless target, he noticed something else. "He ain't got his rifle. He lost his damn rifle!" Seeing an opportunity to enjoy the execution even more, he got up from his position behind the forge and walked blatantly out into the street, his rifle trained on the defeated policeman. Mace walked out to stand beside him, his rifle aimed at Tom as well. He would respect Lynch's claim to take the shot, but he would not hesitate after that shot was fired. Hannah was not so intrigued by the slaughter of the helpless victim, but she decided the sooner the foolish men satisfied their desire for fun, the sooner they would get back to the more important business of finding Will Tanner.

"You ain't so sassy-mouthed right now, are you, Injun?" Lynch taunted. "I'm gonna place my shots real careful, so you don't die on me too quick." He raised his rifle to his shoulder again and took aim. The rifle shot rang out before he pulled the trigger, causing him to hesitate, confused. Standing beside him, Mace collapsed and crumpled face-first in the street. The next shot grazed Lynch's shoulder before he realized what was happening and managed to dive back to the cover of the forge. "What the hell?" he shouted. "Where'd it come from?" To answer his question, two more shots in rapid succession snapped through the open shed where they had taken cover.

"From the corral!" Hannah shouted back as she ran to her horse and scrambled up into the saddle. Whipping it violently with the reins, she galloped away from the back of the shop. As quickly as he could, Lynch was in the saddle and galloping off after her.

Standing beside the corner of the corral by the stable, Will threw two more shots in the direction of the departing outlaws, but they were already too far away. He had intended to get closer to the burning building before making his move. But he had been forced to take the first shots from the edge of the corral when Tom Spotted Horse was forced from the office and lay defenseless in the street. Due to the distance, he had to make sure his first shot counted. It had just been Mace Weaver's bad luck that placed him standing beside Lynch, and consequently, in the direct line of Will's fire. Even at that distance, Will might have downed Lynch as well, had he not turned abruptly when Mace was hit. But at least he had prevented them from executing Tom.

Cranking a new cartridge in the Winchester as he ran up the street to check on Tom and the two outlaws lying in the street, Will tried to get a look at the two galloping toward the creek, but they were too far by then. When he reached the blacksmith shop, he checked the outlaws first to make sure they posed no further threat. They didn't. Will's shot had hit Mace in the side, breaking his ribs and striking his heart, and the other man had caught the brunt of Tom's shotgun blast. He turned to see Tom Spotted Horse propped up on one elbow, gazing at him with eyes glazed in disbelief when he realized he was not going to die after all. Will went to the wounded man then and knelt beside him. He didn't have to ask if Tom's wound was serious—it was fairly obvious that the Chickasaw policeman's hip might be shattered. "I'd best get you to a doctor," he said, even though there was none in Tishomingo that he was aware of.

"Take me home," Tom gasped painfully. "Sarah will ride to get Leon Coyote Killer." He lay flat on the ground then, exhausted, having forced himself to make it to this point. Will nodded. When he looked around at the burning police building, he became aware of a handful of people who appeared now that the shooting was over. He couldn't help wondering where they all were while Tom was under attack by the four outlaws.

"Damn," Wilbur Greene exhaled, gaping at Tom's bloody hip. "That looks pretty bad. Good thing you came along when you did."

"Yeah," Will replied. "Too bad there wasn't anybody here to help him." He stared in the direction the outlaws had fled. He wanted to pursue them before they had a chance to get too far, but he couldn't leave Tom Spotted Horse in his condition. "Go back to the stable. Tom keeps his horse there, doesn't he?" Wilbur nodded. Will continued, "Saddle it and bring it along with my horses." He took another look at the injured man. "He can't sit a saddle. We're gonna need a wagon. Can you help me with that?"

"Sure can," Wilbur replied. "I'll hitch it up and drive it out to Tom's for you. His cabin ain't half a mile from here."

"Good man," Will said. "We need to get him some help. He's bleedin' pretty strong still." Wilbur responded with a vigorous nod and ran to fetch his wagon.

"Take me home," Tom reminded him. "Sarah knows what to do."

"I will, partner," Will said. "Just hang on." He stayed by his side there on the cold ground, close enough to feel the heat from the burning building thirty feet away. Although obviously in pain, the Chickasaw policeman remained alert, his eyes clear as he studied Will's face. Thinking it a good idea to try to keep him that way, Will talked to him, trying to keep his mind off his terrible wound if he could. "Was this the same bunch you telegraphed Dan Stone about?"

"Same bunch," Tom answered. "They come for you."

"You say they were lookin' for me?" Will asked, and Tom nodded slowly. That caused Will to pause and wonder. Why would a gang of outlaws that had been operating in Colorado and Kansas be looking for him? He was certain that he had never seen the men now lying dead in the street. *Jack Lynch,* he repeated the name to himself, but he could not remember ever having any contact with a man named Jack Lynch. What bothered him the most was the fact that he might not recognize the man if he met him unexpectedly. For that reason, it was crucial that he should go after him while he had a trail to follow and before it became too old to read. He looked down at Tom Spotted Horse and considered telling Wilbur to haul the wounded Chickasaw to his cabin while he started after the man he now assumed was Jack Lynch. It was only for a moment, however, because he felt it his obligation to see that Tom was taken care of properly and to render such help as Tom's wife needed. After all, Tom got shot because he was standing in the way of these killers coming after him. Probably, it would be quicker if he went to get Leon Coyote Killer, so Tom's wife could take care of her husband. Even as he thought it, he wondered why Tom wanted to send for the Choctaw man. Will knew Leon as a resident of a small Choctaw farming community called Switchback Creek, halfway between Atoka and Tishomingo. He had not been back to Switchback Creek in quite some time, but he did recall Jim Little Eagle telling him that Leon was acting in a minor capacity as a medicine man since the death of old Walking Crow. Jim had said that Leon had been very close to Walking Crow and had learned a few of the old man's rituals for driving away a bellyache or pulling a sore tooth. Still, Will was a little doubtful. Applying an herb for a sore tooth was one thing, treating a serious wound like Tom's was quite another.

While Wilbur went back to the stable, Will left Tom's side for a few moments to collect the weapons and ammunition from the two bodies. There was always the obligation of burying any outlaws that were killed by a deputy, so Will offered the owner of the feed store Mace Weaver's .44 and holster to do the job. He gladly agreed to do it.

It took Wilbur about a quarter of an hour to return with his wagon, but he had thought to fork a bed of hay into the bed of the wagon to make for a more comfortable ride for the wounded policeman. He also brought a horse blanket to keep him warm. As gently as they could manage, Will and Wilbur lifted Tom and placed him on the bed of hay. Try as they might, they could not pick him up without causing him a tremendous amount of pain. The Chickasaw Indian never made a sound, but the pain was obvious in his face. It was replaced by an expression of surprise when a barrage of shots inside the burning building began. The fire had evidently found the gun case with the ammunition in the cabinet below it. There was not much danger of getting hit by a bullet, but the sound was enough to encourage them to step lively. Will quickly untied

Buster from the wagon tailgate and climbed into the saddle, and they were off to Tom's cabin. Behind them, the few spectators backed away from the burning office to give it more room, but remained to watch it burn.

While he rode beside the wagon, Will could not help feeling amazed by the confrontation just concluded and the unlikely coincidence that had placed him in a position to prevent Tom's death. When he had followed the trail of the four outlaws that Tom had pointed out, it had indeed led in the general direction of Atoka. But after reaching the river, it doubled back in the opposite direction. He had followed it for a mile or more before he lost it at a river crossing and was unable to find it on the other side. Left with no trail to follow, he had decided to head back to Tishomingo, since that was the general direction the tracks led before he lost them. It was lucky for Tom that he did, because there had been no help in the small settlement for the outgunned lawman.

Sarah Little Foot stood in the front yard of her little cabin on the bank of the creek, watching the wagon and the man on horseback approach. She had been concerned ever since hearing the gunshots from the town half a mile away, concerned for her husband. There were many shots. That was not good, and she feared that

Tom might be in trouble. The arrival of the wagon she now saw, seemed to confirm her fears. As it drew closer, she recognized Wilbur Greene on the wagon seat, and Will Tanner on the horse. She immediately frowned. Like her husband, she was not inclined to be cordial to Will, or any of the white deputy marshals who imposed their authority over the Indian police.

At first, she thought Wilbur was driving an empty wagon when it rolled up to her front door. She gasped in alarm when she saw the body lying in the hay. "Tom!" she cried out at once.

"He ain't dead," Will quickly informed her. "He's bad hurt, but he's alive."

She responded to his statement with a look of scorn, as if the deputy were to blame for Tom's injuries. She rushed to the side of the wagon to find her husband silent, but very much alert. Obviously in pain, but with eyes open and steady, he said, "Will Tanner saved my life. We owe him thanks." Uncertain, she looked back at Will, but said nothing, then turned her attention back to her husband. She pulled the horse blanket back to examine the wound and was immediately alarmed by the look of it. "Get Leon Coyote Killer," Tom muttered, his voice barely audible as he became weaker.

In obvious distress, Sarah said, "Leon cannot fix—wound too bad." She looked directly at Will when she replied to her husband, her eyes pleading as she spoke. "We need white man doctor take a look."

Will was not really surprised to hear her say it. He knew Leon Coyote Killer would be hard pressed to take care of a wound that serious. He looked over at Wilbur, who was still seated on the wagon. "There ain't no doctor in Tishomingo, is there?"

Wilbur slowly shook his head. "Nearest doctor is ol' Doc O'Shea over near Durant," he said, "twenty miles from here." He watched Will as the deputy looked at Sarah, then Tom, and finally back to him. He knew what he was thinking. "That's a day's drive with a wagon," Wilbur said before Will could ask the question. "I ain't got nobody to take care of the stable. I can't leave for a whole day to go over there and another day to get back."

Will thought about the two fleeing outlaws, getting farther and farther away, and their trail getting colder and colder. It was going to be a hell of a job running them to ground if he lost that trail, seeing as how he couldn't identify them by sight. He looked again at the suffering man lying in the wagon and knew there was really no decision. Dr. O'Shea was a competent physician when he was sober. Unfortunately, he was drunk most of the time, but he was the only reasonable option they had. "Looks like I'm gonna need to hire your wagon and team of horses," he said.

He dismounted and walked up beside the wagon. "You reckon you can hold up for twenty more miles?" he asked Tom.

"I can make it," Tom replied, but not without strain in his voice.

"All right, then," Will said, and turned to Sarah Little Foot. "Get whatever you need for a couple of days, 'cause we're headin' for Durant as soon as we can get started. We'll drive right on through the night, so we can be there in the mornin'. I got a packhorse loaded with enough supplies to last me more'n a week, so it oughta do for us if we have to stay for a couple of days."

He didn't miss the look of gratitude on Sarah's face as she hopped to it. "I drive wagon," she announced, which surprised him. It was a welcome statement because he much preferred to be in the saddle. She hurried to put out her fire and close up the cabin after loading clothes and blankets into the wagon.

In order to save them the time to drive back to town, Wilbur volunteered to walk back to Tishomingo. "I reckon I can walk half a mile," he said. "That ain't much, but it'll help a little." Will took him up on his offer, and they set out for Durant with Sarah Little Foot confidently driving the two horses and Will riding along beside her, his packhorse following.

CHAPTER 11

Doc O'Shea squinted through bleary eyes that refused to focus on the ray of sunshine that beamed through the ragged hole in the window shade. After several attempts to force his puffy eyes to remain open, he was finally successful to the point where he could look around him to discover where he had awakened on a morning that felt like so many other mornings. In a few more moments, he was able to see objects in the room more clearly and was relieved to see that he was indeed in his very own room behind his tiny office. He could remember very little of the night just passed. He very rarely could on any morning, for that matter, but he had almost made it back to his bed, judging by the overturned chair between the bed and where he lay on the floor.

"God, I need a drink," he uttered, feeling as if his mouth and throat had somehow grown a thick layer of hair while he slept. *There's a bottle in the cupboard,* he thought, and struggled to get up from the floor, making it to his feet on the second attempt, with help from the iron bedpost. After stumbling across the room to the cupboard, he found the bottle. It was empty. "Damn," he swore. "Somebody's been in my room."

Still a little unsteady, he made his way into

his office and gazed at the clock on the wall. It was not yet eight. The Texas House was open for breakfast, but the clubroom in the back of the building would not be open for another two hours. That was when Sheldon Tate opened it to accommodate club members. As a rule, alcoholic beverages could not legally be sold in Indian Territory, but the law was somewhat lenient with private clubs as long as they were restricted to members of the local business community. The Texas House was so named because Texas was where Sheldon Tate was from. And it was not a very well-kept secret that membership was restricted to any non-Indian within the continental United States. "Damn," Doc O'Shea muttered again, "at least I can get some coffee and maybe a little hair of the dog."

It was reassuring to find his hat hanging on the hall tree by the front door, for it had not always found its way home with him. As he placed it on his head, his attention was caught by the framed diploma hanging on the wall beside the tree. *Oliver Halloran O'Shea,* it read, *Jefferson Medical College.* He paused only briefly to consider it. Too much had passed since that time—a marriage that had failed, a career that was destroyed when he was banned from practicing medicine in Wisconsin, all because of drinking. The thought of it only made him need a drink more. *Medicine,* he thought, *I need my medicine,* and out the door he went, almost colliding with Myra Skinner, a middle-aged widow he employed as a nurse, cook, and housekeeper.

Myra stepped back and gave him a look of disgust, but since it was one he was accustomed to seeing from the patient woman, he responded with a smile. "You look like something the cat dragged in," she said.

"And you look especially fetching yourself this morning," he returned with a disarming smile.

"Where are you going?" Myra asked. "You look like you need some strong coffee. I'll put on a pot."

"Don't trouble yourself, Myra darling," he said. "I'll get a cup at the Texas House. I'm going that way anyway."

"Yeah, I ain't surprised," she replied, well aware of the "coffee" he was going for. "I'll make a pot of the good kind of coffee, and you can have a cup of that when you come back."

"Why, that would be lovely," he said, flashing another smile for her. "You're a regular angel." Then he tipped his hat to her and ambled unsteadily on his way to Texas House. This was where Will found him.

Sheldon Tate looked up from his breakfast when the tall sandy-haired lawman walked in the front door of his dining room. "Well, ain't seen you in a while," Sheldon said. "What brings you to town? You lookin' for some breakfast?"

"I'm lookin' for Doc O'Shea," Will answered. "The lady that works for him said I'd find him in your place." He looked around at the empty dining room. "Has he been here?"

"He's here," Sheldon said, and nodded toward the door at the back of the room. "He's doctorin' a hangover with the hair of the dog that bit him."

"Well, I need him to treat a patient," Will said, and headed toward the door.

"You know I don't sell no whiskey," Sheldon called after him. "There's just some I offer friends and members of the club."

"Yeah, I know," Will said, and opened the door. Inside, he found Doc seated at a table with a bottle of whiskey in front of him and a glass half-full. The doctor looked up slowly, too hungover to be startled.

"Well, if it isn't Deputy Marshal Will Tanner," Doc announced grandly. "Sit down and have a drink, Marshal."

"Thanks just the same, Doc," Will replied. "And you've had a-plenty, too." He took the glass sitting before Doc and tossed the contents on the floor, at the same time grabbing the bottle from the table. "You've got a patient to tend to, and I need you sober."

Looking in alarm at the wet spot on the plank floor, Doc seemed at a loss until he regained some composure. "I'll be happy to see your patient," he said. "I'll be in my office around ten o'clock. Bring him in then."

"There's a badly wounded man waitin' in your office right now, and he can't wait any longer to be treated, so get on your feet," Will ordered, "and I'll do my best to try to sober you up."

"I don't need your help, sir," Doc insisted. "I'm as sober as a judge right now. So I'll have that bottle back. I've already paid for it." He held his hand out for the whiskey.

Will grasped his wrist and jerked him up out of the chair. The surprised doctor was able to remain on his feet, although more than a little wobbly. Will released his wrist and watched to see how drunk he really was. "Come on, Doc," he said. "I think with a little help you might make it." He reached down and picked up Doc's hat from the table and plopped it down on the confused man's head. Then he grabbed the back of his coat collar and walked him out of the room. "You'll get your bottle back after you've done a good job on Tom Spotted Horse." He walked him through the dining room, where Sheldon Tate sat astonished, a fork full of fried ham suspended before his mouth. Outside in the cold morning air, Will hurried the doctor along up the street, still holding him by the back of his coat collar.

"I would ask you to slow down a little," Doc

complained. "My legs are not nearly as long as yours." He almost stumbled, but Will caught him and kept him going. "I'm thinking I must report your outrageous conduct to the district office in Fort Smith."

Will had no patience with a man of Doc's skill and training who drowned it all in a bottle. And at the moment, he didn't give a damn if he contacted Dan Stone or not. When they struggled past Dixon Durant's general store, the horse trough near the corner of the building caught his eye. That might help, he thought, if it doesn't kill him. He grabbed the back of Doc's neck and plunged his head into the water, breaking through a paper-thin film of ice on the surface. Flailing helplessly, the doctor struggled frantically, but was unable to escape the powerful hand that held him submerged in the icy water until he was snatched out gasping and sputtering for breath. "No!" he screamed when Will, still holding him by the neck, threatened to repeat the treatment. "I'm sober! I'm all right now!" he cried out in alarm, terrified that the stoic lawman might drown him.

Will doubted the icy plunge was enough to sober O'Shea, but he was satisfied that it was enough to set him on the road to getting there. "All right," he said. "Step lively now and we'll get you home before you catch pneumonia." He picked up Doc's hat, which was floating on

249

the water, and clapped it down on the shivering man's head, causing him to shutter anew.

"Oh my stars!" Myra Skinner exclaimed in disgust. "What was it this time? You're soaking wet!"

"He decided to clear his head in the horse trough," Will said. "What he needs now is a dry towel and shirt, and about a gallon of hot coffee. How's Tom doin'?"

"He's no better than he was when you brought him in," Myra said. "And he's no worse, either. I cleaned him up a little with his wife's help, so he's about as good as we can get him before Doc examines him."

Will took a look at Doc, who was still dazed from the dip in the horse trough. In a moment, he recovered his senses enough to threaten Will. "Your superior in Fort Smith will receive my full report on your barbaric behavior. I doubt you'll be a deputy marshal much longer."

"Marshal Daniel Stone is the man you wanna contact," Will replied. "He's my boss. Now how 'bout it? Can you get yourself sober enough to take care of Tom Spotted Horse?"

Doc didn't answer for a long moment. When he did, he replied softly, "I can," suddenly losing his initial outrage and beginning to get a grip on his intoxication. He gave Myra Skinner a questioning glance then.

Understanding his unspoken question, she

responded, "On your operating table. I'll get you a dry shirt and some coffee."

"Better bring the pot," he said, becoming more sober by the second, only because he had not had time to drink much of the bottle of whiskey before Will found him. His major problem at the moment was a splitting headache, a result of the prior night's indiscretions. Turning back to address Will, he said, "I've got work to do, and I can't do it with you standing around in the way. So go somewhere and come back later this afternoon." Nodding toward Sarah Little Foot, he said, "I'll do what I can for your husband, ma'am. Of course you're welcome to stay."

"Fair enough, Doc," Will said. He looked at Sarah then. "You want something to eat? Want me to build you a fire, so you can fix something?" He knew she had not eaten since the night before.

She shook her head. "I not hungry. Maybe I cook you something?"

"For goodness' sakes," Myra said. "If she wants something, we can fix it in the kitchen."

" 'Preciate it," Will said. "I'll get outta your way now." He left the wounded policeman in the care of the half-sober doctor, knowing he had no better option. He could only hope O'Shea could sober up enough to treat the unfortunate Indian policeman. After taking care of the horses, he thought he might as well go back to the Texas House to get some breakfast. But first, he decided to go to the telegraph office and bring Dan Stone up to date on the search for Jack Lynch and his men.

At the telegraph office in the small railroad station, he wrote out his message as briefly as possible and gave it to the clerk to send. "I'll be in town a while in case I get a reply. I'll either be at the Texas House or the doctor's office." After his message was sent and paid for, he headed back to the Texas House to see if Sheldon Tate had a decent cook. Much to his satisfaction, it turned out that Tate's cook knew how to rustle up a breakfast of bacon and eggs that equaled those fixed by Ruth Bennett. The thought triggered another, one that he purposely tried to keep in the back of his mind. *Most likely Sophie cooked a big breakfast for her husband, Garth, on this morning as well. When,* he wondered, *am I going to quit thinking about Sophie Bennett? I mean, Sophie Pearson.* He was spared from lingering on these thoughts when Tate's cook, Beulah, brought the coffeepot around again.

He was still drinking coffee, and his breakfast dishes cleared away, when a young boy from the telegraph office found him with a reply from Dan Stone. Stone instructed him to continue his search for Jack Lynch and emphasized the need to take him alive if possible. It was the response he expected, however, it was the second part of Stone's message that struck a sobering note.

RECEIVED IDENTIFICATION OF MAN YOU KILLED IN FRONT OF JAIL STOP PRISONER RELEASED STATE PRISON NAMED MIKE LYNCH STOP SON OF MAN YOU LOOKING FOR STOP DEPUTY BOB HARDY FOUND DEAD IN WOODS OFF LITTLE ROCK ROAD STOP HARDY'S HORSE FOUND DEAD NEAR WARD'S CORNER STOP THINK LYNCH RESPON-SIBLE STOP

"Well, I'll be damned." Will exhaled slowly. "Bob Hardy dead. The son of a bitch killed Bob Hardy—no wonder he didn't wanna go to jail." He had never worked with Bob Hardy, but he knew who he was. *That explains a helluva lot,* he thought then. Little wonder Lynch wanted to find him. But how did Jack Lynch find out that he had killed his son? This put a different light on things. He was not only the hunter, he was the hunted as well. It might explain the blood lust with which Jack Lynch went after Tom Spotted Horse. So now his pursuit of the outlaw had become a personal thing. It might make it difficult to honor Dan Stone's request to capture Lynch. This new turn of events made it even more urgent for him to get on the trail of the two outlaws that had fled Tishomingo. Even if he could start after them right now, he would be a day behind. That is, if they had decided to run, instead of seeking the revenge Jack Lynch desired. The problem that presented itself immediately was what to do about Tom and his wife. He got up at once, paid for his breakfast, and hurried back to the doctor's office.

Sarah Little Foot found herself in a most confusing and fearful condition. Like her husband, she had never had a great deal of trust in the white man. And now she was forced to trust the fate of her husband to the hands of the drunken white doctor. Although reluctant to defy her instincts, she was less distrustful of the deputy marshal, Will Tanner, since he had taken it as his responsibility to take Tom to the doctor. Even more, Tom had told her that Will had saved his life, so she was grateful for that. She decided that Will Tanner was a good man. But that didn't prevent her from distressing about the care Tom was receiving from a man who had shown no sign of compassion for his serious condition. She had been especially alarmed when Doc applied the ether that put Tom to sleep, thinking that the doctor had killed him. It had taken Myra Skinner some time to calm her down and reassure her that Tom was only asleep so that Doc could go in after the bullet. Sarah was reluctant, but could see that there was nothing she could do about it, so she decided to trust Myra. It was only after Will returned and checked on the progress of the operation that she decided Tom was in good hands.

Doc spent a great part of the morning trying to dislodge the bullet that had buried itself deep in the muscle around Tom's hip bone. When Will stuck his head inside the heavy curtain that closed off the operating table from the rest of the office, Doc gave him a curt, but encouraging, report on the patient. "He's better off than you thought. That bullet did a lot of damage, but it didn't break his hip as it first appeared. And it's a damn good thing it didn't because I probably wouldn't have been able to fix it." He paused to scowl painfully. "Especially with this god-awful headache," he continued. "Now get the hell outta my surgery, so I can finish this mess."

"Will he walk again?" Will asked.

"Not for a couple of weeks," Doc answered. That sounded like good news to Will, so he pulled his head back from inside the curtain. "I'm gonna need that bottle you took," Doc yelled after him, "just as soon as I finish him up."

"Soon as you finish," Will assured him, and went through the office to the living quarters behind, where he found Sarah and Myra seated at a small table near the stove. As he stepped inside, Sarah looked up at him, her eyes pleading for reassurance. "Good news," he said. "Doc says his hip ain't broke. It'll be a couple of weeks, but he oughta heal up enough to walk and ride again."

Sarah's troubled frown relaxed immediately. "You are good man, Will Tanner. I think your words are true."

"And mine ain't?" Myra huffed. "I've been tryin' to tell you Doc knows what he's doin'." She paused, then added, "Drunk or sober." She had been trying to keep the Indian woman from worrying so much, afraid she might get some crazy notion to rescue her husband. *I hope to hell Doc doesn't lose him now,* she thought. *That woman might try to scalp all of us.* Since Sarah seemed to have calmed down, Myra got up and went back to see if Doc needed her. "There's coffee on the stove," she said as she closed the door.

"No thanks," Will replied. "I drank about a gallon of it at the Texas House."

It was another hour before Doc came into the kitchen, leaving Myra to clean up after the surgery. He told Sarah she could go in and help clean up her husband. "He survived," he said, still grumpy, but seeming more sober. "But I don't know how. I gave him enough ether to kill him. You can carry him back home. Best take a bottle of laudanum with you to help him with the pain. He's gonna have a lot of pain for a few days, but don't go lettin' him drink a lot of that medicine. A teaspoon or two at a time. Give him too much, you could kill him." He paused and waited for her questions, but she was too confused to ask them. She looked at Will for help, and he nodded and said he would make sure she understood what to do. Looking back at Will then, Doc had a question or two. "Who's gonna pay my bill?"

"I reckon I am," Will said, "if it ain't too much." Sarah understood that question. She said nothing, but looked at the tall deputy with undisguised appreciation. She scurried off to the office to take care of her husband.

Doc grunted his approval. "Now, where's that bottle of whiskey? I need something to fix this infernal headache."

"I reckon you earned a drink," Will said. "I gave the bottle to Myra." Doc's face sagged, knowing Myra would hide it from him in an effort to keep him sober. "She put it in that cabinet behind that tin of lard," Will continued, unable to keep from grinning at the triumphant smile that immediately replaced the frown on Doc's face.

Although Sarah and Will were both eager to lay Tom in the wagon and start back for home, Doc insisted that they wait until Tom was fully conscious, so he could evaluate his handiwork. Once he decided the wound was sewed up properly and Tom was going to survive the wagon trip back to Tishomingo, he discharged his patient. "Take him outta here, and don't go tellin' all those crazy Indians over there that I'll treat all their ills unless you plan to keep payin' my bills."

"Thanks, Doc," Will chided. "Don't forget, Dan Stone is the man you wanna talk to in Fort Smith."

"I ain't forgettin'," Doc snorted. "Maybe one day I'll get you on my table."

"That'll be the day," Will replied.

It was a late start, but they finally set out for home in the late afternoon. As before on the trip to the doctor, Will planned to travel straight through the night with one stop to eat and rest the horses. However, because of the obvious discomfort their patient was suffering by the motion of the wagon, Will decided it best to stop for the day when they were about halfway back. *Another day lost,* he thought. So they set up camp when they came to a stream with a good flow of water, and Sarah built a fire to cook supper. Tom didn't feel much like eating, but he was well enough to drink some of the coffee Sarah brewed. The delay was difficult for Will because he couldn't help thinking about the cold trail he had to follow once he got Tom and Sarah home safely. He had no choice, however, for their safety held priority over running Jack Lynch and his gang to ground. In the back of his mind he kept a cautious thought about the man he was hunting. There was still the possibility that Jack Lynch was looking for him.

For that reason, he had helped Sarah make a bed for her and Tom under the wagon in case they had visitors during the night. In the meantime, he positioned himself between them and the wagon road they had been traveling. He intended to stay awake most of the night, counting on Buster and the other horses to alert him in the event he dozed off. He figured that when he got Tom and Sarah back to their cabin they'd be safe because Lynch might be looking for him, but he should have no reason to go after Tom.

CHAPTER 12

"Look comin' yonder!" Tater Smith exclaimed when he spotted the two riders approaching. Rubin looked toward the bluffs where Tater pointed. He saw Lynch and Hannah riding their horses hard. The two outlaws in the abandoned trading post stared out the window looking for others, but there were only two riders. "Where's Mace and Rafe?" Tater wondered aloud.

"Uh-oh," Rubin muttered. "They went lookin' for Will Tanner. Looks like they mighta found him." He remembered well the fateful encounters with the deputy that had taken the lives of his brothers. It was best to avoid the man if at all possible because something bad always happened. Almost certain he knew what Lynch and Hannah were going to report, he followed Tater out the door to meet them.

"We got ambushed," Jack Lynch blurted as soon as he reined his horse to a stop and dismounted. "They got Mace and Rafe. We didn't know they was all set up waitin' for us."

"Was it that deputy, Tanner?" Tater asked. "Did he get both of 'em?"

"No," Lynch said. "That damn crazy Injun shot Rafe." He raised his arm to display the ragged holes in his coat. "He damn near got me with the same shotgun blast, though." He went on to describe the confrontation in front of the Chickasaw police office and the consequent flight to save his and Hannah's life.

Rubin looked to Hannah to hear his sister's version of the ill-fated attempt to corner Will Tanner. "That's pretty much what happened," Hannah said. "We smoked that damn Injun out in the street. Mace put a bullet in him and he was crawlin' like a sick hog, but Lynch took so long to finish him off that we got ambushed while he was flappin' his jaws about what he was gonna do." She shifted her eyes toward Lynch and smirked. "I reckon it was Tanner," she went on. "The shots came from down near the stables. We had to get outta there in case he had a posse with him. I didn't wait to see if he did or not." She paused to reconsider. "Now that I think about it, there weren't that many shots fired. I think maybe we ran too soon. It mighta been just one rifle doin' the shootin'."

"There was a helluva lot of shootin' goin' on before that," Lynch said. "And we burned the Injun's shack down before Mace got shot. If it was a setup ambush, they sure waited a long time to spring it. We mighta cut and run too damn quick at that, but Hannah took off and left me to deal with 'em by myself. I didn't have no choice except to take off after her."

Knowing there was no sense in continuing

261

a blame game back and forth between herself and Lynch, Hannah said, "We need to decide what we're gonna do now. Maybe we oughta go back there. I'm thinkin' now that Tanner was by himself, and he just happened to come along after we smoked that Injun out. It was nothin' but pure luck. He had us standin' right out in the middle of the street without any idea he was around. One thing for sure, that Injun policeman is finished, so it'll still be Tanner by himself. It'll be a different story when there's four of us goin' back after him."

"Damn, I don't know," Tater fretted. "That man ain't nothin' but bad news. Maybe we oughta just get outta here and ride on up in the mountains, like we talked about before."

"He killed my boy," Lynch insisted, lest they forgot. "He's gonna have to pay for that."

"And Rafe and Mace," Rubin reminded him. "Besides, if you never saw him, like you said, you don't know for sure he ain't got some help. Tater might be right, maybe we oughta go up in the mountains and get the hell away from this place."

Hannah listened without commenting until Lynch began to get heated up when it appeared that no one else seemed to suffer the loss of his son as much as he. Turning the small, smooth pebble over and over in her hand, the one she carried to remind her of her vow to her father, she spoke up then. "You ain't the only one lost family 'cause of this man," she said to Lynch. "Me and Rubin have more to settle with Will Tanner than you do. Our three brothers, Levi, Buck, and Luke, were all killed by that devil. And our pa died because of him, just as sure as if he had shot him down. So me and Rubin are goin' lookin' for Mr. Will Tanner, and that's a fact." She nodded solemnly at her brother, expecting a response equally determined. Instead, Rubin shifted his gaze, avoiding her eyes. "Ain't that right, Rubin?" she demanded.

Rubin shrugged, not wanting to buck his sister's resolve, but still concerned about the risk of another meeting with Will Tanner. "Why, sure, Hannah," he replied. "I'm as anxious to settle with Tanner as you are, but I wanna be smart about it. He's done killed enough of our family, so we gotta be careful how we go after him. Right now, he's lookin' for us, too. Maybe we oughta lay low for a bit, like Tater said, let him think we're gone from here. Then jump him when he's give up lookin' for us." When he saw Hannah's frown, he quickly added, "We gotta get him, though. I'm just sayin' let's be careful about it."

"Shit," Hannah blurted, disgusted with her brother's lack of passion. "I'm goin' after that son of a bitch just as soon as my horse is rested up, and you're goin' with me. You owe it to Pa and your brothers."

Tired of listening to what had turned into a family squabble, Lynch interrupted. "You two can argue about that after we take care of our mutual problem. And the best way to do that is for the four of us to ride into that town and find him before he comes lookin' for us. There ain't gonna be no arguin' about it, either."

"Is that a fact?" Hannah responded at once. "And who said you was callin' all the shots?"

Lynch, already steamed up considerably, responded in kind. "I say I'm callin' the shots, that's who. I was callin' 'em a helluva long time before you and Rubin came along, wantin' to join up with my gang, and that's the way things are gonna stay. Ain't that right, Tater?"

"I reckon you've been the leader of the gang, all right," Tater replied, although with not much enthusiasm.

"Your gang, huh?" Hannah huffed. "I'm lookin' at your gang. Ain't but two of you left. Maybe you ain't been so good at callin' the shots." She looked at Rubin again. "Be ready to ride as soon as my horse is ready to go," she said. "Might be just the two of us, but if we go about it a little more careful, we'll get the jump on him this time." Having laid out her intentions, she led her horse toward the barn.

"What if he comes chargin' in here before we're ready to ride?" Rubin called after her.

"Then I reckon we'll have his funeral out here,

instead of in town," Hannah called back to him without turning around.

Jack Lynch stood tongue-tied for a few moments, frustrated and fuming to see his authority challenged by this infuriating woman. He inwardly cursed the day he had crossed paths with Hannah Cheney. He dropped his hand to rest on the handle of his .44 as he watched her walk away. She was a mighty tempting target, and he thought of the satisfaction he would enjoy when he silenced her impudent mouth permanently. The only thing that caused him to hesitate was the fact that he might need an extra gun in another confrontation with Will Tanner. He was still thinking it over when he glanced toward her brother and discovered that Rubin was studying his hesitation intently. He realized then that any move against Hannah would have brought instant retaliation. "I reckon your sister's right," he said to reassure him. "We need to rest these horses up some before we ride into town. If he's got up a posse, we might need fresh horses after we take care of him." He took his horse's reins in hand and followed Hannah to the barn.

It was almost dark when the four outlaws pulled up at the head of the short street that ran through the town of Tishomingo. At Lynch's insistence, they paused to take a good look before riding boldly up the street as they had before. "I swear,"

Tater exhaled when he saw the burned ruins of what had been the Chickasaw police shack. The charred timbers of the building were still smoldering, left unattended now that the flames had died, the few spectators having returned to the routine of the day.

After a few minutes with very little sign of life in the town, Hannah grew impatient. "I didn't ride over here to sit lookin' at this mud hole. Come on, Rubin, we'll look in the stable first. This is where he was hidin' when he started shootin' at us." She didn't wait for his answer, but nudged her horse with her heels. Rubin followed dutifully.

"Hold on," Lynch said, and kicked his horse to catch up with her. "Don't be runnin' off on your own.

Wilbur Greene walked out of the back stall to find himself facing the four sinister visitors crowded together in the small confines between the stalls. Startled, he backed against the rails of the stall, dropping the bucket of grain he was carrying. Thinking he might be facing his demise, he stood speechless until Hannah spoke.

"Will Tanner," she demanded. "Where is he?"

"He ain't here," Wilbur blurted. "He's gone."

"Gone where?" Lynch pressed, looking around him in case of an ambush. "Look in them stalls, Tater." Back to Wilbur, he pressed, "How many men's he got with him?"

Not wishing to answer the outlaws' questions,

but afraid not to, Wilbur said, "There weren't nobody with him. He went to take Tom Spotted Horse to see Doc O'Shea, down in Durant."

"When he shot Mace Weaver, he didn't have nobody with him?" Lynch asked. He wanted to be sure Tanner was alone in this hunt.

"No, sir," Wilbur replied. "Wasn't nobody in this town helpin' him." He wanted to make that perfectly clear to them.

"I told you," Hannah scoffed. Back to Wilbur, she asked, "How long ago did he leave?" When Wilbur told her that Will had left town right after she and Lynch had, she scowled while she tried to decide what to do. "How far is Durant?" When told it was twenty miles, she cursed and said, "Hell, he's already there." Wilbur saw no need to tell them that Will had carried Tom to Durant in a wagon and had gone to Tom's cabin before he started out.

"Well, it's too late now," Lynch said. "He ain't likely to come back before mornin'." He jerked his head around to look Wilbur in the eye. "He is comin' back here, ain't he?"

"For a fact, I don't know," Wilbur replied, knowing that Will would surely be back to return his wagon. "I ain't sure where he was headed after he took Tom to the doctor."

"We're wastin' our time," Lynch declared. "He won't be back till tomorrow. I'm goin' back to our camp. We'll find Mr. Tanner tomorrow." He didn't wait to hear Hannah's opinion. "I better not find out you've been lyin' to me," he said to Wilbur, "or I'll be back to pay you another visit. And it won't be as friendly as this one." He backed his horse out of the stable then and started back to the trading post on Blue River.

Tater followed at once, and after a minute's hesitation, Hannah followed, too, seeing no sense in staying. Lynch was probably right. At the earliest, he would not return until the next morning, but she felt sure he would bring Tom Spotted Horse back home. *And I'll be waiting for him,* she vowed silently.

As she had promised herself, Hannah was waiting for Will's return the following morning. She had selected a spot in a grove of cottonwoods on the bank of the creek that ran through the settlement. She could build a small fire there without being seen. From this position, she could observe the comings and goings easily. Rubin was with her, although with some reluctance, since she had routed him out well before daylight and ridden out without telling Lynch what she was up to. She had told Rubin that she was tired of arguing with Jack Lynch. "We don't need him and Tater to do what we've gotta do," she said. "Tanner's by himself. Me and you can damn sure take care of one man, as long as we don't let him get the jump on us."

The morning drifted into midday with no sign of the deputy and the wounded Indian. Hannah cooked some bacon to eat with the coffee she kept heated in the coals of her fire. Both hers and Rubin's impatience became strained when the afternoon passed without a trace of the hated lawman showing up. Finally, it occurred to her that Tanner might have taken Tom Spotted Horse to his home instead of bringing him back to Tishomingo. She was at once disgusted with herself for not thinking that in the first place. "Damn it all," she suddenly exclaimed, startling Rubin, who was stretched out by the fire. "He wouldn't have brought that Injun back to town." She gave Rubin a kick on the bottom of his boot. "Come on, we've got to find out where that damn Injun lives."

Since the post office was closer to their camp than the stable, Hannah went directly there, just catching the postmaster as he was in the process of locking his door for the day. Hearing the two horses pull up behind him, John Barton turned, preparing to explain that the post office was closed. He recognized one of the riders as a member of the outlaw gang that had attacked Tom Spotted Horse and immediately froze.

"You can keep yourself from gettin' shot, and save me the trouble of wastin' a cartridge on you," Hannah told him, her .44 already leveled at him. "All you have to do is answer one simple

269

question. That Injun policeman's got a cabin somewhere around here. Where is it?"

There was no hesitation on Barton's part, who was now staring fearfully at two guns trained on him. "Straight up the creek," he blurted, "half a mile where the creek forms a bend around a low ridge, log cabin settin' on the inside of the bend."

"Be sure you're tellin' me the truth," Hannah threatened. " 'Cause if that cabin ain't where you say, you'll be seein' us again."

"It's there," Barton replied, his eyes wide with fear, afraid to breathe until the two turned abruptly and rode off in the direction he had indicated. He exhaled in relief only after he felt sure they were gone for good. He wished Tom Spotted Horse no further grief, but he was not willing to risk his life for him. *The grumpy Indian doesn't like white folks, anyway,* he thought, absolving himself of guilt.

"There it is," Rubin said when they came to the bend in the creek. He pulled up and drew his rifle from the saddle sling as Hannah pulled up beside him. There was no apparent activity around the log cabin, and there was no smoke from the chimney. But they remained where they were, watching it for a few minutes before approaching it. "There ain't nobody there," Rubin said when he spotted the padlock on the door. With some sense of relief, he turned to his sister, who was frowning upon this discovery. "Whaddaya wanna do now?"

"I don't know," she replied, and nudged her horse to go forward, riding up to the cabin door. She dismounted and walked around the cabin, peering in the two small windows before declaring, "Nobody here and there ain't been nobody here for a while. The doctor musta kept him in Durant."

"Maybe the Injun didn't make it and they stuck him in the ground over there," Rubin suggested. "If they did, then there wouldn't be no reason for Tanner to come here to the Injun's cabin."

"Maybe," Hannah allowed. The situation only served to increase her frustration and intensify her desire to settle with Will Tanner. After a few moments trying to decide what to do, she said, "I reckon we can watch this cabin for a while to see if anybody shows up." It was disappointing news for Rubin, but he said nothing. Just as they had done in town, they picked a suitable spot to keep watch on the cabin and wait.

After a couple of hours, even Hannah's patience waned to the point where she decided their wait was in vain. "We might as well go on back to the river," she announced. "Ain't nobody comin' back to this cabin today." Unaware that their intended victim had stopped halfway between Durant and Tishomingo that day, just ten miles away, they rode back through the little settlement to be sure. The first things they spotted were Lynch's and Tater's horses tied up in front of the stables.

"Well, I swear, Tater," Jack Lynch taunted as he walked out of the stable. "Lookee here. I do believe it's our partners. They didn't run for the hills after all." Addressing Hannah then, he demanded, "Where the hell have you two been?"

Hannah said, "Lookin' for Will Tanner, while you two were layin' in your bedrolls sawin' logs." She went on to tell them about finding Tom Spotted Horse's cabin. "He didn't bring the Injun back home. I don't even know if the Injun's dead or not. And Tanner ain't showed up here all day, so I don't know what the hell he's up to." She nodded confidently at Rubin. "One thing I know for sure, is that Tanner will be back lookin' for us. So I think we'd best split up, two of us wait here in town, and the other two wait for him to show at the Injun's cabin. Whaddaya say?"

"As good as any, I reckon," Lynch said, since he had no plan of his own. "Tater and I can wait here in town, since you two know where that cabin is." That was all right with Hannah, so they parted again after agreeing that there was very little use in staying late that night. Both parties agreed to call the watch off after hard dark set in and return to the hideout on the Blue River. By that time, they figured Tanner would have rid himself of the wounded Indian and started

272

tracking them. "And if that's the case, then it ain't gonna be long before he thinks about checkin' that old tradin' post we're holed up in."

"Let him come," Hannah sang out right away. "Save us the trouble of tryin' to run him down."

"You know, we keep talkin' about that jasper comin' after the four of us without no help a-tall," Tater said. "Maybe he ain't as dumb as we think he is. Maybe the reason he ain't showed up here is because he's gone for some help." There was a long moment of silence while the other three considered that possibility.

"He wouldn't have to go no farther than Atoka for the Choctaw Lighthorse lawman," Rubin said.

"More'n likely he's already telegraphed Fort Smith to send a posse of deputies over here," Tater said.

"He killed my son," Lynch reminded them once again, but the prospect of a posse of lawmen on his tail caused him to waver. It would take a while for a posse to get there, if they started out from Fort Smith. The problem was he didn't know when they would have started out, or for that matter, whether the posse had to come from Fort Smith. There were the Indian policemen to consider, as well as a troop of soldiers from Fort Gibson, even though that army post was about as far away as Fort Smith. "I reckon it would be the smart thing to make sure we know about any posse before we go after him," he finally decided. "Won't do us no good to ride blind into an ambush of lawmen."

"Until we find out what he's gonna do, I vote we go on back to the tradin' post right now, get our possibles packed up, and head up in them mountains northwest of here," Tater said, "at least till we find out what he's gonna do."

"You vote?" Lynch responded. "When did we start votin' on anything? I'm the one givin' the orders around here."

"He might be right," Hannah said, to Lynch's surprise, since she had been hell-bent to settle with Tanner from the beginning. But she had been thinking about the clashes her family had with the somber deputy down in Texas. Will Tanner was a loner. "But we might not get the chance for a decent shot at him if he's ridin' in the middle of a big posse," she said. "He will come after us, and if he brings a posse and we ain't here, most likely he'll come alone when his posse quits. And if we go up in the Arbuckle Mountains to that hideout you were talkin' about, he'll have a helluva time tryin' to get to us without us seein' him comin'."

Lynch understood what she was thinking. "That is a fact," he said. "That cabin sets halfway up a mountain, at the bottom of a waterfall, and the only way to approach it is up a narrow trail through a rocky draw."

"That cabin's about a thirty-five-mile ride from

here," Rubin said. "What if he don't come after us?"

"He'll come," Hannah replied, confident that she knew the man. "And when he does, we'll kill him."

"How's he gonna know where we went?" Tater asked. He had proposed going to the Arbuckles for the purpose of avoiding the rogue lawman.

"We won't take any trouble to hide our trail," Hannah said. "We'll just lead him right into a trap."

Lynch nodded in agreement, feeling confident now that there was a plan instead of their running all over looking for each other. Still, he had to question. "It's a good plan, but ain't worth a damn if he don't come after us."

"He'll come," Hannah insisted. "The man's a hunter, he can't help himself." Her steady confidence in her opinion was enough to convince the others. At once, they were all in accord. The bickering between Hannah and Lynch disappeared for the moment as the four of them mounted up and rode out of Tishomingo, heading back to Lem Stark's old trading post on Blue River.

Intent upon giving themselves plenty of time to reach the hideout in the mountains, the four outlaws were packed up and on their way early the following morning, after a night with very little sleep. They took turns standing watch in case the relentless deputy showed up, but there was no sign of him when the morning sun spilled over the silent river bluffs. So it was a somber party of partners that rode single file along the bank of the river. Hunters or hunted, they were not certain. Their plan to retreat to the mountain hideout to wait in ambush for Will Tanner was based on nothing more than speculation, for they were only guessing on whether they were running from a posse or one lone lawman. They could not even be sure Tanner would trail them to a hideout, tucked away in a narrow canyon that very few people knew about. Although unwilling to admit it, Jack Lynch could not deny having deep concerns about the man who might be chasing them. The more he found out about Will Tanner, the more he began to wonder how he could show up in the middle of Indian Territory right where he was. Tanner killed his son, and now he was coming after him, one dead body at a time, just as he had with Ike Cheney and his sons. Lynch still blustered about his determination to avenge his son's death, but he couldn't rid his mind of the feeling of being stalked by an agent of the devil. The more he thought about it, the better he liked the idea of holing up in a well-fortified cabin in the mountains. As far as his partners were concerned, both Tater and Rubin were convinced that Will Tanner was an agent of the devil, if not ol' Satan, himself. And they were of the opinion that to run was the most sensible course for them, and hopefully Tanner would not find them. Of course, neither man would admit to having those feelings. Of the four, Hannah was the only one truly committed to avenge her father and brothers, no matter how dangerous their adversary.

Will pulled Buster to a stop in the trees that lined the bank of the creek while he took a good look at the cabin in the bend. There was no sign of anyone, or anything unusual, so he nudged the big buckskin forward and rode up to the cabin. The lock was still in place on the door, but there had been visitors, judging by the hoofprints around the cabin. And when he dismounted to inspect the droppings left behind by one of the horses, he determined the visit to be no more than a day earlier. There was little doubt as to who left the tracks, but maybe they would not be coming for another visit. He decided they would most likely check in town after they had found no one at Tom's cabin. The notion was confirmed when he did a quick scout around the cabin and saw that the tracks leading away from the cabin seemed to lead toward town. Figuring it safe for the time being, he climbed back into the saddle and went back to wave Sarah on in with the wagon.

Even though Tom tried to tell him he was all

right, and he should not waste any more time there, Will would not leave until he had helped Sarah settle her husband in. Then he took the time to split some firewood to make sure she had plenty for her stove. At Tom's insistence, he left them then, after making sure the wounded policeman had weapons and ammunition. With his horses tied to the tailgate, he set out for town with Wilbur Greene's wagon. He left behind him two grateful friends who had one less white man to dislike.

As he had when approaching Tom Spotted Horse's cabin, Will pulled the wagon up short at the edge of town to take a good look to make sure he didn't drive blindly into a welcoming party hosted by the four outlaws. Judging by the number of horses tied up at the hitching rails, he was satisfied that the four outlaws were not there, so he drove the wagon on in to the stables.

"Man, am I glad to see you," Wilbur Greene exclaimed when he walked out of the stable to meet Will. "They were in town lookin' for you."

"How long ago?" Will asked.

"Yesterday," Wilbur said. "The four of 'em were here. One of 'em's a woman, but she's tough enough to be a man."

Wilbur's remark was enough to make Will wonder. Tom Spotted Horse had originally reported seeing four men when he spotted their camp. There was no mention of a woman. Since then, two of the outlaws were killed in the attack on the Chickasaw policeman's office. But Wilbur said there were four riders who came looking for him the day before. Where did the other two come from? It was something to keep in mind. There might be more in the gang than he thought, so he planned to proceed with caution. And the first thing to do was to find out where they were camped, for as often as they showed up in town, it could not be far away. There had been too many comings and goings in the little town during the past few days, so if there was a fresh trail to follow, there was little chance of finding it. So he was just going to have to scout for likely camping spots within a half-day's ride. *And that might take forever,* he thought. Then Lem Stark's old trading post on the river came to mind. The old store had been empty for some time now, and he silently chastised himself for not checking it out to begin with. Any number of outlaws knew about Stark's place over the past few years. It figured that Jack Lynch knew about it, too. With the sudden feeling that he was wasting time, he said a quick good-bye to Wilbur Greene and climbed back into the saddle.

CHAPTER 13

It had been some time since Will had followed the old trail along the bank of the Blue River to the path down through the bluffs to Lem Stark's trading post. But the violent confrontation that had taken place remained in his memory like it was just yesterday, so the evil that had dwelt there seemed to still be hovering over the store and barn. Thinking it best to leave the trail about one hundred yards short of the path that led to the front door, he guided Buster slowly along the river's edge, remaining in the cover of the trees. When he was within fifty yards of the barn, he dismounted, tied his horses there, and proceeded on foot.

Reaching the edge of the clearing, he knelt to take a careful look before going any farther. There was no sign of anyone, no horses in the corral, and no smoke coming from the chimney. He remained there for a few moments more while he scanned the yard from the front of the trading post to the back of the barn. There was no one there, and he had been so sure that this was a most likely place for the outlaws to hole up. *Damn,* he cursed silently, thinking of the time it would take to scout for another campsite. *Hell, this is the most likely place to camp,* he told himself, and rose to his feet. Cautious by nature, he held his rifle ready to fire in case this seemingly deserted trading post was in fact a cleverly arranged ambush. When he felt satisfied that there was no one there, he left the cover of the trees. There was no reaction from any quarter, so he walked across the yard to the store and went inside.

"Maybe I was right after all," he muttered after a brief look around the front room, for there was evidence that someone had been there, as recently as the night before, judging by the ashes in the fireplace. Raking them aside with his fingertips, he found them still warm deep down. "They were here," he announced quietly, but there was no evidence that indicated they were planning to return, for they had left nothing behind. He made a quick search of the rooms behind the store, which he remembered were Lem Stark's bedroom and kitchen where his bony little Chickasaw wife, Minnie Three Toes, cooked for him and his sons. He cautioned himself not to distract himself with thoughts of things that had happened there before and get back to the business at hand. And that was Jack Lynch and his three partners, so he decided to scout the area around the barn and corral and hope to find fresh tracks that might tell him which way they went when they left. He walked back across the clearing to get his horses.

He was in luck, for he found fresh tracks from at least half a dozen horses leading away from the river, up through the bluffs, and heading straight west. There was no apparent effort to disguise their trail. It almost seemed an invitation for him to follow at his risk. Since they held a four-to-one advantage, he wasn't surprised.

The trail continued west with a slight tendency to bear northward for about fifteen miles until coming to a wide creek just short of an old trail that led toward the Arbuckle Mountains. The mountains could clearly be seen in the distance, rising no more than five hundred feet above the horizon. Heavily forested, the gentle foothills gave no indication of the many hidden springs and caves to be found in the mountains beyond them. Seeing that the riders he followed had evidently paused by the creek to rest their horses, he decided to do the same. He took advantage of the time to build a fire to cook a little bacon for himself in the same ashes of the fire built by those he followed.

When Buster and the packhorse were rested, he started out again, crossing the creek and continuing on until striking the common wagon trail north to the Arbuckles. Here he took a little extra time to make sure the tracks didn't continue westward, in case they were intent upon making it only appear they were taking the trail to the mountains. As before, there seemed to be no attempt to disguise their line of travel, so he felt their intention was to seek the cover of that small range of mountains with its many hidden cuts and canyons. He hoped that they were counting on his not knowing of the log cabin built tight up against a seventy-foot cliff where a busy waterfall fell to a sizable pond below.

As he followed the wagon trail that led through the foothills to the south of the mountain range, he remained alert for a small game trail that crossed the common track. It was a trail that he had followed once before when tracking another gang of outlaws. And if Lynch took this same game trail, Will would almost guarantee he was heading for that cabin at the waterfall.

In time, he found the game trail. The bushes where it crossed the wagon track had grown since he had first discovered it, but it appeared that the trail was still used by the herds of mule deer that roamed the heavily forested hills. The freshest tracks he found, however, were left by the shod hooves of horses. He knew then that there was only one place the outlaws were heading. He also knew that he could not follow that trail to the cabin sitting deep in a canyon, backed up against the cliff. No wider than the space necessary to allow horses and riders to travel it single file, the trail was easily watched by anyone standing on the front step of the cabin.

It had been quite a while since he had traveled this part of the Chickasaw Nation, but the circumstances of that particular time would always remain in his memory. Two good men were killed on that occasion, one of them was Fletcher Pride, the veteran deputy marshal who had taken him under his wing and broken him into the Marshals Service. Now almost two years later, he found himself once again trying to figure out how to ride into that canyon alone to arrest four outlaws. But it was too late to think about going for help. Jim Little Eagle was the closest but he was sixty miles away, so there was really no option except to go it alone. *It's gonna be the same way I did it last time,* he thought, *on foot.* And that meant leaving his horses hidden in the fir trees while he climbed up a ravine whose steep western wall formed one side of the canyon. With a new feeling of urgency, he nudged Buster to break into a lope as he guided the big buckskin toward the base of the ravine.

By the time he reached the entrance to the canyon, the sun had already started to sink behind the mountain. But even with the prospect of darkness on the way, he was not inclined to ride up the narrow trail. So he led his horses up into the trees at the base of the ravine and tied them there. After a quick check to make sure his rifle was fully loaded, he started up the steep side of the ravine on foot. When he figured he was about as high up as the pond and the cabin beside it, he paused to listen for the sound of the waterfall for a few moments before climbing to the rim of the ravine, where he had a view of the canyon below. With no real plan of attack decided upon at this point, he took the time to look the situation over. Even in the darkness settling into the canyon, he could still see well enough to note the horses in the small corral close up beside the cabin. *Good,* he thought, *they're all here,* assuming they were still four in number, leading two packhorses. There was no sign of anyone outside the cabin, and there was a healthy fire in the fireplace, judging by the dark cloud of smoke rising from the chimney.

It occurred to him then, that although he was 90 percent sure the people in the cabin were Jack Lynch and his gang, it would be best to make sure before he made any attempt to act. Although he had come into contact with Lynch's men, he had never been face-to-face with Jack Lynch, having seen him only from a distance when he shot at him in the street at Tishomingo. He wasn't certain he could identify him. He glanced up at the fading sky and decided he'd better slip over the side of the ravine and make his way down the steep side of the canyon before it became so dark he couldn't see. So he pushed on over the rim of the canyon, and as carefully as he could, lowered himself crawling and sliding in the patches of loose gravel, his rifle in one hand and his free hand grasping at the small fir trees to slow his descent. *Damn!* he expressed under his breath when he finally reached the floor of the canyon, apparently without alerting anyone inside the cabin. After a moment to stop and listen for any sign of activity inside, he moved to the edge of the trees, some fifty feet from the cabin. There remained an open space before him filled with nothing but the stumps of trees, the logs from which were evidently used to build the cabin. The log cabin had only one door and two windows, one in the front, and one in the back. To confirm his targets, he decided to make his way to the back window.

By this time, it was dark enough deep in the canyon to allow him to move quickly through the stump-filled yard without much chance of being seen, unless he was just unlucky enough for someone to happen outside. Sliding up close beside the back window, he peeked cautiously through a crack in the closed shutter. The light was not good in the room, but he felt sure the tall, wide-shouldered man standing near the fireplace was the same man he missed with his second shot fired from the corner of the stables in Tishomingo. There were two others sitting at a table in the middle of the room and it was hard to tell if one of them was a woman. As far as number four, Will's vantage point did not allow him to see that one. *Well,* he thought, *I reckon I've run them to ground. Now what the hell am I gonna do with them?* The problem was how to avoid facing all four of them at the same time, and that wasn't going to be easy, especially since he was going to try to arrest them if possible. One thing he knew for sure was that he was going to have to draw them out of that cabin, so he backed away from the window to seek the cover of the trees again while he decided how to go about it.

Inside the snug log cabin, Jack Lynch cursed when he reached for the coffeepot sitting in the coals in the fireplace. "Damn, that's hot," he exclaimed.

"What did you expect?" Hannah retorted. "I left that rag on the floor beside it. I didn't think I'd have to tell you to use it to pick up the pot." She walked over from the corner of the cabin she had claimed for herself as soon as they had arrived, picked up the rag, and refilled her cup. Then she tossed the rag to Lynch. "We could use some more wood for the fire," she said, but was met with no response when none of the men volunteered to fetch it. Tired of expecting much voluntary help with the chores, she just shook her head in disgust and went to get it herself. There was a sizable stack of firewood on the small porch where it could remain dry, so it was really not much of a chore. And it was right outside the door, but when she stepped out on the porch, she found that all the firewood was gone. Surprised, she went back inside. "What happened to the firewood?" She looked accusingly at Tater and Rubin, still seated at the table. "I thought you were gonna cut enough wood to take us through the night."

"We did," Rubin answered her. "It's right there on the porch."

"The hell it is," Hannah said. "Not a stick of wood left. You musta been in a big hurry to get in here and set on your behind."

"Hell," Rubin said, "we split up enough wood to take us to tomorrow afternoon. You musta been feedin' that fire way more than you needed. There ain't no way we coulda used all that wood." Not trusting his sister's report, he got up from the table. "I'll go get the wood," he said, and went out the door. In a few seconds, he returned, a look of astonishment on his face. "I swear, she's right. There ain't no wood left."

"Well, you'd best get your behind out to that woodpile and split some more," Lynch ordered. "You and Tater was supposed to do that job. It's gonna get mighty cold in here tonight if that fire goes out."

"Hold on a minute, Jack," Tater said. "Rubin's right. We split up enough wood to last a couple of days. Somebody took that wood offa the porch."

"Who the hell's gonna steal the wood offa the porch?" Lynch retorted.

"Will Tanner is who," Tater said. "That son of a bitch has already found us." He looked around him as if expecting someone to grab him at any minute. "Drop that bar on the door," he said, then got up and dropped the heavy bar on the door, himself.

"He couldn't have caught up with us this fast," Lynch said. "We don't know if he'll even be able to find us at all. This place ain't that easy to find." Even as he said it, he couldn't help but harbor some doubt.

"Then, what happened to the firewood?" Hannah asked. She was not so sure that Tater was wrong. Will Tanner was a different breed of devil.

"I don't know," Lynch replied, clearly trying to keep from becoming rattled by the simple, but mysterious theft of the wood. "Maybe an Injun sneaked up here and took it."

"I'm tellin' you, there's somethin' scary about that man," Rubin cautioned. "He don't work like a regular lawman. Besides, if it was an Injun, he'd most likely go after the horses. He wouldn't be stealin' the damn wood."

That simple observation caused them all to think about their situation and wonder if they were, in fact, in a dangerous position or not. Finally Hannah tried to put things in perspective for them. "You men are lettin' that deputy spook you. He ain't but one man, and there's four of us. If he had a posse with him, they'd have surrounded this cabin and started yellin' for us to come out before they started shootin' the place up. A posse woulda played hell tryin' to slip up that narrow trail without us hearin' 'em in the first place. So if he's out there, there ain't no way he can come and get us without gettin' himself shot. I thought that's what we came up here for in the first place—to set up an ambush. Hell, let him come."

"I reckon you're right," Lynch said. "We've got the upper hand on this game he's playin', but I'm thinkin' we might better check on the horses, in case that is some Injun snoopin' around out there."

"What about the firewood?" Tater asked, still uneasy about that strange little incident.

"Damn the firewood!" Lynch exclaimed, frustrated now by something he had no answer for. "Like Hannah said, if it's Tanner snoopin' around out there, we've damn sure got him outgunned. You and me and Rubin will go out back to make sure the horses are all right, just in case it is an Injun. Come to think of it, it might be a good idea for one of us to stay with the horses to make sure nobody steals 'em. We can spell one another off until mornin'." He was about to continue when he was suddenly interrupted by Hannah.

"Listen!" she exclaimed, holding her finger to her lips to silence him. "Listen," she scolded, holding up her hand when they did not respond at once. When the men realized what she wanted, they all stopped talking and listened for whatever had caught her attention. In a minute they understood, when the clear call of a nighthawk was heard. In a few minutes' time, they heard it again, only this time it seemed to come from behind the cabin.

"Injuns!" Tater exclaimed in a loud whisper. "They're goin' after the horses!"

There was no necessity for anyone to wait for orders—they immediately snatched up their rifles, all aware of the fact that they'd be in a hell of a fix without their horses. "Get out there before they run off with 'em," Hannah cried. "I don't fancy travelin' outta these mountains on foot."

In a show of bravado, Lynch told Hannah to stay inside the cabin while the men took care of the Indians. She made no objection because she already intended to stay inside, not being anxious to step outside in almost total darkness. Lynch went to the door and lifted the bar, but eased the door open slowly, lest there be something outside waiting. When there was no reception of any kind, he pushed the door wide and stepped outside. He had to pause for a few moments before his eyes adjusted to the darkness, the only sound to reach his ears that of the constant waterfall from the cliff above them. After the moments passed, he decided there was no one waiting to take a shot

291

at him. "Come on," he said, and stepped down off the porch, hoping they were not already too late. Rubin and Tater followed close behind him and they heard the bar falling into the two angle iron brackets on the inside of the door. "Leave the damn bar off the door," Lynch called back to Hannah. "We might need to get back in a hurry." There was no response from inside, and there was no sound of the heavy timber being lifted from the door, either. "Ornery bitch," Lynch mumbled before turning his focus upon the corral and the small barn beyond. "Keep your eyes peeled," he cautioned. It was unnecessary advice, for both Rubin and Tater were already straining to see in the darkened canyon as they followed close on Lynch's heels.

The cabin was only a few steps away from the corral, but there was no sound that told them the horses heard them coming. "Oh Lordy," Tater gasped when they found the corral empty. All three men immediately dropped to a knee and looked frantically all around them, but there was nothing and no one there. Not sure what to do, they backed up and huddled together. "We're in a heap of trouble now," Tater moaned, still suspecting it was Will Tanner's doing. "Whadda we gonna do? He's done run our horses off."

Lynch was every bit as desperate as his two partners, but he attempted to maintain some sense of control of their situation. "Whaddaya mean, he? We don't know it's Tanner," he said. "If it was him, we'da most likely got shot at. Looks more like some Injuns snuck in here and stole the horses. You heard 'em callin' back and forth between each other, didn't ya? What we've gotta do is get on their trail before they get very far, and hope there ain't too many to handle."

"Get on their trail?" Tater retorted. "I can hardly see my feet in this dark canyon. How the hell are we gonna track our horses?"

It was hard to argue that point. Lynch was at a loss for an answer for a few moments while he thought about it. Rubin spoke up then. "It might be hard to find any tracks before daylight, but there ain't but one way outta here, unless they led those horses straight up the side of this canyon. And I believe we'da heard 'em if they tried that."

"Well, now, that sure makes sense, don't it?" Tater allowed. "But what did they want with the firewood?"

"I don't know," Lynch replied, tired of hearing the question, "and I don't give a damn. Let's get down that trail. They ain't been gone very long. Maybe we can catch 'em before they get to the mouth of the canyon. If we don't, we ain't got a chance of gettin' our horses back." He was thinking their only hope was the fact that the trail was too narrow to permit the horses to pass any way other than single file. And that might enable them to catch the horse thieves before they managed to get them all through. "Come on!" he yelled again, and started running toward the trail out of the canyon. When they ran past the cabin, he paused just long enough to tell Hannah what was going on and gave her instructions to remain there to guard the cabin. He was thinking the Indians might already have their horses and he didn't want to give them the chance to double back and steal everything else. All their saddles, extra ammunition, and supplies were in the cabin.

Down the trail they shuffled, as quickly as they could in the dark confines of the narrow canyon, barely able to see more than fifteen or twenty feet in front of them. Halfway down, the passage shrank to its tightest place, where a massive shelf of rock jutted out from the steep side. This was the place Lynch was desperate to reach, for it was the one place on the trail that might slow the horse thieves up. If the Indians were already past that point, he knew there was little chance he would catch them, and the four of them would be in dire straights for certain. Just before reaching the spot where the trail looped around the jagged rock, he stopped suddenly, causing Tater to bump into his back. "Hush up!" Lynch whispered. "Listen."

"We caught 'em," Rubin whispered, for they could hear the sound of their horses bunched up in the trail ahead. "They can't get out. Somethin's got 'em bottled up."

"Careful," Tater warned. "We don't wanna let 'em hear us comin'. We don't know how good they're armed."

"That's a fact," Lynch seconded. "Take it real slow."

They inched cautiously along the canyon wall, their rifles ready to fire the moment they saw the first Indian. After moving a few feet farther, they began to make out the dark forms of the horses as the confused animals struggled to move past one another, stymied by the confines of the cramped passage. "What the hell? . . ." Lynch uttered suddenly, for there was no sign of any Indians. But the passage was so dark they couldn't be sure the Indians weren't hiding among the horses. "Watch 'em, boys," he warned. "They might be waitin' to jump us." They stood ready, watching the tangle of horses, but there was nothing to indicate the presence of any Indians. Finally, Lynch proclaimed, "There ain't no Injuns in here. They musta got spooked when the horses wouldn't pass on through the canyon." As he spoke, one of the horses backed away from the others, turned, and padded slowly back toward the three men. It was soon followed by another.

Confident now that there was no one in the narrow passage but the horses and the three of them, Tater made his way through the remaining horses to get to the front of the bunch. He was halfway convinced that one of them may have stumbled, maybe getting trampled by those right behind him, and consequently created the blocked trail. When he worked his way through to the lead horse, however, he found the animal standing, unharmed. "I swear . . ." he started, then called back, "Whaddaya make of this, Lynch?"

"Make of what?" Lynch replied as he and Rubin worked past the horses to join Tater, who was gaping at the two stout tree limbs blocking the passage at its narrowest point. Considerably less dumbfounded than his simple partner, Lynch yelled, "Look out!" He instantly raised his rifle and looked frantically from right to left, knowing at once that they had been led into a trap. Startled by Lynch's sudden outcry, Rubin tried to run back the way they had come, but was hampered by the horses, still bunched up, and blocking the passage. In panic, he backed up beside Lynch and Tater.

"I expect we can make this a whole lot easier if the three of you drop those rifles on the ground," Will said. His voice, though calm and solemn, seemed to cut through the darkness like the shaft of an arrow, startling the three trapped men.

"The hell you say!" Lynch exclaimed, and fired his rifle in the direction he thought the voice had come from. His shot caused an immediate reaction from Tater and Rubin, both men firing their weapons in aimless panic, hoping to hit something, if only by accident. Their reaction resulted in frightening the already confused horses blocking the trail.

"You're all under arrest, and if you do like I tell you, nobody has to get killed," Will said when the horses settled down again, his voice still patient. "But the first one who cocks his rifle again is gonna get shot, so drop 'em. I ain't gonna ask you again." Knowing there was no chance of chambering another cartridge before he could pull the trigger, they did as he commanded.

"Tanner, is that who you are?" Lynch asked. He had no intention of surrendering that easily. He was wearing a Colt .44 on his hip, and he figured he had a chance if he could determine where the deputy was hiding. He seemed to be directly above them, but it was too dark to see him. But if he could get him to talk some more, he thought he had a pretty good chance of hitting him. "I figured you'd show up here, but I didn't expect you before tomorrow. They told me you're the one who shot my son down in the middle of the street, over in Fort Smith. I expect you didn't give him much of a chance, either."

Will was not inclined to have a conversation with the man, suspecting Lynch's taunting was a ploy to expose his position. But he couldn't resist answering the charge. "He drew on an officer of the law. Don't make the same mistake." As soon as he said it, he quickly rolled over on the rocky shelf he was lying upon in time to be out of the way of the shots Lynch immediately fired at the sound of his voice. Without hesitation, Will fired in return, putting a .44 slug in Lynch's shoulder, rolling back to his original position as soon as he pulled the trigger. His quick reaction saved him from being hit by the shot Rubin fired at his muzzle flash. Before Rubin could fire a second shot, Will knocked him down with a .44 slug dead in the center of his chest. He was still determined to take Jack Lynch back to Fort Smith for trial, so he had aimed for the shoulder. In Rubin's case, he had not had the time to be so accurate, what with the sudden jostling of the startled horses when the shots went off. With a third cartridge already chambered, he aimed his Winchester at Tater, ready to fire again, depending upon the outlaw's reaction. Having witnessed the lightning-fast response to his two partners' attempts to resist, Tater immediately threw his hands up in surrender. "Unbuckle the belt and let it drop," Will ordered. Still being jostled about by the frightened horses, Tater did as he was told, then stepped back against the tree limbs blocking the trail. He figured it was a long way back to Fort Smith and maybe there might be opportunities for escape somewhere on that ride. There could be a hangman's noose waiting in Fort Smith, but it was a better gamble than the one Rubin Cheney had just taken. His decision was a wise one, for the phantomlike lawman suddenly dropped down from the dark ledge above to land astraddle one of the horses, then slid off to face the confused outlaw. "Sit down next to him," Will said, and motioned toward Lynch, who was lying back against the side of the passage, groaning in pain. Then he checked to make sure Rubin was dead and not playing possum.

Once he had picked up their weapons, including the pistol that had dropped from Lynch's hand when he was shot, Will methodically emptied all the rifles and pistols and wrapped the ammunition in Rubin's coat to protect it. Then he laid the weapons in a pile and put the bundled cartridges on top to shield them from the weather. The weapons were too much to carry while trying to march two prisoners back to the cabin. When he had secured all of the prisoners, he figured to come back to pick them up. For now, there was little else he could do, so he started the confused horses back toward the cabin. At the narrowest point in the trail there was not enough room for the horses to turn around, so he had to back the lead horses until there was room. Soon all the horses were on their way back up the trail. The last one to leave was carrying Rubin's body. He then ordered his prisoners to get on their feet. "I can't get up," Lynch complained. "I'm wounded, bleedin' bad. I can't walk."

"I shot you in the shoulder," Will said. "You

ain't hurt that bad. Ain't nothin' wrong with your legs. Give him a hand," he said to Tater. To be sure, he asked Tater who the man was that he had killed.

"Rubin Cheney," Tater answered.

"Cheney?" Will repeated, surprised. That put a new twist on the story. He knew that there was one of the Cheney boys who had fled from Texas with his sister and the old man. So that meant there was no one left of ol' Ike Cheney's offspring but the daughter, Hannah. And it figured that she was the woman Wilbur Greene had reported to be riding with the three outlaws. It also solved the puzzle over where the two extra outlaws had come from after two of the original four had been killed. It was not the only puzzle to figure out, however, for he could not account for the old man, himself. Where was Ike Cheney? When he peered through the crack in the window shutter, he had been able to count only three people, and he had been certain that he was trailing four. Maybe there were really five, and Ike was inside the cabin with Hannah. *What about her mother?* he wondered. Was she in the cabin, too? "If that's Rubin Cheney, then I reckon the woman in the cabin is Hannah Cheney," Will said. "Is anyone else in there with her?"

"Nah," Tater answered at once. "Ain't nobody in the cabin but Hannah."

"Shut your mouth," Lynch growled painfully

at Tater. "You don't hafta tell him nothin', you damn fool." Tater shrugged indifferently. He didn't see that it made much difference if the deputy knew there wasn't anyone in the cabin but the woman.

"Your friend there is Jack Lynch," Will said. "What's your name?"

Tater paused to think about his answer. After a moment, he answered. "Wilfred T. Hancock." He had started to answer "John Smith," but decided he might as well name himself something fancy. And the fanciest name he could recall at the moment was that of the president of a bank Scorpion Jack Lynch and his gang had robbed in Kansas.

Will snorted, almost chuckling. He would have bet on *John Smith*. He had to give him credit for originality, however. "What's the *T* stand for?"

"Tater," was the immediate reply, without thinking about it.

"All right, Tater," Will said, "help your friend along, there, and start walkin' back up that trail." With his Winchester aimed at their backs, he followed the two outlaws up the narrow passage. He still had major problems to overcome and he knew he was extremely lucky to have succeeded to this point. Luck had been a big factor in the shoot-out just completed, and he was still counting on luck to enable him to capture the woman holed up in the log cabin. *It might not be so easy,* he thought, remembering the fury of Hannah Cheney when he confronted her in The Cattleman's Saloon in Texas. His plan was to tie Lynch and Tater up in the small barn while he attempted to get Hannah to surrender. And the first step to complete was to get them in the barn without Hannah taking a shot at him when he crossed the clearing. At least, he still had the advantage of darkness. But he had to admit that Dan Stone might be right in always trying to convince him that he was at a disadvantage when tracking outlaws alone. *Right now,* he thought, *I'd even welcome ol' Alvin Greeley with his sagging shoulder to give me a hand.* Jim Little Eagle would have been his choice, and he knew that he should have taken Jim's offer to help before coming after Lynch.

His luck was still holding when they reached the waterfall and the pond, for the horses were milling aimlessly around the cabin. Whether that distracted the woman holed up inside or not, Will couldn't say, but there was no indication he and his prisoners were seen when they crossed the yard to the barn. Inside the small shedlike structure, he wasted no time tying his prisoners to two separate poles that supported the roof at each end, using the rope he had left there before when he had let the horses out of the corral. He took a quick look at Lynch's wound. The bullet had made an ugly hole in the right shoulder, just below the collarbone. There was already some swelling, but the bleeding had slowed to a stop. Will decided it was not a threatening wound and could stand to wait a little while before receiving medical attention. This in spite of Lynch's moaning and insistence that he needed help. Will had other things on his mind: Hannah Cheney holed up in a stout log cabin.

There was no question of surprising her, since she had certainly heard the gunfire coming from the canyon, so he decided he might as well give her a chance to surrender peacefully. Taking cover behind one of the more sizable stumps that filled the yard, he called out to her. "Hannah Cheney! There ain't any of your friends left to help you! So come on outta there with your hands up. You're under arrest. Surrender without causin' no fuss and I'll make it as easy on you as I can." There was no answer, so after a long moment, he called out again. "Whaddaya say?" He was answered by three quick shots from the door, the shots humming around him a little too close for comfort. Then the door was slammed shut and bolted again. "That's what I thought," he muttered with a sigh of disappointment. He had hoped he wouldn't have to try his next attempt to empty the cabin, since he was not that confident in the chance of success.

By this time, the heavy darkness began to fade with the approaching sunrise. Securely tied to the two poles in the small barn, the two prisoners could see what was taking place near the front of the cabin through the gray light. "I reckon he found out it's gonna take a helluva lot more'n invitin' her politely to come outta there," Tater was moved to comment when Hannah's answer was delivered by her daddy's Winchester.

"Best thing that could happen for us is for the son of a bitch to break in that cabin and the two of 'em to shoot each other," a bitter Jack Lynch snarled.

"That'd be good, wouldn't it?" Tater agreed. "But we'd still need somebody to untie us." He was about to say more, but hesitated for a moment when he saw Will roll away from the stump protecting him and make a dash to the front corner of the cabin. "He's gonna try to get in!" he exclaimed. "Ain't gonna be easy. That cabin's pretty stout." He paused again. "Wait a minute," he started, caught up in the actions of the deputy. "What the hell's he doin'?" Then answering his own question, he reported, "He's fixin' to crawl under the porch." At that, both captives were straining to see what was taking place under the cabin. It had been built on a gentle slope back up against the cliff, causing the porch to be a couple of feet high where it joined the front wall, while the back sill sat firmly on the ground. "Well, I'll be go to hell," Tater said. "So that's where our firewood went."

Lying for the most part on his belly, Will pulled the firewood he had previously stashed under the porch to form a fairly large circle over the stack of kindling he had cut with his hand ax on the other side of the ridge where his horses were tied. He placed the kindling under the front sill of the cabin, hoping it would catch strong enough to feed on the cabin floor. It all depended upon whether or not he could get his kindling to burn. There was enough draft under the cabin, caused by a gentle breeze, to make it difficult to keep a flame going long enough to start the kindling, and he had only three matches. He usually relied on a flint and steel to start his campfires, but he hoped he wouldn't have to resort to that.

His efforts were rewarded, however, for the firewood Rubin and Tater had split caught fire with no hesitation, and soon he had a healthy fire blazing under the front of the cabin. He began to expand the firewood out to make the burning area as wide as he could reach under the floor. It soon got to the point where the fire was too hot for him to stay, and he had to retreat from the flames, which now showed a keen appetite for the floorboards above them. He backed out cautiously, pausing only a moment to listen before exposing his backside to the open air to make sure Hannah wasn't standing with the door open, waiting for him.

"Damn!" Tater exclaimed when smoke began

billowing out from under the porch. "He's fixin' to smoke her outta there!"

Impatient with his simpleminded partner, Lynch bellowed, "He's burning the place down, you damn fool! All our stuff is in that cabin." He strained helplessly against the ropes that held him tight against the post as a large patch of flames became visible under the middle of the cabin. When Tater realized what he was saying, he began to yell for Hannah to come out. "She ain't gonna come outta there," Lynch said, so Tater began yelling at Will to get their saddles out of the cabin. Satisfied with the progress of the fire, however, Will moved around to the rear of the cabin, anticipating what he figured Hannah would likely try.

Inside the cabin, Hannah was rapidly losing her confidence to sit tight and force Will to come in after her. Dark heavy smoke was boiling up through the cracks between the floorboards, already filling the cabin with thick, hot air, making it difficult to breathe without coughing. It was obvious that he was going to burn the cabin down with her in it. As the situation became worse and worse, she began to panic when she could now see the flames licking through the edges of the boards. In a frantic effort to extinguish the fire, she picked up the bucket of water near the fireplace, left there to cook with in the morning. She dumped it in the middle of the floor where the flames were most evident. It only made her conditions worse, for it generated black clouds of smoke to mushroom up between the boards, causing her to back away until she was stopped when she bumped into the wall. There was no hesitation now—it was getting more and more difficult to breathe. She had to get out of there!

Doing her best to hold her breath, she retained enough courage to escape without surrendering to the hated lawman, determined to fight her way to freedom. She dragged her saddle to the back window, pushed the shutters open, and threw it outside, along with her saddlebags. In the process, she almost tripped over Rubin's saddle, so she took the time to throw it out the window, too. Thinking it enough to take care of her brother and herself, she climbed out on the windowsill and lowered herself to the ground. As soon as she felt her feet touch the hard cold ground, she turned to collide with the solid form of Will Tanner. Her first reaction was to raise her rifle to protect herself, but he blocked her arm and wrenched the weapon from her hands. Like a trapped wildcat, she tried to strike him, but he locked his arms around her, pinning her arms to her sides. Then he picked her up and walked away from the burning cabin, ignoring her kicking and threats.

"I saved a piece of rope just for you," Will told her when he plopped her on the floor of the barn, facedown. She did her best to resist, but he managed to quickly bind her wrists behind her back, then tie them securely to a length binding her ankles. In a matter of seconds, she was subdued and defenseless with no weapons save her mouth, and Will was very careful not to come too close to that.

"You son of a bitch!" she spat.

"Yes, ma'am," he replied in mock politeness. "You just make yourself comfortable while I go see if I can save another saddle, so one of you won't have to ride bareback." Confident that she was unable to move about, he ran back to the cabin. As well as a couple of saddles, there had to be other things he could save from the fire, like weapons and cartridges. The fire was building rapidly at this point, having caught onto the walls better than he had really expected, so he had little doubt now that the cabin was going to be completely destroyed. The fire's center was already consuming the door of the cabin, so his only point of entry was the rear window that Hannah had come out of. He grabbed the top of the frame and swung his legs over the sill to land on the floor. The air was too thick to breath and the floor beneath his feet felt like a hot griddle, causing him to look around him quickly. In the smoke, he could make out the form of one saddle, but the other one was already scorched by the flames that were advancing toward the rear wall. He grabbed the one good saddle and pushed it through the window. Then he began to throw anything useful he could get his hands on after the saddle—saddlebags, cloth sacks, a box of .44 cartridges, and that was about all he had time for before he had to give in to the smoke. So the next thing out the window was his long frame.

Back in the small barn, Hannah craned her neck to look around her. Seeing Lynch tied to the ridgepole, she sneered, "You did a helluva job of savin' the horses."

"You ain't sittin' so pretty, yourself," he replied. "We got hemmed up in that damn narrow canyon. There wasn't nothin' we could do about it, specially since I took a slug in my shoulder. He got the jump on us. Tater can tell you that."

She struggled to roll over so she could see the other end of the barn. Seeing Tater tied to the rear ridgepole, she asked, instantly alarmed, "Where's Rubin?"

"Dead," Tater answered. "He tried to draw on Tanner, but he warn't fast enough. Jack's right, we was bottled up with the horses and we couldn't see where he was." Then in an effort to give her some condolence, he added, "Too bad about your brother. It took some guts to make a play like that, even if he did get hisself killed."

The news of Rubin's death struck her like the

heavy blow of a hammer. She had never been particularly fond of any of her brothers, but Rubin was the eldest of the four, her mother's firstborn. And now he was gone. All the men in her family were gone, killed one way or another by the hand of Will Tanner. "That murderin' bastard," she muttered, barely audibly, suddenly feeling vulnerable for the first time since she could remember. She struggled furiously against the ropes that restrained her, but the deputy had not been careless in tying his knots. Finally she relaxed, surrendering to her predicament. Then she heard the voice behind her, calm and patient.

"Just as well you settle down and quit fightin' it," Will said. "You'll just be givin' yourself rope burns." He had paused to watch her struggles to be sure he had not been careless when he had hurriedly tied her hands and feet. As damnable as the woman was, he couldn't help feeling a modicum of sympathy for her. He supposed that she had not had many opportunities to take the right path, what with growing up in a family like the Cheneys, where wrong was considered right. He walked around her so that he could speak directly to her.

"Looks like you got the best of me again," she said. "And I blame myself for not lookin' where I was goin' when I came outta that window. So now what are you fixin' to do, kill me, like you did with all the men in my family?"

"I reckon that'll be up to you," Will said. "Depends on how much trouble you cause. What I'm aimin' to do is take you down to Atoka, where you can wait till I can get a wagon to take you and your two friends on to Fort Smith. That'll be easier on all four of us. You cause no trouble, and I won't make it hard on you." Then something she had just said occurred to him. "Whaddaya mean, all the men in your family? Your pa ain't dead, is he?"

"Hell, yes," she shot back. "And it's on your soul, 'cause his heart gave out on him because of you murderin' his sons. You might as well have put a bullet in his brain."

He didn't respond for a few moments while he considered that. Ike Cheney was dead? So there was no longer any threat from the old cattle rustler and murderer. That is, if he could believe her story. She could be telling a tale just to take the pressure off her father. Somehow, though, judging by the bitterness in her voice, he thought she might be telling the truth. Consequently, he again felt a spark of compassion for her loss of family. Even so, he deemed it prudent to watch his back, in case the ghost of the old man came back to rescue his daughter. "What about your mama?" he asked. "Is she dead, too?"

"None of your business," Hannah replied.

"Reckon you're right," he said, then as the first rays of the sun broke through the fir trees

311

to throw flickering imps of light dancing along the waterfall behind them, he gave them his marching orders. "We'll be movin' outta here as soon as I catch up the horses and get the saddles on 'em. We've got about a sixty-mile ride to Atoka and I aim to make it in a day and a half."

It took a little longer than he figured to get ready to depart. After retrieving Buster and his packhorse from the ridge where he had left them, he rounded up the rest of the horses. By the time he had saddles on three of them, and the packhorses ready to travel, it was midmorning. Needing some of the rope to use as lead lines for the horses, he untied Tater and Lynch and cuffed their wrists with a couple of sets of hand irons and chains he carried on his packhorse. It was still some time before noon when they filed out of the canyon, leaving the burnt remains of the outlaw hideout smoldering behind them. Led out by the big buckskin gelding, the three prisoners rode in single file behind Will, their hands bound together behind their backs. Behind them, also on lead ropes, came the packhorses with Rubin Cheney's horse trailing the lot.

In another minor fit of compassion, Will had dragged Rubin's body over to a gully and covered it over with rocks from the base of the cliff. He could not be sure if it was a wasted gesture or not because there was no apparent reaction from Hannah, her face remaining expressionless when they rode past the makeshift grave on their way out. "Ain't you gonna give us somethin' to eat?" Tater asked as they passed by the narrow point in the canyon where they had been corralled and captured.

"When we rest the horses," Will replied. "Nobody's done enough work to be hungry by now, anyway."

"My shoulder's painin' me awful bad with my hands locked behind my back like this," Lynch complained. "I ain't sure I can stay in the saddle unless I have my hands free to hold on."

"Then I reckon you'd best get a good grip with your knees," Will said. He suspected Lynch might have come to an erroneous assumption, caused by the slight consideration he had shown Hannah for the loss of her brother. *This is gonna be a long trip,* he thought.

CHAPTER 14

Will figured they had covered about twenty miles when they came to a slow-moving creek that looked to be a good place to water and rest the horses. He was hoping to make about forty miles before stopping for the night. This time of year the days were shorter, so it would be pushing it to try to make the forty miles unless he moved on after a short rest. He considered it for a moment, then decided he couldn't drive the horses that hard. Even though his task was a difficult one, he had no choice but to transport three prisoners with no prison wagon and no help. The first problem came up right away. "I gotta pee," Hannah announced when he started to help her out of her saddle.

Of the many arrests he had made during the last couple of years, this was the first time he had been called upon to handle this problem. He hesitated for a moment before replying. Looking around him at the trees and the berry bushes growing beside the creek, he said. "All right. As soon as I make sure your friends are comfortable, I'll take you over there in those bushes."

"I can't pee with you watchin' me," Hannah informed him. "And I sure as hell can't pee with those two buzzards gawkin' at me."

314

Her remark stumped him for a moment, then he replied, "We'll work it out. I ain't gonna watch you." He reached up and took her arm to help her down. When she was on the ground, he untied her hands. She immediately began rubbing her wrists. "Now, while I take care of them," he said, nodding toward the two outlaws still sitting on their horses, watching him intently, "you can pick up some of those dead limbs and get a fire goin'." He immediately saw a gleam of inspiration in her eyes, and knew what she was thinking. "Build your fire right between those two cottonwoods yonder." He pointed to two sizable trees about twenty feet apart. "And, miss, I'll be watching every move you make while you're doin' it. You make one wrong move, and I will shoot you. You can count on it." The gleam in her eye faded as quickly as it had appeared. She was convinced that he meant what he said. When she seemed to accept his promise, he stepped back and gestured toward the trees. She proceeded to gather wood for a fire. He was somewhat surprised that she didn't answer his threat with her usual defiant retorts.

While keeping a close eye on the woman gathering firewood, Will pulled his two male prisoners off their horses, one at a time, and handcuffed them to the two trees he had pointed out to Hannah. Confident that they weren't going anywhere, he took care of the horses while

Hannah built her fire. When she had a healthy blaze going, he said, "All right, that looks like it's goin' pretty good. I'll take you so you can pee now."

"I told you," she replied at once, "I can't pee with you gawkin' at me."

"Damn it, I ain't gonna gawk at you," he shot back, getting a little irritated by her insinuation that he might. "You just do what I tell you and won't nobody see your precious bottom." Having little choice, other than wetting herself, she reluctantly submitted. Using the rope he had tied her with before, he looped a knot around her boot with one end of about a thirty-foot length. Leading her over to a clump of bushes, he said, "You can crawl in there behind those bushes and do your business. If I feel any slack in this rope at any time, I'm comin' in there after you. You understand?" She nodded, realizing finally that he intended to give her the privacy she demanded. "Now, in case you get some crazy idea in your head, I can tell you that I know the difference between an empty boot and one with a foot in it." She nodded again, after just having considered that possibility. "And when I say, 'bush,' you damn sure better shake some of those leaves, so I can see 'em. All right?" Once again she nodded. "All right," he said. "Now get along, we need to cook something to eat."

"He must figure himself to be some kinda

gentleman," Tater observed as he and Lynch watched the procedure taking place at the edge of the bushes. "If I had a gun on that woman, I wouldn't go to all that trouble to suit her fancy. I'd tell her to pee or bust, specially that woman."

"If he don't watch hisself, that woman will get the drop on him," Lynch said, his words still strained with the pain in his shoulder. "And when she does, we'll see what she does for you and me. I don't count on nothin'. She's as likely to take off with everythin' and leave the two of us tied to these trees."

"Man, I hope she don't do nothin' like that," Tater said. "Hell, she needs us. She can't go it alone, a woman like that."

"Ha," Lynch snorted. "A woman like that? You mean a bitch rattlesnake like her."

Their discussion ended with the emergence of Hannah from the serviceberry bushes. Will waited while she untied the rope from her boot, then they walked back to the fire, which was well along by then. Will told them that he planned to free them long enough to let them eat, while he would stand guard with his rifle and six-gun. "Hannah is gonna do the cookin'. I'm afraid it's gonna be pretty skimpy chuck: fried sowbelly and some hardtack, unless she wants to make up some pan biscuits. There's a small tin of lard on one of your packhorses and I've got some flour. And there's a little sack of sugar, in case she'd rather make some slapjack. We've got a coffeepot and a gracious plenty coffee, so we won't starve to death."

"When do *we* get to go to the bushes?" Tater asked.

"After you eat," Will said. In case they were giving thought to the possibilities of escape that might offer, he added, "I'll be goin' in the bushes with you, though."

To their surprise, Hannah made no objections to her job as cook. As Will suggested, she used the flour and lard, and mixed up some simple pan biscuits. Will freed his prisoners while they ate, sitting opposite the fire from them with his rifle ready. When they had finished the meal, he handcuffed Hannah to a tree while he marched the men into the bushes to fulfill their contract with nature. On the part of the two prisoners, there were no thoughts toward making a run for it because it was far too easy for Will to cut both of them down before they could get more than a few yards away. When they were done, he marched them back to their respective trees and secured them again before freeing Hannah to clean up the pan and coffee cups. Again he was surprised by her reaction. He had anticipated her refusal to cooperate, but she did his bidding without objection. It seemed to him that she had accepted her captivity, although it was hard to imagine such a change in the woman, based on his past experience with her. He decided that she could be up to something and might require even closer surveillance, so he considered himself as having been warned.

When Hannah had finished with the cleanup, he secured her once again to her tree while he took another look at Lynch's wound. There was some swelling right around the wound, but there was no sign of infection as yet, so he decided it would do to just bandage it and let the doctor in Atoka take the bullet out. "You gotta do more for me than stuff that damn rag in my shirt," Lynch complained.

"It'll hold till we get to Atoka," Will said. "If you behave yourself, I'll get the doctor to take a look at it." He glanced up to catch Hannah gazing intently at him, as if judging his every action. It was hard to guess what she was thinking, he thought. In his limited experience with the female gender, he had to admit that it was hard to guess what any woman was thinking.

Under way again after the horses were rested, Will led his column out due east as before with a little over two hours' travel before the sun settled down on the horizon behind them. Camp that night went pretty much as their rest stop had. With long experience of sleeping with one eye open, he had little trouble from his prisoners. They were an odd trio, with Lynch scowling painfully, Tater almost lackadaisical, and Hannah strangely calm. In fact, it was hard to imagine her as the same Hannah Cheney who had appeared to be the most aggressive of Ike Cheney's brood. Will wondered if the loss of her father and all four of her brothers in such a short period of time might have had a sobering effect upon the young woman. Possibly she was realizing the path she had chosen to follow had brought nothing but pain and heartache, now that it was too late to go back. Again, he felt compassion for the unfortunate daughter of an evil outlaw. Maybe she had no choice in the life she was forced to live. It was a cruel way to end up at her age, with her whole family wiped out, but she had to be responsible for the life decisions she made for herself. Away early the next morning, Will planned to jail his prisoners in Atoka before the sun set again.

It was close to sunset when Jim Little Eagle returned to his cabin on Muddy Boggy Creek, just north of Atoka. He stepped down from the saddle at the corner of the corral, then paused when he saw a string of riders approaching from the west. In a moment, he was able to recognize the lead rider. No one sat a horse quite like Will Tanner, tall in the saddle, with his hands almost resting on the saddle horn. It was also easy to identify the big buckskin gelding the broad-shouldered deputy rode. *Looks like Will's been busy,* Jim thought when he saw the three riders behind him, their hands behind their backs, their horses on lead ropes. He looped his reins over a rail of the corral and walked out in the yard to meet his friend.

"Hi-yo, Will," Jim greeted him. "Whatcha got there?"

"Howdy, Jim," Will returned. "I brought you some guests for that little jailhouse of yours. I'd like to leave 'em with you till I can get a wagon sent over to transport 'em to Fort Smith."

"I thought you didn't like to bother with a jail wagon," Jim said.

"Most of the time I don't," Will said. "One prisoner ain't that much a problem, but with three to keep an eye on, it's a sight easier with the wagon, so I can keep 'em chained up."

"Is that the gang Tom Spotted Horse reported over near Tishomingo?"

"Yep," Will answered, "what's left of 'em. One of 'em's got a bullet in his shoulder that could stand some lookin' at. Is Doc Lowell still here?"

Jim took a step aside to get a better look at the three prisoners. "Yeah," he answered. "Doc's still practicing medicine off and on." He paused for a moment when he looked at Hannah. "I'll ride into town with you and we'll put your prisoners in the jail, but you know there ain't but that one-room cabin. You gonna put the woman in with the two men?"

"I've been thinkin' about that," Will replied, and glanced briefly at Hannah, who appeared anxious to hear his answer. "I'm hopin' we can find someplace else to stick her."

Jim's wife, Mary Light Walker, who had come from the house to hear the conversation, spoke up at that point. "What she do? She kill somebody?"

Will stroked his chin while he considered the question. He had no idea what Hannah Cheney had done before she crossed his path. "Well," he answered, "not that I know of." He paused, then added, "But she's threatened to."

"She can stay in smokehouse," Mary said, knowing Will would provide the money to pay for her food. "I feed her."

"That sure suits me," Will said. "That all right with you, Jim?"

Jim shrugged. "I reckon. I've got a good padlock I can put on the door. It oughta be all right if she ain't gonna be in there too long. I don't know of any other place to hold her right offhand."

"I fix," Mary said when it appeared that they all agreed. She went at once to the barn to fetch some hay for a bed while Will got a couple of blankets that Hannah had used for her bed the night before.

Lynch and Tater watched sullenly as the special preparations for the female prisoner took place. Finally Lynch could hold his tongue no longer.

"How 'bout my shoulder? I need to get some doctorin' done pretty quick. I'm in a heap of pain. Throw her in the damn smokehouse and let's get goin'."

"If you're in that much pain," Will said, "maybe you want me to dig that bullet outta you. I guarantee I can get it out, but it'll be a helluva lot worse than Doc Lowell doin' it, so you'd best just quit your bellyachin'." That was enough to quiet Lynch while they waited as Mary Light Walker filled a bucket of water at the pump, then carried it into the smokehouse. When she was ready, Will pulled Hannah from her horse and led her to the smokehouse door, where he freed her wrists and waited for her to go inside.

As she stepped in, she startled him with a softly spoken remark. "Thank you for not lockin' me up with them." Once again he was astonished by the change in the seemingly contrite young woman. He only nodded in reply. Then after Mary demonstrated how she could easily pass a plate of food under the door, without having to unlock it, Will decided the arrangement would work. He untied the packhorses, pulled their packs off, and turned them out in Jim's pasture, along with Hannah's and Rubin's horses. Left with only the two men to concern him, he stepped up into the saddle, and with Jim Little Eagle beside him, headed toward town.

• • •

Dr. Franklyn Lowell went to answer the knock on his front door. When he opened it to find Jim Little Eagle and another man standing on his front porch, he guessed somebody had gotten themselves shot. That was about the only occasion when the Choctaw lawman called upon him, but the tall man standing beside him didn't appear to be wounded. "Jim," Dr. Lowell acknowledged. "What can I do for you?"

"Howdy, Doc," Jim said. "We locked up a couple of prisoners we'll be holding till we can get 'em transported to Fort Smith. One of 'em's got a bullet in his shoulder. Reckon you could take a look at him?"

Lowell assumed then that the man with Jim was a lawman as well. "I suppose you're a deputy marshal," he said, looking at Will.

"That's a fact, Dr. Lowell," Will answered, "Will Tanner." He had never had occasion to come in contact with the doctor before, but he had heard Jim talk about him. No one in the tiny railroad town knew for sure, but there was speculation that Doc, like Doc O'Shea down in Durant, had gravitated to Indian Territory after having lost his license to practice medicine in one of the northern states, some said Chicago. With no family, Doc kept pretty much to himself while maintaining a modest practice, setting a few broken bones and spooning doses of cough syrup to the farmers' children. It was rare when one of the Indian families consulted the stocky little man with the full white beard and matching hair.

"Will Tanner," Lowell said. "I've heard the name. I suppose you'll be responsible for my fee."

"Reckon so," Will answered.

Lowell turned back to Jim. "I'll treat him, but not down in that rat hole you call a jail. You'll have to bring him here."

"I'll bring him," Will said.

"Well, hurry up then," Lowell prompted. "It's almost time for my supper, and Lottie closes the kitchen at six," he said, referring to Lottie Mabry, who ran a diner next to the rooming house her husband owned.

"Right," Will replied.

The two lawmen returned to the jail and Will placed Lynch's hands in the handcuffs again. Jim gave Will the key to the padlock on the door and the two lawmen parted company, Will back to the doctor, and Jim back to his cabin. "Mary will have something for you to eat when you get done here," Jim said. "They oughta be all right till morning. I'll bring 'em something to eat then. They've got water in that bucket."

Overhearing their parting words, Tater called out from inside the dark log structure. "Hey, we ain't had nothin' to eat since noon! It's a long time before breakfast." When there was no response to his complaint, he added, "Don't take too long with that doctor. It's kinda spooky in this dark hole. I can't see my hand in front of my face."

"Bring him in here," Doc Lowell said to Will when he returned with his wounded prisoner. Lowell led the way to his examination room off the living room and directed the scowling patient to sit down on the table. "You'll have to take those hand irons off of him, so I can move his arm." He looked Lynch directly in the eye as he instructed Will. "Shoot him if he tries the slightest thing."

"I'd be glad to," Will replied, and sat down on a chair in the corner of the room to watch the procedure.

"Ain't you gonna give me nothin' for the pain?" Lynch asked.

"You won't need anything," Lowell said after examining the wound. "It'll be over before you get a chance to hurt much." The doctor had a small supply of chloroform, but he was reluctant to use it on an outlaw, thinking the man probably deserved to hurt a little. He thought it more prudent to reserve his anesthetic for his law-abiding patients. A reason closer to the actual fact of the matter was the approaching closing time at Lottie's Kitchen, and the added recovery time for his patient to recover from the drug. So, determined to finish before suppertime, he went to work on Lynch's shoulder.

As the doctor promised, the operation didn't take long, but it was not without considerable pain, so much so, that Lynch passed out during the deepest probe for the .44 slug. "It was a little deeper than I thought," Lowell commented casually, but it's out and he oughta be all right, if he keeps it clean." He went to the sink and pumped some water into a basin and proceeded to clean his hands. "Three dollars oughta do it."

Will thought it a bit too high, but paid him without complaint. He figured he'd sell one of the captured horses to pay his expenses. He cuffed Lynch's wrists again, ignoring the gruff outlaw's usual protests of pain. In a slight fit of compassion, he stopped by Lottie's Kitchen and bought some biscuits and ham, feeling an obligation to feed his prisoners. With the two of them secured for the night, he returned to Jim's cabin on Muddy Boggy Creek.

"You think they hang that woman?" Mary Light Walker asked as she offered Will more coffee.

"I don't know," Will said, "maybe, maybe not. I reckon it depends on what Judge Parker thinks." He thought about his initial encounter with the vengeful hellion in The Cattleman's

Saloon in Sulphur Springs. He remembered diving for cover behind a table when the enraged woman came through the door shooting wildly at him. Thinking of her recent behavior, it was difficult to believe a person could change so completely without getting struck by lightning or something. He shrugged. "She sure rode with a ruthless bunch."

Mary nodded thoughtfully. "They her brothers," she said. "She don't have no choice."

"Well, maybe," Will said. Mary had obviously been talking to the prisoner while he and Jim were in town.

Mary continued. "All her family gone, four brothers and father, all gone. Mother all she got left. Now mother won't have nobody."

This caught Will's interest. "Did she say her mother's still alive?" He had wondered about that before.

"Mother live with sister and her husband on Blue River, near Tishomingo. She don't know her whole family dead."

Will found himself in a conversation he wasn't comfortable with. Evidently, Hannah had struck a nerve in Mary's motherly instincts. And he had to admit that he had felt some compassion for her, but everybody is responsible for the choices they make in this world, he told himself. *It's best you remember the wild-eyed hellcat that emptied a six-gun in your direction in The Cattleman's,* he thought. He found himself wishing to hell that she was not in the picture for the simple reason she made transporting his prisoners difficult. It would be far less complicated to handle prisoners who were all male, even with a jail wagon. Seeking to end the conversation with Mary, he concluded by saying, "I ain't in the judgin' business. It's just my job to catch the lawbreakers, and Hannah Cheney was ridin' with one of the worst bunches. They just happened to be all one family." He got up from the table. "I reckon I'll head out to the barn and get to sleep now. Thank you for the fine supper. I 'preciate it."

Before he unrolled his bedroll in Jim's barn, he checked on Buster to make sure the buckskin was all right. While he stroked the gelding's neck, he thought about the talk with Mary Light Walker about his female prisoner, and he decided to check on the smokehouse to make sure Hannah was securely locked in for the night. His inspection found everything tight and the padlock on the door. He paused to listen for a moment. Everything was quiet, so he turned to go back to the barn. He had taken only a step when he was stopped by a faint noise he could not at first identify. It had come from inside the smokehouse, so he paused and listened more intently. After a moment, he realized what he had heard. It was the soft sound of weeping, like that a child might make if alone and afraid.

Hannah Cheney crying? Surely he was mistaken. He quickly walked away as quietly as he could, scarcely able to believe it.

It was a while before he finally fell asleep that night. His mind was occupied with events that had taken place that day . . . and Hannah Cheney. Mary Light Walker talked about the woman as if she was a victim of her family. But Mary had never seen Hannah with blood in her eye, as he had. He didn't know why it bothered him. He had never concerned himself with the fairness of life, and why outlaws chose to break the law. His job was to put a stop to their lawlessness. "To hell with it," he muttered. Finished with cluttering his thoughts with the reasons for people's actions, he turned on his side and went to sleep.

The next morning, Mary was already cooking breakfast by the time he came out of the barn. "I didn't mean for you to go to so much trouble," Will said. "But I'll pay you for the food for my prisoner and me."

"Never mind," she said. "You always bring gifts when you come. I not charge for you or the woman. Maybe you leave some supplies to feed her while you wait for wagon."

"I changed my mind," Will said. "I ain't gonna wait for a jail wagon. That would take too long. I'll take her off your hands this mornin'."

This surprised both Mary and Jim. "You not

gonna telegraph Fort Smith for a wagon?" Jim asked. "What you gonna do?"

"I decided it doesn't make sense to wait that long for a man to drive a wagon over here. It's my fault for not bringin' one in the first place." *Dan Stone would be the first to tell me that,* he thought. "You go on into town and I'll be along later. I'm gonna pack up the horses I'm gonna take with me. Whaddaya say I leave that extra horse here with you?" He was referring to the horse Rubin Cheney had ridden. "That'll make up a little for your trouble."

"Well, sure," Jim replied. "That's generous of you, but I'll help you saddle up."

"I can handle it," Will said. "I'd appreciate it if you'd ride on in and get my two prisoners ready to ride."

"Whatever you say," Jim said. "I'll go pick up their horses at the stable."

" 'Preciate it. I might be a while, but I'll be along. Ain't no hurry."

After Jim left, Will saddled Buster and Hannah's horse and loaded the pack saddles on his packhorse and the packs that belonged to Lynch and Hannah on one of the other two. He was ready then to take charge of his prisoner again. Mary followed him to the smokehouse and stood aside while he unlocked the door. "I feed, but she not eat much," she said. Will nodded, gave the key for the padlock to her, and told Hannah to come outside. He watched her closely as she walked out, squinting to adjust her eyes to the early morning light.

"Time to get goin'," Will said to her, and waited for her defiant response, but there was none.

Without a word, she dutifully put her hands behind her back to be handcuffed, her head bowed slightly. When Will had clamped the hand irons closed, she looked up briefly at Mary and said, "Thank you."

Mary nodded and replied, "Good luck to you."

All the while, an astonished deputy marshal stood silently witnessing the quiet exchange between the two women, still finding it hard to believe the transformation that had seemingly occurred in Hannah Cheney. Evidently, talking with Mary had caused Hannah to take stock of where her life choices had taken her. Thinking he was wasting time then, he took Hannah by the arm and led her to the horses saddled and waiting. Mary stood in the yard, watching them ride away, Will leading with Hannah's reins tied to his saddle, and the packhorses following behind. *It's going to take them a long time to get to town, going in that direction,* she thought.

Mary was right, it would indeed take them a long time to reach town, had they continued on that course, but Will had another stop in mind. Hannah felt some concern, for she had a notion that Atoka was not due west from the cabin. She had watched through a crack in the smokehouse door when Jim Little Eagle had departed, and she was certain that he did not ride in this direction. She figured it would do her no good to point that out to Will, however.

Will continued for over an hour in the same direction, holding Buster to a fast walk, until coming to a shallow creek. He pulled the buckskin to a halt and dismounted, then reached up to help Hannah. Unsure, but knowing she was helpless to resist, she allowed herself to be helped down. "Stay there," he ordered, then he untied one of the packhorses and retied it to Hannah's saddle. When that was done, he came back and freed her hands. "Your mama's alive?" he asked. Hannah nodded slowly. "In a cabin on Blue River?" She nodded again. "You think you can find that cabin?"

Her eyes suddenly lit up in surprise. "Yes, I know where it is. It's my aunt and uncle's place." She hesitated before asking, "Are you gonna let me go?"

"I reckon," he said. "But I don't know why. I reckon your mama's lost enough of her family, and she most likely needs your help now. As far as I'm concerned, you never rode with your pa and your brothers. Now, get goin'."

She didn't waste any more time, but climbed up in the saddle immediately. Giving him one long look, she said, "Thanks, I'll never forget you for this." Already feeling like a softhearted fool, he made no reply and instead slapped her horse on the rump. As she galloped away, she thought, *I knew he had a conscience.*

Will turned Buster back toward Atoka, turning his actions in the last couple of hours over and over in his mind. Right away, he was undecided how he was going to explain to Jim Little Eagle. He had always been honest with the Choctaw lawman, but he was reluctant to admit to him that he had just decided to set Hannah free because he had destroyed her family and her mother needed her. And yet, he didn't care for the idea of making up a story about how she somehow escaped. *Maybe I'll just tell him she tried to run and I had to shoot her,* he thought. *Jim would never believe that.* Another thought struck him then. *I wonder if I had given her a gun if she would have tried to shoot me?* He shook his head, trying to rid his brain of the troubling thoughts. "Well, ain't nothin' I can do about it now. What's done is done."

Seeing the horses tied in front of the jail, Will turned Buster's head toward them. Inside the small room on the side that served as an office, Jim saw Will approaching, so he walked out to meet him, a look of surprise on his face. "You change your mind?" he asked when Will pulled up and dismounted.

"No," Will replied. "I'm headin' out as soon as I can get those two ready to go. Did they eat yet?"

"Yeah, I had Lottie fix 'em some biscuits and gravy," Jim said. "What happened to the woman?" He saw the hesitation in Will's eyes and came to a quick assumption. "Did you have to shoot her? Did she try to run?"

Again he hesitated. It would have been easy to simply say yes to both questions and maybe that would be the end of it, if Jim didn't press for more details. "No," he finally said. "She didn't run. I put her on her horse and sent her to find her mama on Blue River. I need to get Jack Lynch to Fort Smith as soon as possible, and I don't need to have a woman on my hands while I'm doin' it."

Jim didn't comment right away, taking a few moments to think about it. When he did speak, it was with an indifferent shrug of his shoulders. "You think maybe she didn't really have anything to do with the robbing and murdering?"

Will shrugged in reply. "Hell, I don't know. Maybe not. I just don't wanna be slowed down by a woman."

Jim nodded. It was easy to see that Will was not completely sure about the decision he had made. "The woman talked to Mary. You know, women talk to other women. Mary thinks the woman didn't do the bad things her brothers and father did. Not much different from Choctaw, Cheyenne, Comanche, any Indian tribe; wives and daughters have no say in what warriors do. They got no choice."

"I reckon you're right," Will said, feeling somewhat better about his decision to let Hannah go free. "Well, it's done, anyway, so let me load up my prisoners, and I'll get on the trail before I burn any more daylight."

CHAPTER 15

"Where's Hannah Cheney?" Lynch wanted to know when she was not waiting with the horses in front of the jail. Will ignored the question while he prepared his prisoners to ride. So Lynch started to protest. "She's as guilty as me and Tater. Why ain't she goin' with us?" He looked from Will to Jim Little Eagle as if demanding an answer.

Will locked the hand irons on Lynch's wrists before pausing to reply. "Because she tried to get away and I shot her," he finally said, thinking that might influence Lynch's ambitions for escape, and Will was sure he had them. He glanced at Jim and noticed the faint trace of a smile on the Choctaw lawman's face. "Climb up in that saddle," Will said to Lynch, and stepped back to give him room. Since it would be a great deal more comfortable for his prisoners, he didn't bind their arms behind their backs. He figured there wasn't much they could do with their wrists handcuffed before them because he intended to lead their horses with their reins tied to his saddle. Even with both hands to grasp the saddle horn, Lynch complained that it was too painful on his wounded shoulder. "Well, if you can't, I reckon there's nothin' we can do about it," Will said. "You'll just have to walk till your shoulder heals enough so it doesn't hurt to get on your horse." He turned his attention to Tater. "Climb on that horse. We're fixin' to leave. Lynch is gonna walk." The simpleminded outlaw immediately grabbed his saddle horn and stepped up into the saddle. Back at Lynch then, Will said, "You're gonna have to keep up. Come to think of it, I'd best tie a rope to your horse, so you won't fall behind."

"Son of a bitch," Lynch muttered under his breath, and reached up to grasp the saddle horn. Emitting a grunt of pain, he placed his foot in the stirrup and swung his leg over to flop heavily in the saddle.

"What I thought," Will remarked. "Might as well tell both of you, the easier you are on me, the easier I'll be on you. And just so you understand, my job is to arrest you and deliver you to the court. Dead or alive, it's all the same to me, so if you try to run, I will shoot you and save the federal district court the expense of a trial." He stepped up on Buster and wheeled the buckskin toward the east. With a tip of his index finger to the brim of his hat, signaling a salute to Jim Little Eagle, he started out, his two sullen prisoners trailing behind. Taking a trail he had traveled more than a few times before, he set out for the Sans Bois Mountains, planning to stop to rest the horses at a spot he had also used before.

It was the middle of the afternoon when they approached the narrow creek that had served him as a campsite once before when transporting a prisoner back to Fort Smith. The sight of the shady creek caused Will to recall that time. Maybe on this occasion, his prisoners wouldn't attempt to escape. Men and horses were both ready for a stop. By Will's reckoning, they had covered about twenty miles since leaving Atoka, and he planned to give the horses a good rest, then make another fifteen or twenty miles before camping for the night. By that time, it would be approaching darkness, and they could cook their supper then. For now, he would let them build a fire for some coffee while the horses rested. "It'd sure be a lot easier to build this fire if I had both hands free," Tater commented.

"I expect it would at that," Will replied, but gave no thought toward accommodating him.

There was barely enough daylight left to unload the horses and gather wood for a fire before Will called for a halt by a stream at the eastern-most foothills of the Jack Fork Mountains. He purposely picked a campsite at the point where he had parted company with Perley Gates some days before. He remembered that there was good water there as well as a grassy slope for grazing the horses. There was also a stand of young pine trees that provided a handy place to secure his prisoners for the night, and that was his first priority. Once they were bound hand and foot, he proceeded to take care of the horses, then went about making a fire and fixing something to eat.

"I thought we was gonna ride all night," Tater grumbled to Lynch, who was tied to a tree a few yards away. "I'm 'bout to starve to death." He tried to shift around to a more comfortable position on the pine needles, in order to watch their captor better as Will went about the business of frying some bacon.

Lynch, who was also watching intently, responded gruffly. "He's gotta get careless sometime. He ain't gonna be able to watch us every damn minute. If he keeps ridin' like we done today, we ain't gonna have more'n two days to figure out how to get him. So we've gotta be ready to jump him when we get our chance."

"How we gonna get a chance to jump him?" Tater asked. "We can't do nothin' tied up like this."

"I don't know," Lynch said. "When we eat, maybe, if he frees our hands like he did when we stopped back yonder. You just make sure you're ready when we get the chance."

"Just be sure you don't do somethin' dumb and get us both killed," Tater said. He was not sure Will would ever be that careless. "You heard what he done to Hannah."

"If he takes us into Fort Smith, we're gonna hang sure as hell," Lynch replied impatiently. "If you ain't figured that out yet, you're dumber'n I thought. So you better be figurin' you've got two days to live or die."

"I reckon you're right," Tater conceded.

Kneeling by the fire, Will was aware of the whispered conversation between his two prisoners. Although he could not hear what they were saying, he could well imagine the topic. Their situation was desperate, and he had no doubts that they would try to escape—it was only a matter of when. This was a clumsy way, and a risky one, to transport two dangerous outlaws, so the outcome depended upon whether or not he became careless. With that in mind, he decided to feed them one at a time, so he wouldn't have to be concerned with watching them both at the same time.

When the meat was done, he dropped a couple of pieces of hardtack in the bacon grease without bothering to break off the moldy edges. He figured that eating a little mold was the least of their worries, and frying it in the bacon grease disguised it, anyway. When he was ready, he called out, "Which one of you wants to eat first?"

"What the hell you mean?" Lynch retorted. "Ain't you gonna feed both of us?"

"Why sure," Will replied, "but only one at a time. So which one wants to eat first?"

"I do!" Tater responded immediately, causing Lynch to scowl at him.

"We're both hungry," Lynch complained. "Lord knows you ain't give us much to eat. You ain't got no worry. We ain't gonna try nothin'."

"I'm glad to hear that," Will said. He went to Tater and untied the ropes binding his hands and feet. Then he propped his rifle against the tree, since he needed both hands to unlock the chains binding Tater's wrists together. As soon as the key turned in the lock, he released it and drew his handgun. "Shake 'em off," he instructed. Somewhat confused by the process, Tater nevertheless shook his hands free and let the manacles drop to the ground. "All right, walk over to the fire and sit down, Indian style," Will said. Knowing what he meant, Tater settled himself beside the fire with his legs folded underneath him. Will holstered his pistol and picked up his rifle again. Then he sat down on the other side of the fire where he could watch Tater eat.

Back at his tree, still fuming, Lynch watched the careful procedure. It was obvious that the deputy intended to take every precaution to minimize their chance of escape. He decided that it was going to be up to him to make the move and take the first opportunity that came along, no matter his odds. "You ain't the only one that's hungry," he yelled at Tater after his partner appeared to be in no hurry to finish his coffee. It was clear to him now that the slow-witted Tater was not going to initiate any attempt on his own. In fact, he seemed content to go along peacefully to his hanging. The thought was enough to cause a sharp stab of pain in Lynch's shoulder, reminding him of his wound again and the handicap it might be. *I don't give a damn,* he thought, *I ain't going to no hanging.*

When Tater finished his supper, Will let him answer a call from nature, holding his rifle on him, even though he complained that he couldn't "go" with somebody staring at him. Will shook his head impatiently, unwilling to go through with the procedure he had followed to accommodate Hannah's reluctance. "Just turn around and pee," he ordered, "or wet your pants later." Tater did as he was told. When he was finished, Will returned him to his tree and secured him for the night. Then he repeated the procedure with Lynch, and unfortunately for the outlaw, there was no opportunity for an escape attempt. When Lynch was put away for the night, Will ate his supper. When he was finished, he led Buster up near the fire and tied him to a tree. Then with his rifle beside him, he settled down for the night, knowing the big buckskin would alert him if anyone was moving around him.

The night passed without incident, and Will had the two stiff and complaining outlaws in the saddle soon after daylight. "We'll ride till the horses need rest, then we'll eat," he said, and they were on their way toward the Sans Bois Mountains to the east. It was obvious to Jack Lynch that Will was going to continue working the horses long and hard in order to reach Fort Smith as soon as possible. And every mile traveled brought him closer to Judge Isaac Parker's court and the gallows that awaited.

Will didn't want to push the horses too hard, in spite of his desire to complete the journey as soon as possible. But he had a specific spot in mind that he wanted to reach before stopping. There was a tree-lined ravine leading down from the southern side of the mountains with a strong stream in the center of it. It was an ideal camping site, as evidenced by several old remains of fires. In this case, it suited Will's needs for a rest stop. There was good water and good grass, plus a stand of oak trees that provided plenty of dead limbs for a fire.

It was past the middle of the morning when they finally reached the ravine, and Will decided he had best allow plenty of time for the horses to rest. When he had taken care of the horses, he allowed Lynch and Tater to have their hands free to eat their breakfast, as he had done the day before. And, as before, he made coffee and cooked their food before he cooked his. When they were finished, he walked them downstream to take care of business, then tied them to a couple of trees in a clump of young pines on the other side of the creek. With a little distance between him and his prisoners, but not so much that he couldn't watch them, he sat down to have his breakfast.

"Looks like there's somebody in our campin' spot, Merle," Winona Sylvester said to her husband.

Merle rose up a little from the wagon seat and stretched his neck in an effort to see better. "Sure is," he agreed. "Feller by hisself, looks like, but he's drivin' a lot of horses somewhere."

"He's just settin' there by the fire," Winona said. "Wonder who he is?"

They usually stopped by this stream to rest the mules on their trip to Tom Beamer's trading post north of the Sans Bois Mountains. They made the trip only twice a year, and on this day they were on their way back to their farm ten miles south of the mountains. "Ain't no tellin'," Merle said, answering her question. "Don't look like nobody I've ever seen before. Might be a good idea to keep on goin' and stop somewhere else."

"He's spotted us," Winona said, for the man by the fire stood up at that point, a rifle in his hand.

"He'd have to be blind not to," Merle said, then called out at once to his mules, "Gee up there." With a slap of the reins, he turned the wagon to the right. But the man was walking at an angle to meet them. "I don't know what he's got on his mind. He wouldn't be the first outlaw on the run to find this part of the territory." Merle thought about whipping the mules up and making an effort to keep going, but he was afraid that might cause the man to use that rifle in his hand. He reached down beside the wagon seat to reassure himself that his .44 and holster were in easy reach. "I reckon we'll see what he wants."

Will lengthened his stride to make sure he cut the wagon off before it came any closer to his camp. Although many people camped here, this was the first time he had ever run into anyone else. *And it would have to be today, wouldn't it?* he thought. He looked back over his shoulder as he approached the wagon and noted that his two prisoners could not be seen under the trees on the bank of the stream. *Good,* he thought, *ain't no use in alarming the lady.* He assumed they had left the common wagon road because they wanted to rest their mules, but it might be better if they didn't know about the two dangerous outlaws by the stream. "Howdy, folks," he called out. The driver pulled his mules to a stop, and Will could see the definite signs of concern in both man and woman. "You lookin' to rest your mules?"

"Well, I had that in mind," Merle said. "But I was thinkin' about headin' a little farther upstream."

"That's probably a good idea," Will said. "There's a nice little clearin' about a hundred yards up that way where you can most likely drive your wagon closer to the water. Most of the firewood here where I'm camped has been used up."

"Yes, sir," Merle replied. "I reckon that's what we'll do."

The uncertainty was so evident in their faces that Will decided he should ease their apprehensions. He pulled his coat aside to reveal his badge. "I'm a deputy marshal on my way back to Fort Smith. You folks got a place around here?"

His comments seemed to immediately remove the frowns from both their faces. "Yes, sir," Merle replied, "about ten miles south of here." His whiskered face broke into a wide smile. "A marshal, huh? For a while there, you had me worried."

"You've got nothin' to worry about," Will said. "Go on upstream and make your camp, and good day to you." He stood watching them as they pulled off, waiting to make sure they pulled on out of sight before he returned to his fire and his coffee.

"What's he doin'?" Tater asked, unable to see beyond the fire Will had built. "He sounds like he's talkin' to somebody."

"I can't see much better'n you," Lynch answered. "I think it's a wagon and he's talkin' to whoever's drivin' it." They listened for a clue, but in a little while, they saw Will return to sit by the fire. "I reckon he sent 'em on their way."

"Wonder how long he's gonna keep us tied up on this damn bank?" Tater groaned after another quarter of an hour or so had passed. "My behind's already gone to sleep."

"Yeah," Lynch replied, "I noticed it was snorin'."

"I can't help it," Tater complained. "It's that damn hardtack he's feedin' us. You fry it in that grease and . . ." That was as far as he got before Lynch stopped him.

"Sssh," he whispered. "What the hell is that?"

"Where?" Tater asked, also whispering.

"Yonder, on the other side of the stream." He nodded toward a clump of laurel.

Following the direction of the nod, Tater squinted to peer at the bushes. After a moment, he saw movement in the leaves. "Somethin's in them bushes," he whispered, "and it's comin' this way. Maybe a deer."

They both stared at the bushes for a few moments, then suddenly Lynch grinned as he caught a glimpse of a calico skirt and a thought immediately occurred to him. "It ain't no deer," he said. "It's an angel come to save us. Just be real quiet and let me do the talkin'." *And hope to hell she don't scream,* he thought.

She didn't. In fact, when Winona parted the branches and saw the two men tied to the trees, she was too startled to make a sound. Much like a deer, she stopped, dead still, her eyes wide as saucers. She was so stunned that she forgot the reason she had sought the privacy of the laurel bushes. "Don't be scared, ma'am," Lynch said, speaking softly so as not to be heard by the deputy seated by the fire some distance away. "I'm Deputy Marshal Tanner, and this is my partner. I'm afraid we've run into some bad luck." He glanced back at the fire, but Will was still sitting there, unaware of the visitor to his prisoners. "Me and my partner were sent to arrest that man you talked to," he said. But he ambushed us, shot me, and captured us both. He hid us down here, so nobody could see us from the trail."

Finally able to find her voice, although still in a state approaching shock, Winona stammered, "But he was wearin' a badge."

"I ain't surprised," Lynch said. "I figured he wanted somethin' with it when he took it off my shirt. Ain't no tellin' what he might do, so I want you to get somewhere safe. That man's a murderer and he said the reason he's got us tied up is because he wants to kill us real slow. But I'm worried 'bout you and your husband. I don't want him doin' you folks no harm. There ain't nothin' we can do to save ourselves, but I'll feel better if I know you got away before he comes after you."

Winona was terrified, but she had always been a strong-willed woman. "Is there anythin' I can do to help you?" she asked.

"No, ma'am," Lynch answered. "The only way me and Tater could have a chance is if we had a gun and somebody cut us loose. Then we might could arrest him and take him back for a fair trial, maybe save some more innocent folks."

Winona's mind was whirling, trying to digest all she had just been told. Deputy Tanner seemed genuine in his greater concern for her and Merle than any he had for himself. So her fighting spirit rose to combine with her Christian faith to bring her to a firm state of commitment. "I can get you a gun," she avowed, "and I can cut you loose. My husband's got a .44 Colt revolver in the wagon and a shotgun, too."

"Oh, ma'am," Lynch said, "I surely wouldn't want you to take any dangerous chances. Our job is to protect folks like you and your husband. It looks like me and my partner was careless, though, and let the outlaw turn the table on us."

"I couldn't live with myself if I was to run off and leave you with that murderer," Winona declared. "Don't you worry about me. I'll be right back."

"Bless you, ma'am," Lynch praised. "You be careful. That .44 would be best. Make sure it's loaded." She was off at once, disappearing in the bushes again.

"I wish you hadda told her I was a deputy marshal, too," Tater said. "You reckon she'll really come back?"

Merle was not sure what to believe when Winona returned, breathless from running through the bushes. He thought at first that something was after her, and he reached for the shotgun in the wagon. When he found out why she had really been running, he was more distressed than had it been a bear chasing her. "My Lord in heaven . . ." he exclaimed, immediately alarmed to find themselves in such a perilous situation. His initial impulse was to hitch up the mules again and drive like hell. But Winona was babbling something about coming to the aid of the law and preventing the murder of a deputy marshal, all the while fishing under the wagon seat for Merle's pistol. When he was able to calm her down enough to explain, she told him of the encounter by the stream.

He was not so ready to accept her belief in the two men she had met. "I don't know, hon, that feller was wearin' a badge, and he talked like a nice-enough man."

"I told you," Winona insisted as she rummaged

through her cookware for a butcher knife. "He said that murderer took his badge." Finding the knife she searched for, she turned back to her husband. "A nice, polite feller. He said his name was Tanner. And that man with the badge sure was in a hurry to meet us and keep us from drivin' on down by the creek back there. And he didn't say anything about havin' two fellers tied up in the trees."

Merle was not sure what to believe at that point. It could be that the situation was exactly as Winona thought. "You say he said his name was Tanner?" he questioned. "I've heard of a deputy named Tanner. This feller you just saw, was he a tall feller?"

Winona said that he sure was. "And he was wounded. That outlaw had shot him."

"I don't know," Merle repeated, wishing they had stopped somewhere else to rest the mules, but reluctantly giving in to the possibility that they had, in fact, landed in the middle of an unlikely situation.

Winona had made up her mind, thinking it was her Christian duty to do the right thing and possibly prevent two senseless murders. "Someday the law is gonna clean out all these outlaws that run to Indian Territory to hide out. And honest folks need to help 'em when we can."

"I reckon you're right," Merle said. His wife's instincts were good about most things, and the more he thought about the situation, the more plausible it became. There was also the damnable impression of fear he would give his wife if he chose to run. Assuming the responsible position then, he said, "Here, gimme the pistol. I'll take it to the deputy. You'd best stay here."

"I'll go with you and show you where they are," Winona countered. Already enflamed with the passion to right a grievous wrong, she had no intention to remain with the wagon. Knowing it would be useless to protest, Merle made no attempt to do so. She plunged into the bank of laurel bushes and he followed right behind.

"Ha, I told you so," Jack Lynch exclaimed softly to Tater when the bushes parted to reveal the man and woman. He instinctively took a quick look in the direction of the campfire and became even more confident when he saw Will walk over to check on the horses. With the deputy distracted for a few minutes, the timing couldn't have worked out better. Looking back in the direction of the laurels, he nodded to Winona and Merle when they hesitated to come any closer. He winked in Tater's direction when he saw the weapons the couple carried. Getting back into character, he greeted them gratefully when they hurried over to the trees. "Lord bless you, ma'am. You can go to work on these ropes." While she attacked his bonds with her butcher knife, he nodded solemnly to Merle. "I'm right pleased to meet the husband of such a brave woman. I just want you to know you're sure enough doin' the right thing—and a righteous thing at that. Is that gun loaded?" Merle said that it was. "Good," Lynch continued. "As soon as your wife saws through this rope, give me the gun, and you two get on back to your wagon. I'll bring your gun back as soon as I arrest that gunman. I don't want you gettin' hurt."

Silent to that point, Tater was unable to resist announcing, "I'm a deputy marshal, too. Ain't that so, Lynch?"

"Yeah, that's so," Lynch snapped, annoyed when his simple partner slipped and called him by his name.

The slipup caused Merle to hesitate. He wasn't sure what Deputy Tanner's first name was, but when he had heard Tom Beamer refer to the lawman, he didn't think it sounded anything like "Lynch." It was of no consequence to what happened next, however, for Winona's blade sawed through the rope at that instant, freeing the outlaw's hands. Lynch reacted immediately and snatched the Colt from Merle's hand. He cocked it and aimed it at the startled farmer. "So far, you've done real good. Don't mess up now and get yourself killed. Get them ropes offa my feet." Merle dropped to his knees immediately and began frantically untying Lynch's ankles.

Gesturing toward Tater, Lynch said to Winona. "Get over there and cut him loose, and don't try nothin' funny, or I'll blow a hole in your husband's head."

She did as he said, but not without comment. "You low-down son of a bitch. I hope you rot in hell."

Lynch snorted, amused. "I expect I might," he said. "Now, hurry up, we ain't got all day."

They wasted no time obeying his command. "Hurry, hon!" Merle implored as he herded Winona back the way they had come. She plunged headlong into the bank of thick laurel, never taking time to worry about the branches that thrashed her face and body. When they were well away from the two outlaws, she slowed to a less-punishing pace, and when she felt sure they were safely away, she stopped abruptly and screamed as loud as she could. "What the hell!" Merle exclaimed, thinking she must surely have lost her mind.

"I'm tryin' to warn that marshal," she explained. "I'm afraid we just caused him to get shot, so we oughta try to let him know somethin's wrong." Before Merle could protest, she screamed again.

"You're gonna get us kilt," Merle blurted. He grabbed her hand and charged through the young oaks beyond the bushes, heading for the wagon. The realization that he was left without a weapon to try to defend Winona and himself was enough to spur him to hitch the mules up and depart. "Throw that stuff in the wagon," he ordered breathlessly, and ran to collect his mules.

"What about the deputy?" Winona cried.

"Ain't nothin' we can do to help him," Merle yelled back at her. "Best now we worry 'bout savin' our own hides!"

"That ol' bitch!" Lynch cursed when he heard Winona's scream ring out through the trees like the screech of a wounded hawk. "I shoulda took that knife and cut her throat. I oughta knowed she might do somethin' like that." He looked frantically back toward the campfire and the horses beyond. "You see him?" Peering toward the clearing as well, Tater strained to see. Like Lynch, he could see no sign of the deputy. "He sure as hell heard her yowlin', but that don't mean he knows what she was yowlin' about," Lynch reasoned. "Most likely he'll think she come up on us and it scared her to scream."

"Maybe so!" Tater responded, still scanning the clearing in the trees where the fire had been built. "I still don't see him, but he's bound to be here pretty quick!" Their problem was compounded by the absence of heavy brush among the young pines where they had been bound. "There ain't nothin' to hide behind 'cept these skinny pine trees," he said as he held Winona's shotgun at the ready.

"Put that shotgun down and back up against that tree again," Lynch directed, thinking quickly. "Put your hands behind the tree, so's he'll think you're still tied up. He won't be able to tell we're loose till he gets too close to run for it. Take some of them ropes and wrap 'em round your boots." Doing likewise, Lynch jammed the Colt .44 in his belt behind his back and stepped back against the tree again. Their ambush set, they waited for the unsuspecting lawman to show up.

Will was inspecting the hooves of the buckskin gelding when he was startled by the sudden scream that echoed through the trees by the stream. His first reaction was to drop to one knee and pick up his rifle, which was lying close by him. Motionless then, he waited and listened. There it was again, and he guessed that the woman had wandered down the stream and come upon his prisoners tied to the trees. "Damn," he cursed softly, thinking that he'd rather that had not happened. Since he could not be sure that was the case, however, he decided he'd better be cautious when he went to find out for certain.

He cranked a cartridge into the chamber of his Winchester and crossed over to the other side of the creek, then started working his way carefully up the bank of the stream toward the stand of young pines. When he was within about thirty yards of the spot where he had secured them, he could see them clearly, and they seemed to still be bound to the trees. And yet, there appeared to be something that didn't look right. They had not sighted him, so he paused to study the scene. After a moment, he saw it. "All right," he called out. "Both of you, step away from the trees and kneel on the ground." He saw both men flinch, but they did not do as he instructed.

"How the hell can we do that?" Lynch called back. "You got us tied up to these trees." He looked toward the sound of Will's voice, trying to spot him.

"I'm not gonna tell you again before I start shootin'," Will replied. When his warning was ignored, he raised his rifle and aimed it at a spot on the tree about a foot or two above Lynch's head. When the Winchester spoke, sending a chunk of pine bark flying, it caused a chain reaction that Will had not foreseen. Frightened, Tater immediately lunged forward to land flat on the ground. Lynch, having seen the muzzle flash in the bushes, reached for the .44 jammed into the back of his trousers and started firing as fast as he could. Will had no choice but to cut him down before one of the wild shots found their target. Struck in his chest, Lynch staggered backward until stopped by the tree. He managed to squeeze the trigger one last time, sending a harmless shot into the ground at his feet before he crumpled, mortally wounded.

In a fit of panic, Tater scrambled backward to

pick up the shotgun he had laid on the ground behind the tree. Will rose to his feet from behind the low bushes that had concealed him and stood ready to fire before the frightened outlaw could bring the shotgun to his shoulder. "Don't try it," he warned. "You'll get the same as him." Tater dropped the shotgun immediately. When he did, Will said, "Now back away from it." Tater did as he was told, having no desire to test the somber lawman.

Will pushed through the bushes, his rifle still trained on Tater. There was no sign of the woman or her husband. Will guessed that they had fled. He walked over to Lynch's body, slumped over at the foot of the tree. Scorpion Jack Lynch had escaped the gallows after all. As Will was about to check to see if he was still alive, Lynch exhaled his last breath before listing over sideways. Will picked up the Colt and stuck it in his belt. This was not the way he wanted this to end. He had been determined to take Jack Lynch in to Fort Smith for trial, and with the outlaw's death, he felt a sense of failure. Looking over at the wide-eyed countenance of Tater Smith, he couldn't help thinking he was a poor symbol of the fierce reputation the Jack Lynch gang had earned throughout Colorado and Kansas territories. *Well,* he thought, *if I can manage to transport him back without killing him, maybe that'll count for something.* Looking at Tater, he was reminded of a hound dog, staring at him with pleading eyes, wondering if he was going to get something to eat, or get a whipping. "Come on," he said, motioning for him to start walking. "I'll tell you the same as I told you when we started out. If you don't make it hard on me, I won't make it hard on you." He nodded toward Lynch. "He made it hard on me." He saw an immediate sense of relief in Tater's eyes as he walked him over to the fire. "I reckon you're the last of Scorpion Jack Lynch's gang."

Tater considered that and decided it pleased him. "I reckon that's right—makes me right famous, don't it?"

Will almost laughed in response. "Yeah, reckon it does."

While they waited for the horses to be rested up to get under way again, the only decision Will considered was whether or not to bury Lynch's body. Since this was a well-known camping spot, he figured it the proper thing to do to at least drag the body away out of sight. Besides, if he didn't put Lynch in the ground, at least the outlaw would have a chance to finally do something worthwhile. Buzzards need to eat. *And outlaws, too,* he thought, so he offered the coffee left in the pot to Tater, who graciously accepted it.

Drinking the last of the coffee and feeling more comfortable because he was no longer afraid he was going to be shot, Tater felt compelled to ask a question. "How'd you know we warn't tied to them trees when you snuck up on us? You couldn't see that good through them bushes."

"You were backed up to a different tree," Will said. "I tied you to the one next to it."

"Damn," the simple man swore.

CHAPTER 16

"Will, is that you?" The voice came from the trees on the ridge above them.

"Yeah, Perley," Will yelled back. "What took you so long?"

There was no answer for a couple of minutes until the elflike little man appeared at the base of the ridge. "Hell, I didn't know who was doin' that shootin'. They sounded mighty close to my camp, so I thought I'd best come take a look—make sure I wasn't about to have company." He favored Will with a wide grin. "I smelled that coffee from the top of the ridge, though. Anybody get shot?"

"You just missed the last of the coffee," Will said. "But I reckon we could take the time to make a little more." While he proceeded to build another pot, he went on to relate what had just taken place there in the ravine. "I wasn't sure you'd be back around here. Last time I talked to you, you said you were thinkin' about movin' your camp north of the Jack Fork Mountains—said the deer were gettin' scarce around here."

"I was thinkin' about it," Perley said. "But don't you know, I came back here night before last and there was a deer eatin' outta my lean-to. I figured that was a sign." He took the empty

362

cup Will handed him, eyeballing Tater as he did. "Looks like you got what you came after," he said to Will.

"Not really," Will replied. "I came after four, but I'm headin' back to Fort Smith with only one." He nodded toward the prisoner, meekly nursing his cup of coffee. "Say howdy to Tater."

Perley nodded to Tater, and Tater proudly responded, "Pleased to meetcha. I'm the last one of Scorpion Jack Lynch's gang. You mighta heard of us."

"Can't say as I have," Perley said. Back to Will then, he asked, "You thinkin' about stayin' here tonight? 'Cause if you are, you might as well ride on over to my place."

" 'Preciate it, Perley," Will said, "But I expect I'd better keep on goin'." He glanced at Tater. "I need to get Tater, here, to Fort Smith before he decides to turn rabbit on me sometime when my back is turned."

"You ain't got no reason to worry 'bout me," Tater declared. "I ain't gonna cause you no trouble."

"I'm glad to hear it," Will said. He studied the simple man for a moment. Tater seemed suddenly older than he had before. His eyes were watery and dull, and his beard and hair appeared to have taken on more gray. It was almost as if the man had aged in just the past few days. Will decided Tater meant what he said about not causing any trouble. Further thoughts on the subject were interrupted by Perley.

"You sure you don't wanna come on over to my place and start out again in the mornin'? I'll bet you ain't had no fresh meat since you were here last time."

"Mighty temptin'," Will allowed, "but I expect I'd better keep movin'." With the demise of Jack Lynch, Will no longer felt the urgency to get to Fort Smith as soon as his horses could carry him. But he had a strong desire to be done with the Jack Lynch gang. So he would take no chances with Tater, but he was certain he was not the threat he was when Lynch was alive to tell him what to do. In a way, Will felt somewhat sorry for the old outlaw, for it appeared that his life had effectively ended when Lynch slumped over at the foot of that tree with a .44 slug in his chest. It was now no more than a day and a half ride to Fort Smith, and Will decided he might as well make use of the daylight still left and deliver Tater to his final reckoning. So he said so long to Perley, and he and Tater started out again, planning to camp for the night twenty miles closer to Fort Smith.

The sun was still high in the sky when they reached Fort Smith the following day. Will had judged Tater's attitude correctly, for he had caused no trouble at all on the ride, seeming to have accepted his appointment with the gallows. He thought maybe it was his imagination, but Tater appeared to sit up tall and proud in the saddle when he was led through the streets of Fort Smith. He even gave a smile and a friendly nod to the people they passed on the street leading to the courthouse. In his few years of experience as a deputy marshal, Will could not recall arresting anyone before who seemed as eager to get to jail. When Will turned him over to Sid Randolph, Tater didn't wait for Will's introduction. "I'm Tater Smith," he informed Sid. "You most likely heard of me, rode with Scorpion Jack Lynch, and there ain't nobody left of the gang but me."

"That so?" Sid replied, and shot a quizzical glance in Will's direction. Like Perley Gates, Sid had never heard of Tater Smith or Jack Lynch. "Well, I reckon we're proud to have you stayin' in our establishment," he said. "I hope your stay is enjoyable." With a grin for Will, he led Tater inside to lock him up.

Well, that takes care of that, Will thought, stepped up into the saddle, and took the horses to the stable where Vern Tuttle took them off his hands. Thinking he might still catch Dan Stone in his office, he walked back to the courthouse to report in. On his way upstairs, he met Alvin Greeley coming down. "Alvin," Will noted politely.

The tall, angular deputy marshal paused

for a moment as if deciding whether or not to acknowledge Will with a greeting. "Tanner," he finally mumbled reluctantly. It was plain for Will to see that Greeley was still steamed over his having left him in Durant, so he continued on up the steps. He reached the second floor before Greeley called after him, "I heard you went to Tishomingo lookin' for four outlaws. Did any of 'em make it here alive?"

"One," Will answered, and kept walking. He supposed he was saddled with the reputation, but he felt no obligation to explain himself to backbiters like Alvin Greeley.

"Damn!" Dan Stone blurted when Will walked in his office. "So you are alive. I reckon all the telegraph lines are down in Tishomingo."

"I wired you from Durant," Will replied, ignoring his boss's sarcasm. "I told you I was goin' after Lynch and his men."

"That's right, you did," Stone said, still with a touch of sarcasm in his voice. "So I expect you caught up with them and they're now downstairs in the jail."

"One of 'em is," Will said. "The other 'uns didn't make it."

Stone favored him with a look of exasperation, although it was not really sincere. He did not believe that Will was prone to kill without an honest attempt to arrest the outlaws he went after. But he wanted to make sure his best deputy understood where he stood on a prisoner's rights. "All right, then, tell me what happened." He listened to Will's account of the entire quest to run Jack Lynch to ground, and he believed him when he said the deceased outlaws gave him little choice in their demise. When Will had finished, Stone told him to go get himself a drink and go on home. "You can lay around that rooming house you live in and wait for that fellow's trial. I don't expect that'll be too long. Judge Parker has been running them through the courtroom pretty damn fast. I think he was trying to clear his calendar before the first of the year. I'll run the paperwork right on over, so you stay close 'cause you'll most likely be called to testify."

The first of the year, Will repeated Stone's words to himself. *Sophie was married to Garth Pearson.* The thought always brought a feeling of melancholy, and now that it was done, it seemed especially depressing. As usually happened, he tried to erase the picture from his mind, never having really understood why the precocious young woman occupied such a great portion of his brain. *I've got no business thinking about another man's wife and that's for sure,* he told himself, and vowed to put her out of his mind. *I'll start with a double shot of whiskey before I go home for supper.*

As was usually the case, Will was greeted warmly by Gus Johnson when he walked in the

Morning Glory. "Figured you was most likely over in Injun Territory, since you ain't been in for a while." Will told him he had guessed right, but didn't offer any details. Lucy Tyler waved to him from a table near the back of the saloon, where she was drinking with a fellow wearing a Boss of the Plains Stetson. Evidently the long-suffering prostitute had a promising customer, and Will was glad of it. He was tired and wanted a drink, a good supper, and a comfortable bed. He knew he could get the last two at Ruth Bennett's boardinghouse, so he finished his drink and bade Gus a quick "Good night," and left for home.

The cold evening breeze seemed to cut right through to his bones as he made the short walk to Bennett House. It struck him as odd that he always felt the cold more when he was back in town. When he bothered to think about it at all, he decided that it was because, when he was in the field, he was thinking less about comfort. With minor thoughts such as this, he was startled when he came to the picket fence in front of Bennett House and saw Sophie busy sweeping the front porch.

She paused to watch him as he opened the gate and walked up the path, the hunter returning home, his saddlebags over his shoulder, his rifle in his hand. "Well, well," she said. "I see you found your way home again."

"Reckon so," he said. "I didn't expect to see you sweepin' the porch, though."

"Why not?" she replied. "I'm the one who usually sweeps the porch before supper. Since Mama hired Margaret, I don't help as much in the kitchen."

"Yeah, but . . ." he stumbled. "I mean, I just didn't figure to see you, figured you and your husband wouldn't be stayin' here with your mama."

"Well, I guess that's where you figured wrong. In the first place, I don't have a husband."

The impact of her statement struck him so suddenly that he had no time to disguise his shock. He thought at first that he had lost track of the date again. "But what about Christmas?" he blurted. "I thought you and Garth . . ."

"We decided that maybe it wasn't the right thing to do," she said. She left it at that without telling him that it was she who called the wedding off, to the dismay of not only Garth, but her mother as well as Garth's parents. It was a cruel thing to do on the eve of the wedding, but after some long soul-searching, she knew that it was more humane than entering a union that was guaranteed to fail. As fine a man as Garth was, she could not agree to a marriage she was not totally committed to. She shouldn't have let it go so far. It had been a cheerless Christmas morning that greeted them after she and her mother argued over the issue well into the early hours. Ruth was forced to admit defeat shortly before it was time to start breakfast for her boarders. Throughout the wrenching discussion, Sophie did not offer the one point that to her was the most telling reason. She never felt the small sensation of excitement in her bosom with Garth that she felt every time she saw the tall sandy-haired lawman striding confidently down the street toward the house.

Her statement rendered the confused young deputy helplessly lost for something to say. Speechless for a few moments, he finally managed to say, "Well, I reckon I'm sorry things didn't work out for you." Inside, he knew he had wished they would not marry, even though he thought he had no right to do so. Feeling totally at a loss for anything else to say that would be appropriate, he shifted back and forth nervously from one foot to the other for a few moments. Finally, he mumbled something about needing to wash up before supper, and went inside the house, leaving her shaking her head in frustration.

Maybe her instincts had been misleading her all along, she thought. Or was his skull too thick to read the signs? *I'll be damned if I'm going to spell it out for him,* she thought. *He's going to have to approach me because he wants to. I swear I'll die an old maid before I tell him how I feel. He's going to have to tell me first.* With that, she made an aggressive sweep with her broom, sending a small pile of dirt flying off the edge of the porch.

At the supper table that night, the other residents of Bennett House were all cordial to the young deputy marshal. The only one who seemed different was Ruth Bennett. He could not put his finger on it, even though Sophie's mother was quietly polite. He caught her gazing at him a couple of times, only to look quickly away when he glanced back. He decided not to waste any more time wondering about it. Women were hard to figure out, anyway. So why not concentrate on the fine supper that Margaret and Ruth had prepared? It was a welcome relief from the almost steady diet of sowbelly and hardtack that had been his for the past several days.

The next day, Sophie and Ruth, too, appeared to settle back to a more normal atmosphere. At least, that was the way Will perceived it. Sophie, especially, returned to her usual lighthearted demeanor, even to the point of teasing about the week-old growth of light blond whiskers on his face. To drop him a hint, she took his shaving cup and his boar's hair shaving brush from his room and set it on the stand in the washroom. He took the hint and made it a point to put them to work. And when he passed Sophie in the front parlor on his way out the door, she commented, "I almost didn't recognize you without all that scrubby hair on your face." He blushed and rubbed his chin.

"Are you leaving town again?" she asked, even though he was not carrying his saddlebags and rifle.

"Nope. I've gotta hang around town till the judge tries that fellow I brought in," he replied. "Don't know when that'll be, but it oughta be pretty soon, accordin' to what Dan Stone told me."

As it turned out, however, Tater Smith's trial was moved back on Judge Parker's docket. Will used the extra days to work with the horses he kept at Vern Tuttle's stable. A couple of them had been idle long enough to need saddle-breaking again. The work caused Will to think about his days at the J-Bar-J when Boss Hightower was still alive. Those were hardworking days, but he remembered it now as a happy time, and he had to wonder why he had decided to leave the ranch to land in the violent business he was now in. *I'll go back to Texas,* he thought, *when the time is right.*

Tater Smith's trial started late one afternoon, and did not take long. Will was called to the witness stand and turned out to be Tater's main defense. He stated his true opinion of the simple man on trial, testifying that Tater would not likely have committed the crimes he was charged with, had it not been for the overbearing influence of Jack Lynch. For whatever reason, Will couldn't guess, but Judge Parker did not sentence Tater to the gallows. Maybe it was the Christmas season. Instead, Tater was sentenced to life imprisonment in the Arkansas State Prison in Little Rock. He gave Will a long, contented gaze as the guards led him out of the courtroom. He imagined he could guess the simple outlaw's thoughts. He could live out his life enjoying the notoriety of being the only surviving member of the infamous Scorpion Jack Lynch's gang.

It was after dark when Will walked down the street to Bennett House. He was surprised to find Sophie sitting in a rocking chair on the front porch, bundled up in a quilt against the cold. "What are you doin' sittin' out here in this weather?" Will asked.

"Oh, I don't know," she replied. "I just felt like I needed some cold air in my lungs, I guess." She got up from the rocker. "How did the trial go?"

"All right, I reckon. They ain't gonna hang him, and I was kinda glad they ain't."

"You didn't get any supper," Sophie said. "I can find you something in the kitchen."

"I appreciate it, Sophie, but I believe I'll walk back up to the Mornin' Glory. I don't know why I didn't just stop there to begin with. Too much confusion in my mind, I reckon. I could use a drink tonight and I'll get something to eat there. Mammy's always got some leftovers and there ain't no sense in you havin' to clean up the kitchen again."

She started to tell him it would be no trouble, but decided he probably preferred to go to the Morning Glory. "All right," she said, "but I don't care if you change your mind." He seemed more quiet than usual, even a little sad. On a sudden impulse, she stepped up close to him and kissed him tenderly on his cheek, then stepped quickly away. "Don't drink too much of Gus Johnson's whiskey," she said. Flushed and confused, he could only stand there and stare at her for a few moments until she told him she would be in the kitchen if he changed his mind about eating. "Go on and get your drink," she said, then remained there on the edge of the porch, watching him until he disappeared up the dark street.

She turned and was about to go inside when she heard a woman's voice from the darkness beyond the porch. "Looks to me like you two are mighty sweet on each other."

Sophie was startled. "Mama, is that you?" She stared at the figure emerging from the darkness and now approaching the steps. "What are you doing out in the yard?" And then she could see that it was not her mother. It was no woman she knew. "Is there something you want?" she asked when the strange woman walked up the steps. In the next moment she was stunned when she saw the pistol in her hand.

"Is there somethin' I want? Yeah, there's some-thin' I want. Do you know what it feels like to have your whole family murdered? I do. Will Tanner murdered my father and my four brothers. Now he's gonna know how it feels, 'cause I'm gonna kill you, let him see how he likes it. I'm gonna let him cry over you for just a little while, then I'm gonna kill him." She raised the revolver and aimed it at Sophie's head.

"Hannah." She turned at once when she heard her name called, but not quick enough to fire before the bullet struck her in her breastbone. One dying attempt to raise her weapon again brought a second shot that struck her in her forehead, and she slumped to the floor.

Terrified, Sophie ran to the safety of Will's arms, and this was where Ruth and one of her boarders found her, her face buried against his chest. "Sophie!" Ruth screamed and ran to her daughter.

"She's all right, just scared," Will said, and released her to her mother's arms.

Behind him, one of Ruth's boarders, Ron Sample, stood dumbfounded, staring at the body lying on the porch, a shotgun in his hands. "Lord a-mercy," he exclaimed. "We heard the shots, so I grabbed my shotgun and come a-runnin'. Who is that?"

"Her name's Hannah Cheney," Will said. "And she wouldn't be here if I wasn't such a damn fool." He thought of the contrite woman who had emerged from Jim Little Eagle's smokehouse, the picture of remorse, a victim of her evil father. *And I swallowed it,* he scolded himself. She almost got her revenge and he nearly lost the one person he cherished most, only realizing that fact at this moment. "You take Sophie inside," he said to Ruth. "It's all over now, there ain't nobody else to worry about." He turned to Ron. "Gimme a hand and we'll carry the body offa the porch. I'll get Ed Kittridge to pick it up." He paused to casually kick a small, smooth pebble off the porch, never giving a thought to how it happened to have landed there.

"It's a lucky thing you were here when she showed up," Ron said as he propped his shotgun against the porch railing and prepared to grab Hannah's heels.

"Yeah, lucky," Will agreed. It was luck, he thought, for the only reason he was there was because of a kiss on his cheek. He had not gotten far up the street when he convinced himself that her kiss was more than a casual impulse, so he stopped and turned around. Maybe he was wrong, and the kiss was nothing more than Sophie being Sophie, and he'd best forget about it, and go on to the Morning Glory. *I need to know for sure,* he had thought, because he was going to go crazy wondering all the time. *It's time I got my nerve up to ask her.* Resolved to do just that, he started back to the house. When he had seen the dark figure approaching the porch, he wasn't sure why, but he knew it was Hannah Cheney. And from that realization, there had been no time for any conscious thought. His natural reflexes took over.

He walked to Ed Kittridge's place of business and rode back to pick Hannah up with him in his wagon. "I'm glad to see you back in town," Ed quipped. "My business picks up when you're in town." Will didn't particularly appreciate Ed's attempt at humor. He had no desire for the reputation. After Ed took the body away, Will went into the kitchen to find something to take the place of that supper he had never gotten around to.

He found Ruth and Margaret seated at the table, finishing the coffee and discussing the events of the evening. They invited him to join them. When he said he could really use something to go with the coffee, Ruth fixed him a plate of biscuits and ham, left over from supper. He asked about Sophie, and Ruth said she had sent her up to her room, that she was still upset after the harrowing encounter with Hannah Cheney. "She'll be all right tomorrow. Don't worry about her." She hesitated for a moment, watching him intently before adding, "You know Sophie." When he got up to leave, she stopped him with a hand on his arm. "Thank you, Will. Thank you for saving my daughter's life." He nodded solemnly in response, again at a loss for the proper thing to say.

Ruth was right, Sophie was her usual spirited self the next morning, bright and cheerful when she saw Will at breakfast. Afterward, when he started to leave for the courthouse, she stopped him at the door. "I guess I was too terrified to know what was happening last night, but I want to thank you for being there."

"You're welcome," he said. "Glad I was there." He thought about the reason he had happened to return to the house last night and decided this was not the time to discuss it. Maybe there would never be a proper time.

"Where are you off to now?" Sophie asked.

"The courthouse," he answered. "I've gotta go see my boss. He's been complainin' that I don't check in with him regular enough."

"Then you'll be back here again?"

"I reckon," he said.

She smiled, thinking they were involved in a cat and mouse game, but she knew in her heart that he was fated to be with her. He just had to work up his nerve to tell her he felt the same. Many things that had happened during the terrible confrontation with Hannah Cheney the night before were vague in her memory. But the one moment she distinctly remembered was when she was protected in his embrace. She was at home there. "Don't be late for supper," she said, playfully dismissing him.

"I won't" he said with a laugh.

Purposefully overhearing in the parlor, Ruth Bennett shook her head, exasperated, knowing there was nothing she could do to prevent her daughter from traveling the same road she had taken. *What the hell,* she thought. *A short time with Will Tanner might be a lot better than a lifetime with a man like Garth Pearson.* The thought brought memories back, both bitter and sweet, yet none that she could ever wish to have missed. And the image of Deputy Marshal Fletcher Pride came to her mind, bold and robust, like a wild mustang, filling the room with his presence. Will might be a little more quiet than that, but she knew that this gentle mountain lion was what her daughter needed. *Lord help her.* She smiled then. *I might as well get used to it.*

ABOUT THE AUTHORS

William W. Johnstone is the *New York Times* and *USA Today* bestselling author of over 300 books, including the series Preacher, the First Mountain Man, MacCallister, Luke Jensen, Bounty Hunter, Flintlock, Those Jensen Boys!, Savage Texas, Matt Jensen, the Last Mountain Man, and The Family Jensen. His thrillers include *Tyranny*, *Stand Your Ground*, *Suicide Mission*, and *Black Friday*.

Visit his website at www.williamjohnstone.net.

• • •

Being the all-around assistant, typist, researcher, and fact-checker to one of the most popular western authors of all time, J. A. Johnstone learned from the master, Uncle William W. Johnstone.

The elder Johnstone began tutoring J.A. at an early age. After-school hours were often spent retyping manuscripts or researching his massive American Western History library as well as the more modern wars and conflicts. J.A. worked hard—and learned.

"Every day with Bill was an adventure story in

itself. Bill taught me all he could about the art of storytelling. *'Keep the historical facts accurate,'* he would say. *'Remember the readers—and as your grandfather once told me, I am telling you now: Be the best J. A. Johnstone you can be.'* "

Books are produced
in the United States
using U.S.-based
materials

Books are printed
using a revolutionary
new process called
THINKtech™ that
lowers energy usage
by 70% and increases
overall quality

Books are durable
and flexible because
of smythe-sewing

Paper is sourced
using environmentally
responsible foresting
methods and the
paper is acid-free

Center Point Large Print
600 Brooks Road / PO Box 1
Thorndike, ME 04986-0001 USA

(207) 568-3717

US & Canada:
1 800 929-9108
www.centerpointlargeprint.com